'The Troubles of Northern Ireland are not over.
This message is so disturbingly, convincingly and
elegantly conveyed in Anthony J. Quinn's first
novel… Beautifully haunting.'
The Times, Books of the Year

'*Disappeared* is a major piece of work. Eerily
tender, a wonderfully wrought classic that is a
landmark in the fiction of Northern Ireland. Line
up the glittering prizes. This one is
going to take 'em all.'
Ken Bruen

'The beautifully written *Disappeared* is much more
than a routine whodunnit as it unflinchingly lays
bare the deep ambivalence that haunts post-peace
process Northern Ireland society as it tries to come
to terms with its violent past. Outstanding.'
Irish Independent

'Quinn enriches *Disappeared* with Irish history and he
does an excellent job of ratcheting up the tension.'
The Rap Sheet

ALSO BY ANTHONY J. QUINN

Border Angels

DISAPPEARED

ANTHONY J. QUINN

A Mysterious Press Book
for Head of Zeus

First published in the United States in 2012
by MysteriousPress.com/Open Road Integrated Media.

First published in the UK in 2014 by Head of Zeus Ltd. This paperback edition first
published in the UK in 2015 by Head of Zeus Ltd.

9 7 5 3 1 2 4 6 8

A catalogue record for this book is available from
the British Library.

Paperback ISBN: 9781781858998
eBook ISBN: 9781784088149

Printed in the UK by Clays Ltd, St Ives Plc

Head of Zeus Ltd
Clerkenwell House
45-47 Clerkenwell Green
London EC1R 0HT

WWW.HEADOFZEUS.COM

For Cathal and Marie
who listened to my first stories with a smile

PROLOGUE

January 20, Washingbay, Lough Neagh, N. Ireland

All winter, retired Special Branch agent David Hughes waited for the sun to shear the black horizon and lift the gloom. The winds had been fierce, blowing the heavy clouds around the sky but never clearing them. Each dawn a dark tinge spread from the east, casting the hills in a murky glow, so that there was not one colorful thing for his mind to take refuge in. The fields around his farmhouse were stark and muddy, lined with the black barbed wire of thorn trees.

That afternoon he was so agitated, he could not settle in the house. The wind from the lough had turned dark again. Dark as night because it closed in and shut out the world, blundering against the stone walls of the cottage, scoring against the roof, scouring the windows, jabbing with its sharp fingers into his mind until he felt the demon shadows dance to the surface.

To calm his nerves he downed a dose of the pills his doctor had prescribed him. The tablets no longer helped him sleep, but they had the effect of postponing the present, reducing him to a numbed and haggard shadow of himself. Better that, he thought, than be prey to the tumult of voices rising from the cracks in his mind.

With grim resolution, he turned on the television and watched a

1

DIY series, followed by a chat show, and then a program about flight attendants. He flicked from station to station, drifting in and out of consciousness. Gradually he subsided back to the present, to the dull order of a winter's evening. Limping slightly, he walked into the kitchen, put on the kettle, and looked out the window.

At the bottom of the garden, he could see the figure of a man signaling wildly with his arms. He had seen him earlier, making his way along the thorn hedge that divided the garden from the farm. Now he was standing under an old oak tree in full view of the cottage, waving his arms in the air as if throwing invisible stones in anger.

David Hughes forgot about his tea and the biscuit he had placed at the side of a saucer. The sight of the stranger had distracted him. In the hall, he wrapped himself up against the howling wind. He was aware from his reflection and the evidence of his overcoat that he had lost weight. Slowly and reluctantly, he made his way outside. The roar of the wind was deafening. It made his head whirl as though he had banged it against something.

It was only when he walked right up to the stranger that he realized the man was shouting. It was the black wind drowning out everything else.

Perhaps I should be more afraid of this stranger than my illness, and the wind that has blown all winter, thought Hughes. I should leave him alone with whatever is annoying him and return to my humdrum evening and the safety of the house. Why bother a tormented man flailing his arms and shouting to himself on a winter evening?

But he felt emboldened by curiosity.

"What's troubling you?" he asked, smiling conscientiously, playing the part of a harmless, hospitable old man.

The man was still gesticulating and shouting, but the sound was smothered by the shadows flying through the air. The wind had taken hold of the branches above them, grinding them together, and the spaces between the branches were filled with the roar of the lough.

The stranger loomed close.

As he spoke, Hughes was aware of the sound of the wind and the branches vanishing, and the dim sky becoming darker. The man's face shone with a cold light.

2

"Do you think we can determine how we live and die?" he asked.

Hughes laughed, deriving a dour amusement from the stranger's question. "Only in the small details," he answered. "We all flow from chaos."

The stranger produced a small metal object from his pocket, and passed it back and forth in his hands like a toy.

"What's that?"

The stranger explained that it was a special type of battery.

"By itself it's harmless," he said. "But it's meant to power the timing device of a bomb that will kill many people. The very thought of it makes me shudder."

"I'm going to make sure I botch this one," he announced to Hughes. "It's going to be the last job I ever do for the IRA."

The stranger's face was very pale. Hughes could see the compassion in his eyes, like that of a father desperate to remove a splinter from his son's thumb.

The details of the story rang a bell. A picture from the past began to form inside Hughes's head.

"Who are you? You can't be who I think you are." Hughes's voice was suddenly aggressive.

The rising moon peeked out through the heavy clouds and then disappeared again.

"Do you hear me?" he shouted. "Who are you? I can't be talking to Oliver Jordan. He's been dead for nearly twenty years."

"I've returned," said the stranger. "I've come back with this black winter wind to sniff out my killers."

The old man stepped back shakily. There had always been something odd about Jordan's death.

"Aren't all murders odd?" the stranger asked, as if listening to his thoughts.

But there had been something particularly disturbing about Jordan's. Not only the failed police investigation, but also the years of silence from Republican paramilitaries. Who would have thought that a bad deed, buried away in the past, would be brought up by a ghost like this on a wild winter's evening?

"You've caught me off my guard," said Hughes, his voice carrying a hint of complaint. "The authorities could never explain your disappearance. What do you want of me?"

He could see the dark bands around the stranger's wrists where his captors had bound him. The picture was now fully formed in his mind. He saw a man tied with binder twine hanging upside down in a cattle shed, burn marks on the back of his hands, clumps of torn-out hair lying on the manure-decorated floor.

"Dead bodies weigh more than live ones," said the stranger.

"I know. I've been carrying the memory of yours for years."

"But you've carried it all the way to a dead end. It's time to go back."

"What do you mean?"

"I want you to go back over the investigation. Tie up all the loose ends. You're the only one left who can solve the mystery of my disappearance."

"Why have you come to me at this stage of my life? Look at me. I'm good for nothing now."

"Even you must have a soul. You must do this for your own salvation."

"But my memory is failing. I lose faces, names, dates, as easily as buttons popping off a shirt. My mind is falling apart."

"If you want to have peace, you'll find a way to remember."

The stranger handed the old man the battery, his first lead.

"Do this for me. On your own. Without the police or anyone else. They'll only hold you back."

"That's how I've always worked," said Hughes. "Alone."

He examined the battery and placed it in his pocket.

The wind rose again, and a hail of thorns flew through the air, pricking the stranger's hands and face.

"Good," he said. "I'll come back in a month's time to check on your progress."

The flow of thorns intensified, scratching the air like the noise of a scythe being sharpened. The stranger's face seemed to wilt under the deluge. He fell back and his body was suddenly swept away like a black blanket into the howling air.

1

One month later, Coney Island, Lough Neagh

"This time they plan to kill you."

Joseph Devine turned his head in the cramped bird-hide to see who had spoken, but there was no one there. His eyes were tired, and were watering in the biting wind that gusted a mile from the gray shore.

"For God's sake, hasn't scaring me been enough?" he whispered.

"Not this time. Not for them. They've waited too long."

"I never harmed anyone," he said. But that was what he always claimed.

All day he had been hiding on an island that was a haven for waterfowl but a precarious sanctuary for a frightened old spy.

Even here, the voice had followed him.

"I've given up informing," he pleaded. "I've stopped pretending to be something I'm not. Can't they see that?"

"Don't you know, Joseph?" goaded the voice. "A spy without an act is very soon no spy at all."

There was nothing more he could say.

He peeped through the binoculars at the scene he feared had been planned as the stage for his death—an empty cottage huddled within a wooded shoreline. It was still difficult for him to imagine that he was going to die now, at this stage of his life, with the Troubles over, and a cease-fire in place.

The voice had him hemmed in with guilt.

"Your conscience has finally worn you out, Joseph. It waited patiently all these years. It had an advantage over you. Time."

For most of his life Joseph Devine had been running from someone or something, the British Army, the Royal Ulster Constabulary, the IRA, strange cars in the rearview mirror, unexpected phone calls late at night, even the shadows at the bottom of the lane. Not that he would ever admit a tremor of remorse for the betrayals he had carried out during his forty-year career, but he had never stopped glancing over his shoulder, looking for the shadows he knew would always be there. When the Troubles ended, and Special Branch effectively retired him, his greatest fear was that suddenly he had eluded even the most secretive of his pursuers. What void had he tumbled into now they were gone? If no one was watching him, he knew he would never be free from himself and the voices in his head.

The plaintive call of a mallard drake cut through the air and, cupping his hands, he made a raspy guttural sound in reply, stringing four hail quacks together quickly, coaxing the anxious bird to return to the hide. He was keeping the creature close by in the hope that it would toll an alarm at the approach of an intruder. He expected even the snap of a twig end to set off a Geiger counter of quacking.

The drake heard the imitation of a hen in distress and, banking hard, turned and flew straight back. About twenty yards from the hide, it fluttered its wings and landed on the water. Devine allowed himself a brief smile at the bird's smooth return.

"That's more like it," said the voice. "Now you're covering the angles. After all, there's no better spy in the world than a wild bird. A master stroke of geometry, Mr. Devine, as Master Brannigan, old Brandy Balls himself, would have said."

With the sky coaxing the last embers of light from the western horizon, Devine lifted the binoculars again and checked the house he had hoped would be a place of rest in his old age. He scrutinized the bottom of the lane, the impassable thicket of blackthorns that bounded the untended garden, the alignment of the ragged curtains in the cottage windows, watching for a sign of the shadows he had been hiding from since he was a teenager.

A hunting gun lay by his side, the thin barrels resting against his stubbled cheek. He cursed, remembering he had not practiced shooting with his new gloves. Their thickness might change the way he held the weapon and pulled the trigger. He stretched his tired fingers, feeling the damp chill that had penetrated even the leather, and tightened his grip on the binoculars.

A straggle of crows spun away from a nearby oak tree and his close-up view of the cottage wobbled. When he refocused, the house still sat softly on the shore. But for the absence of smoke curling from the chimney, it was an image of domestic peace. The crows settled down and night leaned along the shoreline. He sighed and dropped his gaze.

"Time to rest now, Joseph," purred the voice. "It's been hard work keeping up the pretense all these years. The effort has worn you out. God knows, it's a miracle how you survived at all."

Barbs of frost rose from the freezing floorboards, sending spikes of cold through his feet and knees. He felt himself sink inward like a hibernating animal, the cold gravity of winter pulling at the core of his being. The strain of the daylong surveillance had taken its toll.

"Close your eyes and sleep, Joseph. You've found the perfect hiding place for the perfect spy."

Although he was sure his enemies were buried in their graves, their ghosts had been patrolling his dreams for years, tormenting him, coming for him at night in flurries like leaves from an immortal tree. His only relief was in playing his favorite record, the earliest present from his father, a scratched recording labeled *Dawn in the Duck-Hide*. Side one was a narrated introduction to fowl hunting, while the flip side played uninterrupted sounds of marsh creatures waking at sunrise.

A keen duck hunter all his life, the recording never ceased to enthrall him. The cries, warbles, and soft ruffling calls soothed his mind, inducing the rush of equilibrium through his veins he had once found in alcohol. It was during one such listening that a solution presented itself as to how he might finally free himself of the past.

He had been deluding himself, however. When the phone rang that morning, a convinced panic took hold of him. The familiar voice at the other end had spoken only a few words, but the call prompted his flight from the confines of the cottage. He knew then without doubt that his enemies were assembling for their final act of revenge.

The back door was stiff with frost, and he had to heave it open with his shoulder. Though his arthritic hands ached, he dragged the rowing boat along a slippery bank to the shore, his breath carving contorted shapes in the air. The sharpness of the morning strained his lungs, and welts of ice cracked beneath his boots, tearing the stillness of the shoreline.

The island. He was sure his pursuers were unaware of the refuge he had created there. He had not survived all these years without at least a vestige of his old craftiness.

The shadows began their pursuit when he was a teenager. He thought the sleek car was lost and its occupants looking for directions, pulling up alongside him as he trudged home from a football match. The driver's window rolling down to reveal a man with a gray face and gray eyes, his voice low and deep as the powerful engine of the car.

"Fancy playing for the opposition, Joseph?" he said with a smile.

His name, how had the man known that? For a second he innocently thought the driver was the manager of the neighboring parish's team.

"Who the hell are you?" he asked.

"That's not important right now, Joseph. Let's just say I'm a scholar and my special field of study is you." His cold eyes narrowed, searching the boy's face for a reaction.

"All I want is a little information about some bad boys, like who's doing what and with whom. We'll look after you, pay you well, sort you out if you get into trouble, help you if the soldiers give you hassle."

He stepped back, his trainers sinking into the roadside mud, overwhelmed with the feeling that he had become a keyhole through which a very bright light was shining.

"No thanks, mate," he said, unable to stop the panic squeezing through into his voice.

The man, whom he came to know simply as the Searcher, nodded slowly and seemed satisfied with his response.

"Fine, no harm done then," he said, rolling up the window. He gave a half-salute and drove off.

But there were more encounters on empty roads, with conversations about uncles who had been beaten up, sick relatives harassed by soldiers, and warnings that he was being followed by paramilitaries. Sometimes promises of money and fast cars were made, sometimes veiled threats uttered, and all the while the Searcher's cold eyeballs stared relentlessly into the boy's, steady as magnetic needles, pointing to the flaw, the line of weakness inside him he had not suspected was there.

In the years of subterfuge afterward, he had grown to realize one inescapable truth—that his first act of betrayal was like a fire that would never completely burn itself out. He had run through his life like a child in a dark forest, longing for an all-consuming betrayal to blaze behind him, burning everything, leaving behind only ashes, no smoke, no sparks, no burning embers, no traces, no shadows, only ashes.

The distant croak of a crow stirred him from a brief and uncomfortable sleep. He listened intently to its pattern. *Caw-aw, caw-aw, caw-aw.* Even though the call was half drowned in the evening fog, he recognized it as the crow's signal that all was safe.

He smiled at the thought of relying on a crow to keep his darkest terrors at bay. On a hunting expedition, he would have thought nothing of blasting it out of the sky.

It was roosting time now, and all along the shore, waterfowl were swarming back to their nests, their calls bubbling up into the gathering night. Closing his eyes, he assembled the roosting calls in his mind, mapping out their locations on the island. In the dark of the hide, his sense of place was delicately rooted by this shifting web of birdcalls, and as he listened to their noises and the twilight ruffling of their wings, he was slowly lulled back to sleep.

A distressed croak from the mallard woke him with a start. The sound filled him with concern, the quack resembling a death cry, a wet gouging sound throttled from the bird's throat. He climbed out of the hide and waded toward the source of the quacking, but the sound had abruptly ceased, swallowed up in the darkness of the freezing night.

Another distressed quack sounded in the undergrowth. This time in the clear air, he heard the crack in the call. A wrong note. A human note. The person imitating the call was an expert but his ears were no longer deceived.

A movement snatched the focus of his eyes and he knew then that a path leading to death had opened up. The reeds moved and he sensed the shadows hasten toward him. Plunging through the marsh to the duck-hide, he caught sight of another shape looming before him. As he wheeled around, he heard a noise that sounded like laughter.

The voice he had heard that morning on the phone spoke in the darkness. It had changed subtly, deformed after all these years with contempt or illness. He tried to pinpoint its location, a black orifice amid the silently moving shadows, directing them toward their prey.

He had not realized his pursuers would be that many. Their number filled him with dread. What if they all wanted retribution, to have him divided up and subjected to their individual versions of hell? How many deaths could a man endure?

He surrendered his last hope when a heavy object struck him across the face and his mouth filled with blood. Another strike sank his left eye into his skull like a nail.

His remaining eye gaped around as the shadows tore at his clothing and rained down blow upon blow, stripping him to his bare skin. And then an executioner's silence as they paused for breath. Holding his naked sides, he tried to roll away, his body doubling up with pain.

"You murderous bastard," said the familiar voice close to his blinking eye, a cold smile drawn across his lips like a visor.

"I never killed Jordan, if that's what you believe," he pleaded.

"But you were in cahoots with those who did," the voice countered, thick with saliva, ready to gobble up the cold dish that was being served.

"I just wanted to help his family. Make amends for what happened."

Too hurt to move he tried to beg for mercy.

"I give up, I give up," he whispered, more in the form of a promise to himself.

But the shadows did not give up until it was almost dawn. Pounding and hacking at his body as if they had been fasting for years from violence to enjoy this feast.

When they had finished their job and left the island, a flock of crows gathered around the victim. As the dawn's stain seeped through the sky, the crows began their scolding, their cries obliterating the usual morning chorus, screaming and condemning the grisly sight before them. But there was no audience left to hear them. A thin rain began to fall, coming down like a curtain over the informer and the island that was a haven for waterfowl.

2

They had told the new police recruit a lot of his time would be spent in the company of drunken people. When he answered the urgent call on Saturday night, he was beginning to realize this was an absurd understatement. The officer had just finished his first tour of the pubs of Armagh City with a colleague. He was feeling irritable, unused to the clamor at closing time, the staggering drunks gaping through the windows of the patrol car, their exaggerated shouting and laughing penetrating the reinforced glass. He could not escape the observation that the throng of young people cavorting down the street was like a poisoned organism celebrating its own death throes.

He had been revolted by the sight of bodily fluids ejected in alleyways and against walls—the bubbling mess of nighttime intoxication washing down the streets of the ecclesiastical city. Sitting in the passenger seat, he had felt like a diver trapped in an underwater cage, flinching at the grinning under-faces of sharks reeling by.

"There's nothing stopping them from partying now," the older officer had remarked.

Northern Ireland's rural towns were no longer mute, inhibited little corners of sobriety and sectarianism. To his colleague, however, the liberated nighttime scenes were a strong endorsement of the curative powers of a little terror. Say what you like about the paramilitaries and trigger-happy troops, they knew how to keep the rabble in their place.

In the quiet of the control room, the new recruit listened to the stricken caller and assumed it was a case of a drunken relative not arriving home. He suspected the caller herself might be intoxicated too. He almost had to hold the phone away from his ear to grasp what she was saying. He fumbled for a notepad. Behind the high-pitched words, he detected a sinewy note of control in the woman's voice, as though her usual self-command had been overwhelmed by a wave of turmoil. The officer took the details and checked the whereabouts of the patrol car.

Then he donned a bulletproof vest and stepped outside into the protective shadow of the watchtower, where he lit a cigarette. The female desk sergeant he would normally have chatted and flirted with at this hour was unfortunately off duty. Dealing with the boredom of the long wait till dawn was a professional technique the young officer had yet to master.

He stubbed the cigarette out and came to a decision. Inspector Celcius Daly always reminded the night-shift officers to phone him if anything unusual occurred, especially at the weekend. By this, he meant to exclude the long tail of alcohol-related crimes. The request, usually delivered with Daly's stray, fatigued eyes sweeping upward as if in prayer, had the effect of motivating the officer to handle alone whatever problems arose. On this occasion, however, the new recruit decided to press ahead and risk Daly's irritation.

Celcius Daly had sat up late drinking whiskey by a turf fire in his father's cottage. The turf belonged to a moldy batch his father had cut the previous summer. The old man had probably handled each piece five times before bringing them home and still they were wet. The damp smoke had filled the room and triggered a coughing fit. Daly had wrapped himself in a duffel coat and made his way out to the open porch, where the air was sharp and clean but cold.

He saw the moon rise and combine with the frost to form a silvery rime on the ridge of potato drills his eighty-two-year-old father had watched over until the week of his death. He refilled his glass and returned to stare at the broken ridges shining in the moonlight like the rib cage of a hungry beast. In his intoxicated state, he must have found the moonlit tableau diverting. It was well after three a.m. before he stumbled to bed.

The phone jarred him from his sleep. His stomach leaped, and he cursed involuntarily. He had just slipped into a remarkable dream—a series of lottery balls swiveling into view, their numbers shining with the luminosity of a premonition. He had watched them drop into place: 49, 11, 21, 7...

On awakening, the first thing he did was write the numbers down on the back of an old photo he found in the drawer of the bedside locker. Unfortunately, the phone had interrupted the winning sequence. He tried to guess the remaining two but the feeling of certainty dimmed. He rubbed his eyes, and the random numbers faded into that elemental pointlessness that permeates everything in the small hours of the night. He realized it was the middle of the night, and he was alone in bed.

Even though it was six months since he had separated from his wife, the loneliness he felt on awakening on nights like these still surprised him. The clock's dim face was the only light in the room—3:50, it read. The bars had long closed and most revelers would have made their way home by now, he thought. A domestic row had ended badly or a drunken street brawl had spilled over into something more violent. Either way, he could expect a dawn of gastric terror. At least he had not slept long enough to feel the jagged impact of a hangover.

He climbed out of bed and listened to the receiver.

"Hello, what is it?"

"I hope I haven't disturbed you, sir," said the voice.

"No, not at all," he replied with a sigh, staring again at the numbers he had scribbled down. For a brief second, he felt cheated. What had it cost him over the years to answer such calls in the night? He thought ruefully of his wife and their impending divorce, and it struck him that a happy marriage was worth more than several fortunes.

"Something unusual has come up."

"Anyone dead?"

"No, no one at all. An old woman rang from Washing Bay. Someone broke into her home by forcing the back door."

"A burglary?"

"No. Some clothes and medication were missing but that wasn't why she was ringing."

"She wants us to help her fill out the insurance form?" asked Daly, a note of irritation creeping into his voice. Why had the recruit bothered him with a botched burglary?

"She was on the verge of being hysterical. I tried to calm her down. She claimed the burglars kidnapped her elderly brother. A man called David Hughes."

Daly paused. "What? Did they leave a ransom note?"

"She didn't say. But she sounded terrified. Her brother is sick. He has Alzheimer's. I didn't know what else to do."

"Any chance he just wandered off while going to the toilet?" asked Daly with exasperation. Unfortunately, they didn't teach police officers common sense at training college.

"She claimed he couldn't have got out on his own."

"OK. Tell your colleagues to wait for me outside the cottage. We'll form a search party. Who knows? Maybe the old man has fallen asleep somewhere. Let's hope he hasn't gone too far."

Daly pulled on some clothes. His mouth was dry and he felt the beginnings of a headache. He had overdone it with the whiskey, he realized as he searched for his rolled-up socks. A glance at the murky reflection in the window was all he wished to see of his appearance.

His father's cottage sat on the southern shore of Lough Neagh. During the winter, the landscape resembled a mini-tundra, filled with migrating arctic geese. The moon had disappeared while he had slept, and he peered blankly through the small window.

The lough was at its darkest and fullest on these early February mornings. The fields and bog land that ran down to the shore were dark too, impossible to read without the guidance of hedges and lanes, and slashed with bog holes deep enough to sink a man right up to the waist. It was a patchwork of life and death that had to be negotiated carefully, even by the young and healthy. At least the weather had been dry, he thought. He hoped the rivers would hold this winter. Only six months earlier, a rainstorm had flooded the lough shore countryside and stranded him at his father's wake. The Blackwater River had burst its banks and swamped the lane to the cottage. The parish church, which lay half a mile away, was cut off completely, rising out of the water on a little island of green.

It was a long wake, even by Irish standards. Through the tiny windows of an upstairs bedroom, the mourners watched the low sky soak up the gloom. When it stopped raining, a strange quietness fell across everything. It wasn't until the following morning when the sun burst through the clouds that the waters receded.

The relief felt by the trapped mourners was palpable as the hearse took off down a lane lined with glinting green holly. Daly accompanied his relatives and former neighbors in the snaking cortege. The wet road in front of the hearse shone like the brightest place on earth. Someone cracked a joke about his father's old car, which had floated out of the yard and ended up in a ruined haystack. Daly remembered how his dad used to rev the guts out of its engine before setting off every morning to Mass.

He forced his feet into a pair of Wellington boots and climbed into his car. At four a.m., the winter darkness beyond the windscreen was all-embracing, a dead-end in the night. He drove along the lough shore until he reached the Bannfoot and then turned left for the motorway. He glanced in his rearview mirror. Not a car in sight. At the roundabout, he turned the heating down and tried to find a weather report on the radio. A husky-voiced DJ was speaking in Irish and playing tracks of Motown music from the 1960s. Fugitive memories of dancing at parish discos scurried along the fringes of his consciousness.

He rolled the window down a fraction to clear his head, and headed west. The old man must have wandered off and fallen into a ditch, he thought. It was probably a journey he had made countless times in the past—an easy scramble over the familiar folds of his fields during daylight, and in full control of his faculties.

He passed a carload of youths. A boy leaned out of the passenger window and made obscene signals at the detective. He was obviously drunk. Daly overtook the car and tried to focus on the task at hand. It would be a small search party, unless they were able to call upon neighbors. He had organized many search parties during his twenty-year career and knew it was common for the missing person's body to be pulled out of a river or lake several days into the search. He hoped they weren't too late, or that at least the protective cloak of senility had prevented the old man from experiencing too much terror.

Daly was surprised by the farmhouse's remote location. If his relatives had lived there, he would have moved them at the first sign of illness into a neighboring village. His headlights lit up a grass-covered lane that didn't look as though it had been used too often. A foot-and-mouth sign saying essential visitors only flashed its warning at them. He drove on; the last outbreak had happened more than three years previously.

3

Daly swept his car into a yard at the back of the farmhouse. An attempt had been made to cordon off the small fields, but the restless winds and the trampling of hungry animals had opened up gaps in the fencing. In places, the ground had turned into a muddy quagmire.

It wasn't difficult to read the signs of infirmity in the untidiness of the yard filled with rusting machinery, the embrace of brambles and weeds throughout the garden, and the fields half lost to thickets of blackthorn. Paint was peeling from the walls and a few tiles had fallen from the roof. It was the same loss of interest and descent into chaos that marked his father's cottage. The lough-shore countryside was full of decomposing houses like these, tucked away amid the gloom of thorn and elder hedges.

A mushroomy smell vied with the oversweet scent of rotten damsons as Daly climbed out of his car. He was confronted by a gaunt woman in her sixties, wearing a voluminous dressing robe. Even in the dark with the wind blowing Eliza Hughes's gray hair across her face, the fear could still be seen shining in her eyes. At first Daly thought she might be deranged, but when she started speaking, her voice was sharp and clear.

"I've checked the outhouses and the fields. There's no sign anywhere. It's no use, he's long gone."

She brought Daly into the house and, flourishing a key, unlocked the door into the missing man's bedroom. It reminded Daly more of an interrogation room than a bedroom, with its bare walls devoid of photos or decoration, the tiny window and the bright shadeless bulb hanging from the middle of the ceiling. In the center of the room was a bed with security bars and a pressure mat laid out on the floor. On a small dressing table, a candle had burned out with a pile of paper ashes stuffed around the wick. Something about the candle struck him as odd, but he could not quite place what it was.

"What happened?" he asked.

"I put David to bed at the usual time, raised the bars, and switched on the pressure mat. It should have triggered an alarm if he slid out."

"And it was switched on?"

She nodded.

"Your brother is an ill man?" asked Daly surveying the room.

"He has dementia. Some days he doesn't even remember where he is and confuses me with our mother. I've asked for more help but you know what social services are like. Anyway, David would never have coped with life in a nursing home."

Daly checked the back door and saw that it had been splintered with a crowbar. It was reasonable to conclude that burglars had indeed entered the property. He took Eliza by the arm and sat her at the kitchen table.

"It appears that your house has been burgled, Miss Hughes. Have you checked your valuables?"

"There's nothing of any worth here. All they took was his medication and clothing," she replied.

"There is also the possibility that your brother woke up in a confused state and simply walked out after the burglars, whoever they were," suggested Daly.

She got up and busied herself making tea. "They've taken him away. They've been watching us for weeks."

"Who?"

"I have no idea. But there was a storm one night last week. A cow broke loose and went on the rampage, tearing up the back garden and knocking over pots. I chased it back up the field and phoned its owner."

She handed Daly a weak cup of tea.

"While I was up there I found a hole had been cut in the hedge. There were cigarette stubs and footprints in the ground. Ever since then I've felt there was someone out in the dark who shouldn't be there."

"Do you have anything of value in the house?"

"Nothing beyond what's sentimental. My brother spent his life going to church, tending his farm, and hunting ducks in the winter. He treated his fields as God's allotment. Work was its own reward."

Daly nodded but thought of all the bachelor farmers who had died leaving a small fortune squirreled away in their mattresses.

"If your brother was taken away against his will, surely he would have made some noise or struggle?"

She looked at him blankly. "Unless he was unconscious."

"Can you think of anyone who might want to do something like this to an old man?"

"No. David kept on good terms with everyone. Before he took ill."

Daly surveyed the sparse bedroom again. Old age had few comforts or pleasant surprises. Perhaps the old man was terrified of illness and death and had done a bunk. Daly thought of all the times he wouldn't have minded dropping out of his own life, at least for a while.

He left Eliza in the kitchen and walked out into the darkness. In the low huddle of outhouses, the beam of his torch picked out rusty chunks of machinery, an overturned rowing boat and farming bric-a-brac. A basket of seed potatoes emptied itself of a colony of mice, and the sinister black eyes of what was probably a rat gleamed at him from the shadows. The smell of turpentine lingered in the air. He found nothing that would help in the search for the missing man.

In the yard, he bumped into Officers Harland and Robertson, who had been checking the fields around the house.

"Nothing to report so far, sir," said Harland.

"Phone the neighbors and let them know that David Hughes is missing," said Daly. "Ask if they've seen or heard anything. And get them to check their outhouses. It's a cold night. If he's out there, he's bound to seek shelter somewhere."

Daly thought that if they didn't find him in the next hour, he would have to bring in tracker dogs and a helicopter to sweep the countryside. Using his torch, he examined the thorn hedge bordering the back garden. His alert eye discovered a gap in the thick branches where the wind blew through unconstrained. He spotted where the branches had been neatly sawn off, the pattern of rings still clear. The gap gave an interrupted line of sight to the cottage's kitchen door.

When he returned to the farmhouse, Eliza Hughes's silhouette was framed in the kitchen window, unmoving. Daly felt spurred to a greater urgency and strode off with his flashlight across the undulating farmland, his feet slipping and sliding into icy mud holes. The moon came out, and its light streaming through the trees was so blue and cold Daly could almost taste it in the air.

His ankle twisted in a hidden ditch, propelling him face first into a blackthorn hedge. He ducked to avoid a jagged branch, and for a second he caught the glint of something in the light of his torch. A pattern of frozen water drops fell from the higher branches and something white briefly hung in front of him before disappearing. He listened intently to a fluttering sound in the swaying trees. Something was caught among the branches. Whatever it was, there was no hint of the old man or his presumed captors. He felt like a dog hunting a scent that had grown cold.

He heaved himself further into the thicket of thorns, and grunted in surprise when he uncovered a secret hollow. What looked like a pair of clown's hands, yellow and enlarged, waved at him. He leaned back in shock, fumbling for his torch. In the beam of its light, he saw that someone had propped a pair of Marigold gloves on a set of twigs. For the first time since arriving at the farmhouse, he felt unnerved. Collecting his wits, he examined the rest of the hedge, finding further objects suspended from branches—an alarm clock, an old battery, bags of nails and wire. His torch scanned the ground and lit up a row of faintly discernible mounds. He knelt down and propped his flashlight against a stone. He wondered, Could they really be what he thought they were? Then he saw the crude crosses at the top of each mound with lettering etched in them. A set of names and dates had been inscribed: OLIVER JORDAN d. 1989, BRIAN AND ALICE MCKEARNEY d. 1984, PATRICK O'DOWD, d. 1985.

The mounds were small, more like a child's attempt at a play cemetery than a proper memorial. He dug at each of them with his bare hands, unearthing nothing but rotting leaves and mud. He felt a curtain shift momentarily, revealing the sinister tableau of a troubled mind. Looking up he saw old newspaper cuttings spiked on thorns, like prayers to a pagan god. Most were shredded by the wind and wet through. He pulled one down. It was an old clipping of a news report about an unexploded bomb. Another clipping described an explosion that had killed a six-year-old girl and a nun.

A surge of adrenaline rushed in his veins. He felt as though he'd accidentally pressed the Up button and ascended the lift shaft into the deranged galley of Hughes's mind. One thing he was sure of, the old man's thoughts had wandered farther than the simple circuit of his fields and orchards.

Back at the farmhouse, he handed Eliza the Marigold gloves.

"I take it these are yours. They were part of some kind of memorial garden in the hedge, complete with makeshift crosses and graves."

She sat down heavily. "Oh dear, David and his demented games."

A look of exasperation filled her eyes. "Inspector Daly, dementia has turned my brother's mind into an amusement park with its own ghost train. It's not just a case of forgetting things and getting lost. The illness makes him perform these bizarre rituals, like hanging up old bits of newspaper in the hedges. He keeps talking about the past, and says he can see ghosts. In the last few weeks, he's started to make crosses out of anything he can get his hands on. Ribbon, sticks, flowers, rope. I try to tidy them up before visitors arrive, but I can't keep track of all his movements. Then there's the messages he writes. Horrible things I can't describe. Filled with curses and threats."

Daly decided to push no further. The woman was clearly in a nightmarish predicament. The sole witness to the twilight of her brother's disorganized mind. He rubbed his eyes and got up to go.

"We'll do our best to find your brother, Ms. Hughes," he promised. Eliza watched him go in silence, gathering her cardigan around her shoulders.

Outside it was still dark and the branches of the thorn trees pawed in the wind. He could see the tracks of light that signaled his officers' searches in fields sloping down to the hidden shore. In a few

22

hours, it would be dawn. If they didn't find Hughes soon, he might die of hypothermia. God only knew what was running through the old man's mind.

The mobile in Daly's pocket rang as he walked back to his car. He hit Answer, not recognizing the number.

"Where's your black suit, Celcius?" asked a familiar voice.

"Anna," he said, dropping into the driver's seat in surprise. "Where are you?"

"In your house. I found the spare key under a cracked paving stone. I've searched your wardrobe and a chest of drawers."

"What are you doing there?"

"My sister's father-in-law died on Thursday, and the funeral is in Dublin this morning. I wanted you to come with me, but it's too late now. I couldn't find your mourning suit anywhere."

"It's at the dry-cleaners."

"I've been thinking of you, Celcius. I wanted you to know that. I have to go now."

"I'm working on a case. Can't you wait an hour?"

The tenderness in her voice was replaced by a familiar heaviness. "No. I have to leave right now. My sister is waiting for me. You're always working on a case."

"Wait. Can you do me one favor?"

"What?" She sighed.

Daly pressed the phone closer to his ear, desperate to prolong the conversation. His breathing grew panicky and dry, as though he were trapped in a cavity of thinning air.

"Can you get me a lottery ticket?" he said just before she disconnected the call. "I have a feeling these might be our lucky numbers—49, 11, 21, 7. You can pick the last two yourself."

There was a pause as she scribbled them down.

When she spoke, the tenderness had returned to her voice. "Is this the new romantic Daly?" she asked.

"What do you mean?"

"The numbers—they're our first date backwards. Seven p.m. on November 12, 1994. I didn't think you remembered." She paused. "I'll call you if they come up. Bye, Celcius."

When Daly returned to his father's cottage, he was greeted by a dawn burdened with the premonition of rain and a hangover. The sun found a gap in the clouds and streaked across the low-lying bog land and hedgerows. He almost felt his way to the front door, taking in razor-sharp details, the bright stone walls, a windowpane burning with the morning light, the whiskey glass sitting in the shadow of the porch, pale with frost.

He sensed her presence within the house immediately. She had spent time tidying the living room, folding away clothes, removing unwashed cups and plates, piling newspapers and CDs into a rack.

He felt a twinge of jealousy that she had devoted time to rearranging the objects of the room rather than waiting for him or continuing their phone conversation. Rather than say a proper good-bye, she had left him this tidy room filled with her perfume and an eerie silence. The memory of her voice rasped against the edges of his hangover. Perhaps he ought to have ignored the call from the police station, stayed among the clutter, and waited for her to appear.

Daly had phoned Anna many times during the first months of their separation, when she was living with her parents in Glasgow. He had been tormented by the thought she was seeing another man. "There's no one else to blame for this but ourselves," she kept telling him. But he had struggled to believe her, convinced by his detective's logic that an unknown culprit had destroyed their romance. In many ways, it had been an irrational response, based on self-delusion and paranoia.

During the first months, he kept expecting the arrival of divorce papers, but none came. He put their house in Glasgow up for rent and applied for a transfer to Northern Ireland. He had hoped for a post in Belfast, but to his surprise was sent to Armagh, where he had grown up. At the time, it had made sense to move into his father's abandoned cottage.

In another phone conversation, he asked her what she wanted from him. She replied he had to prove that he had a world outside his detective's life. Living in Glasgow, amid the churn of promotion and paperwork, he came to the grim realization that the request was impossible to grant. She might as well have asked him to prove the existence of a fourth dimension. Now he suspected he might be capable of fracturing time itself, without hesitation, to preserve what he had found with her.

He went into the kitchen and opened something from a tin. He was too tired to read the label, but it smelled like something Anna would have fed her cat. After a few mouthfuls he got up, leaving a fork sticking in the tin, and dragged himself off to bed.

4

The nameless voice at the other end of the phone spoke briefly before replacing the receiver. Father Jack Fee listened to the blunt facts stripped of any semblance of tragedy and slowly put down the phone. It was five a.m. and he was sitting in his cold study. He had served in a border parish as a curate during the Troubles, and knew what the messenger was referring to. He understood the authority in the caller's voice, even though the message was inconclusive, and might even have been an elaborate prank. It was very sad and, more than sad, disturbing. He walked over to his desk and wrote down the message. It was his priestly duty to follow the instructions, though it was a responsibility they had never prepared him for in the seminary.

In a tree on Coney Island the body has been left for you.

It sounded like a clue in a gruesome game of treasure hunt, he thought. By the time he had dressed, washed, and collected his prayer book and oils, it was dawn. He opened the front door and walked outside. The morning smelled of damp moss. A few specks of rain fell from the low clouds that dragged across the sky. Clouds move with such a silent, enviable sense of purpose, he thought.

A cataract had left the priest almost blind in one eye. It meant he was no longer fit to drive and had to rely instead on one of his parishioners for lifts. On this occasion, however, he decided to spare his regular driver the ordeal. Praying to Saint Christopher, he drove his ten-year-old Renault out onto country roads crusted with potholes, toward the ring of town lands known as the Munchies.

In all, he had administered last rites to six murdered men. The phone calls had directed him to where their bodies lay in deep ditches or lonely forests, binder twine tied around their hands and fertilizer bags placed over their heads. The men had been branded informers, very much an endangered tribe during the Troubles.

During the bad years, he had imagined his parish not so much a sanctuary for a God-fearing flock but as a no-man's-land between two armies, an arena for IRA ambushes and British Army patrols. The normal standards of right and wrong did not apply to his parishioners, only what was necessary or unnecessary for survival.

He drove through a forest of dense birches and came out at the town land of Derryinver with its expansive view of Lough Neagh. He swung the old car through a series of bends that the locals claimed would knock the devil out of a heretic, and, with gears grinding, passed by Maghery Church. The vague outlines of the Sperrin Mountains were visible in the distance, capped with snow. He sped along as the road rolled through a landscape that was a sniper's puzzle of thick thorn hedges and slanting fields.

It was fitting that this would be one of his last missions before retirement. The entire forty-eight years of his vocation had been a sad trajectory through the purgatories of this accursed province. Perhaps when he looked back from his deathbed, he might come to realize that the Troubles had saved his ministry, especially toward the end, the confessed crimes of his parishioners winding around his soul like a nest of snakes. It had been easy to distinguish good from evil, and prevent, or at least delay, his own slide into spiritual indolence.

Pulling into Maghery Park the car skidded slightly on an untreated patch of ice. A fisherman, pulling in his boat at the nearby pier, looked up and waved at him. Disguising his unease, Father Fee got out and asked after the man's mother, who had been seriously ill.

It had been a long, dark winter with too many heavy skies. However, at the lough shore, the sheen of light filled his eyes, making his cataract weep. The bright swell of water lapped against the fisherman's boat, casting arcs of light over his shadowy form.

The priest asked the fisherman to ferry him across to Coney Island. Then he sank heavily onto the wooden seat, knocking the holy oils and water bottle in his pocket. He was glad the sun was shining as they rowed out. The fisherman's oars dipped just deep enough to catch scoops that were more sunlight than water, the brightness momentarily dispelling any dreaded thoughts of what was to come. For a while, it was enough to watch the fisherman as he rowed, and with whom he felt solidarity. Fishers of men, fishers of lost souls, he thought to himself. He exchanged a few words about the weather, determined not to make the mistake of communicating the reason for his trip, or the anxiety he felt.

He was used to finding the bodies of informers left discreetly in half-sheltered places, clogged with weeds and briars, the corpse facedown and hidden from view. It had been difficult to locate the monstrosity in those humdrum scenes, his eyes eased by the sight of blossoming flowers and birds flashing through the hedgerows. When he stepped onto the island, he quickly found that this occasion was different. The person who had dumped the corpse had a showman's talent for the macabre. The corpse was propped grotesquely in the hollow of a tree, the head and shoulders slumped with a look of haggard exhaustion in the grizzled face. Immediately he recognized the body as one of his elderly parishioners, and a regular Mass-goer at that. He had not seen him for weeks, which had been unusual.

The priest shook his head sadly. Another piece of human flotsam washed up from the great shipwreck of violence they called the Troubles. Although the bombings had stopped more than a decade ago, it was still an unpleasantly recurring fact that his priestly life was hemmed in by sectarianism and murder.

Often, when he looked down from the altar at his small congregation, Father Fee thought of his parishioners' fears and hopes, their homes and families, the little crosses they carried on their backs and in their hearts. Since the cease-fire, many paramilitaries had gone to ground along the lough shore—entire families of them, in fact. Some of them forged new careers in politics, others took to alcohol, and a few found God. The religious ones were the men whose minds were mangled by what they had seen and done. Through the sacrament of confession he extended God's forgiveness to them, and in doing so, in their unstable state, he became someone to whom they had to prove themselves constantly. They were his lost flock of sheep, turning up faithfully at all the weekday Masses, giving large donations to the collections, even offering to send him on holidays to Rome and the Holy Land. At funerals, they placed their rough hands on his shoulder and whispered, "Well done, Father."

During the Stations of the Cross, he could see them gathered behind his shoulder, reflected in the glass-covered paintings of Christ's ordeal on Calvary.

His cataract smarted as he watched them from the altar.

He saw the cold-eyed blackmailer sitting behind the mother with a young child, and in the back pews, beside the elderly couple with all their sons in America, the murderer who had no heart.

Their terrible crimes echoed constantly in his mind.

And then there had been Joseph Devine.

Father Fee had been drawn by something like tenderness to his pensive face, tilted upward to the statue of the crucifix. An old man struggling with his conscience. All his effort narrowed down to a final battle with the voices in his head.

His mind went back to Devine's last confession. It had been an unusual exchange between a confessor and a penitent. Devine had begun by describing his inability to feel joy at the christening of a friend's granddaughter.

"I didn't feel anything, Father," he had whispered. "It was an effort just to smile. I couldn't even bring myself to hold the baby in my arms."

Father Fee had paused, unable to supply a comforting response. Although they were separated by the metal grille, Devine's face felt very close. On his breath, he smelled the stale whiff of alcohol.

"Is what I am afraid of true?" Devine asked him.

"What are you afraid of?"

"That I'll never be at peace with myself."

The question worried Father Fee. He rubbed his bad eye before answering.

"Why wouldn't you be at peace? God is full of forgiveness. All you have to do is make a full confession in the presence of the Lord."

"I do that every month, Father."

Father Fee paused again.

"You're not telling me the truth," he chided. "You haven't come here today to talk about a christening. There's something else troubling you. I don't know what it is. Perhaps you are too ashamed to say. I don't know. The only one who knows is you. And God."

He waited for the words to sink in.

"Nothing else troubles my conscience, Father," replied Devine, a note of defiance creeping into his voice.

"Then why are you here?"

And then the words that Father Fee was expecting came. It was gratifying to discover that shame still had power. Of course, it depended on the community you sprung from, how important its opinion was to you. Informers in this part of the world were regarded as the lowest of the low. Father Fee had heard it said that if you raped your next-door neighbor it would soon be forgotten, but if your grandfather was an informer you would be an outcast all your life.

In the semidarkness of the booth, the priest felt Devine's eyes fix on him.

"I thought I could leave my past deeds behind me, but the voices won't go away. I was a spy for the British security forces. I did it for the money. Men were killed because of the information I supplied."

Father Fee absorbed the revelation. He sighed in preparation for what was to come.

"How often did this happen?"

"Too often to remember."

"And did you feel any remorse for your actions."

"At the start, yes, I felt guilty. My conscience rebuked me. But after that, the sense of shame went. You see, the men I helped kill were violent and dangerous. None of them were innocent."

A moment of tiredness overcame the priest. He felt as though he were trying to force his way out of a bad dream.

Devine waited patiently for the priest's absolution, but instead Father Fee closed his eyes. His parishioners' hunger for absolution felt like something bottomless he had to feed forever. The priest's mouth was dry, and his head throbbed. He did not feel able to continue with the usual words of the sacrament. Light trickled under the door. He looked at his hands and was surprised to see they were shaking. Perhaps this ought to be my last confession, he thought. Tomorrow I will ring the diocesan secretary and ask to be allowed to retire.

At last he spoke. "Usually for penance, I would suggest prayer, but in your case, I will make an exception. You have come here seeking some form of redemption, but forgiveness is not that easy. Before I can absolve you from your sins, you have to make amends for what you did."

He had then outlined the unusual task he had in mind for Devine's penance.

"After you have done this, you may return to this booth and I will continue with the holy sacrament of confession," he told him.

He blessed Devine and closed the metal grille. The confession was over. He could hear Devine splutter and struggle to say something like a puzzled child running out of questions to ask.

Afterward he felt a strange exhilaration. After years of dutiful obedience, of deferment to the will of God, he saw this digression from the rite of confession as a form of emancipation. He no longer had to make things better for men who had murdered or assisted in murder.

Standing over Devine's dead body, the priest reasoned to himself that everything had happened as was destined. True, he had not envisaged that Devine would end up being murdered, but he saw the workings of some kind of mysterious, possibly even divine justice that enabled him to be the first to find his body. Now he could give Devine last rites and complete the act of confession.

The priest knelt down and, gingerly placing his hand on the man's forehead, uttered the words he had said so many times before.

"May God Almighty have mercy upon thee, forgive thee thy sins, and bring thee to everlasting life."

The prayer took just a few seconds. Afterward he turned to rest his eyes on an ancient hydrangea shrub, covered in sodden masses of last year's flowers. The branches were bowed with the weight, unable to cope with the abundance of dead blooms. He wondered why nature did not just allow the shrub to scatter its huge flowers when they faded, and lighten its load. He felt a great need for some sign of spring, a fresh snowdrop petal or a leaf bud unsticking itself, but the shrub was as useless to him as all the years of baggage inside his head.

His eye with the cataract filled with water, and then his good eye began to smart in sympathy with the bad eye. Devine's body swam into vision like a thorn that could not be extracted.

5

The fisherman advised Celcius Daly to sit back and enjoy the view as they pulled away from the rickety jetty. The shoreline became wilder as they rowed out, clearing the inlet to head north into the great gap of water called Lough Neagh. Soon Daly could see the outline of Coney Island, and as the boat drew closer he made out the burnt stump of a large oak tree struck by lightning. A group of men and women, some wearing forensic suits, were foraging their way through twists of blackened wood. As the fisherman steered the boat past a bed of reeds, a tern flew at them with increasingly fretful pipings.

The sleek, sculpted fiberglass of the police launch, the only boat the force had in service, took up most of the tiny landing jetty. Daly managed to jump ashore without breaking a leg, glad to be reacquainted with surefootedness.

"As a rule, corpses don't make any sound," warned the pathologist, Ruari Butler, as he sauntered over to greet the detective. "But I'm afraid this one's a little unusual in that regard."

He took Daly on a tour of the murder scene with an exaggerated propriety, as though he were a guide at a National Trust property. Daly fumbled as he stepped over the tape, stumbling in the big man's wake.

At first glance, everything looked aboveboard to Daly's eyes. The body of a barefoot, elderly man sat propped within the scorched stump of a tree, his face untroubled, the mouth slightly open and the tongue sticking out, like a creature trying to escape the death of its host. The smell of rotting sloe berries flavored the air, and bluebottles droned above the corpse like a deep snore. No outward sign of evil, he remarked, the death a tragic accident that had happened to an old man who might have normally walked this way barefoot and rested in the hollow of a tree every morning.

But on closer inspection it was evident that parts of the corpse had been set alight, making it difficult to distinguish between human sinew and burnt wood. The victim's blackened limbs, shriveled after the fire, were entwined with charred branches as though his body had twisted itself around the remains of a burnt deformed twin. An examination of the head revealed multiple bruises and patches of sticky blood. The back of the scalp was a mangled flap of gristle.

Around the corpse, hardworking, competent professionals waltzed about, snapping photographs, mopping hairs and microscopic pieces of evidence from the undergrowth, collecting and cataloguing a brutal segment of the past that they would eventually waltz off with to fill the shelves of a police laboratory.

Butler was talking to him, but Daly could barely follow the words as he took in the scene before him. Some detectives sucked up the details of gruesome murder like efficient vacuum cleaners, but Daly was not one of them. Butler noticed his discomfort. To help him regain his composure the pathologist turned to the view of the Armagh shoreline and began listing the distant town lands, Clonmakate, Columbkille, Maghery, Derrylileagh, as if for his own amusement.

The tremor of squeamishness that passed through Daly's gut was nothing to his sense of professional rivalry when it came to dealing with the macabre, and he felt a twinge of annoyance at Butler's tactful distraction.

"How long has the body been here?" he asked, turning toward the pathologist's composed profile.

"Fortunately, the victim has been found before serious decomposition could set in or the local wildlife have had their wicked way with him."

"You're telling me it could not have worked out better for him?" Daly's voice was stony.

"To a degree. A wildlife preserve is not a good place for a murdered body."

"Where is a good place?"

Butler stepped gingerly around the lumps of wood, unperturbed by either Daly or the corpse, his features concentrating on the process of thought and deduction. Death simplified things, like mathematics. Working out how it happened meant seeing things clearly and being objective; dropping the veils of sentimentality.

"At least he got a priest's blessing," remarked Daly.

"Kindly performed by a Father Jack Fee from Maghery. Do you know him?"

"No, no. I'm not a regular Mass-goer. But I will look him up."

"He says the dead man was Joseph Devine, a devout parishioner. Mr. Devine had no next of kin, apparently. The wallet in his jacket held a driving license and a few bank cards."

The ripples of wash from a passing motorboat splashed urgently against the jetty. The two men watched the boat frisk the island's rocky shoreline and then disappear from view.

"The victim was killed by brute force and a series of blows to his skull," Butler continued. "His limbs were also set alight, possibly as a means of torture. The sap in the tree acted as a form of fuel. We'll never be able to supply you with an exact time, but roughly speaking he's been dead for no more than twenty-four hours."

Butler prodded the victim's chest with a pair of forceps. There was a wheeze and then a series of sounds caught in the corpse's throat. A reedy, birdlike gurgle. It was one of the strangest noises Daly had ever heard. High-pitched, savage, inhuman.

He glanced at Butler with an almost pleading look. "What the hell was that?"

"You don't recognize it?"

Butler pushed the corpse's mouth ajar. He had already given the throat a meticulous examination. Using the pair of forceps, he whisked out a small metallic object with a practiced motion and held it up to Daly.

"A duck whistle. Wedged above the voice box."

Some of the tension eased from the detective's face.

"From the trauma in the area it looks as though it was forced in while the victim was still alive."

"Gives a new meaning to croaking it."

Butler ignored the remark. He paused for a moment, using a measure of his theatrical talent to regain the stage. "The way the body has been left in plain sight in such a dramatic fashion and the fact that a priest was informed of its location suggests the involvement of paramilitaries."

"We've no evidence to substantiate that yet," grunted Daly.

"Either way, the media will swarm all over this one."

Daly shrugged. "Perhaps the attention will bring forth some leads."

"Here's one for you. His death meant a lot to his murderers."

"How come?"

"Burnt and tortured and then beaten to death, a duck caller lodged in his throat. In my experience, not a common way for a victim to be dispatched. A bullet to the head is much simpler and more efficient."

Daly grumbled. "So our prime suspects are a group of paramilitaries with macabre imaginations and an interest in duck hunting."

Butler bared his teeth in a half grin. He went back to working on the corpse while Daly set off to explore the rest of the island, glad to escape the sight of that sinister tree stump. He ought to have remained and given the crime-scene technicians a hand, but he needed to clear his head. Besides, Butler was in charge and would ensure no stone was left unturned.

Back at the shoreline, he took a deep breath of the lough air and watched the cloud shadows shuffle across the water. Farther south, he could see the purple-gray gloom of the Mourne Mountains retreating into the horizon along with the disappearing winter light.

Coney Island was a wild, weird place, visited only by fishermen waiting out a storm or adventurous bird-watchers. It had been used as a place of refuge by the O'Neill chieftains during the Elizabethan wars, and was named after a witch who was supposed to have been a spy for the British queen. The story went that she had poisoned Red Hugh O'Neill while administering aid to a battle wound. A witch, a murderer, and a spy, thought Daly. Mrs. Coney made Mata Hari sound like a Girl Guide.

He followed the shoreline and began to plan the investigation, setting out the different stages. After examining the crime scene, they would start questioning people who lived or worked near the lough. They would try to work out how the dead man came to be on the island, how the killers got there and made their escape. Had anyone noticed anything strange? Any unusual boats or vehicles in the vicinity? The lough shore had two tightly knit communities, one of Protestants, the other of Catholics, both sides wrapped fiercely in a web of mutual suspicion. Anything odd within the visible rim of the horizon would have been noted by someone.

He reached a shingle beach of perfectly rounded boulders and, picking his way over them, idly wondered if he could manhandle a few of them into the fisherman's boat. They would help decorate his father's ruined garden. A seagull dove into the water and resurfaced with a wriggling eel. The lough was teeming with life, and murder, too, he thought. The civilized land across the lough might just be a figment of his imagination.

Northern Ireland was no longer a bad place, he reassured himself. Bad food, maybe, and some bad people, but the peace process was beginning to undo a lot of the harm of the past forty years.

The shingle beach gave way to a deep bed of reeds, which reached out into the distorting mirror of the lough, and he shivered. The murder had been an unusually cruel one, and he feared the investigation might be long and difficult. The killers had taken risks, secure in the knowledge they would not be disturbed on this uninhabited island. Had they lured their victim here to this water-haunted island or arranged a rendezvous?

He noticed a track of broken reeds and freshly disturbed mud leading into the reed bed. As he approached, a flock of ducks clattered from their nesting positions. They were swift, elusive creatures, their bodies adapted for the quick getaway. He stopped for a moment, mesmerised by their shaking ripples and reflections. The easiest way to retrieve order from chaos, he realised, was to wait for stillness to settle.

In the heart of the reed bed, he came across a bird hide. It was a lot less drafty and more sophisticated than the ones he remembered as a boy. Inside it, he found a pair of binoculars. Bird hides were really human hides, he thought, designed to conceal the idiotic behavior of ornithologists and duck hunters. The binoculars were surprisingly powerful, not the antiquated set he was expecting. Through them, he scanned the shoreline, a twisted bank of roots and rocks hovering above an exact reflection of itself. He didn't have a pad or a pencil to record the creatures in his sights, but then a spot of bird-watching wasn't on his to-do list. His gaze rested on a rundown cottage, half hidden in the trees, the back door slightly ajar. Other than the dwelling there appeared to be no signs of human life along the shore.

Daly blinked. The memory of the dead man's face was so barbed he could see its outline transposed onto the shadowy trees and their watery doubles. He put the binoculars down. He wasn't even sure what he should be looking for. He might as well have been scanning a fairy-tale picture-show for the traces of an evil monster.

He stepped out of the hide and followed the path back through the reeds. A bedraggled, bloodstained object caught his eye. He pushed it with his boot, thinking it was a dead bird. But instead it was the first clue that might identify the attackers. He lifted what looked to be a bloody diving glove and dropped it into a forensic bag. Perhaps the wearer had removed it for a better grip. The attack had been meticulously planned and laborious to implement, he realized. He wondered how long it had taken for the victim to die.

By the time the fisherman returned Daly to the mainland it was late afternoon and lights were beginning to twinkle in the cottages. A cloud of midges greeted them as they stepped ashore. The fisherman told him they weren't as bad as the summer variety. These ones had only one set of teeth.

6

A throng of white-suited scene-of-crime officers was pressing through gaps in the blackthorn hedge as Daly drove up the lane to the remote cottage. He exchanged almost invisible nods of recognition with the uniformed men who lined the driveway, and caught a glimpse of Det. Derek Irwin giving a rusted wheelbarrow a bored kick.

The cottage belonged to Joseph Devine, and Irwin had been marshaling the SOC officers since seven that morning.

"I thought you'd left us in the lurch," Irwin greeted Daly. He had not visited the murder scene, so its shadows were absent from his lively features. In fact, a ripe tantrum was about to burst inside him.

"This is great. I thought you were in a hurry to get started this morning. After your phone call I left without getting a bite of breakfast."

In the glare of his petulance, Daly's profile was a lump of blunt granite. He barely spared Irwin's outburst the space of an eye blink.

"No need to panic," he said. "Devine's murderers haven't just slipped out the back door with minutes to spare. No crime in real life is ever that easy."

Irwin scowled and brandished his mobile phone, which had started ringing. "Social call," he declared, tilting his long curly head, and then with the tiredness and irritability vanishing from his voice: "Poppy, hi. Hey, hope I didn't wake you getting in last night. It took ages to get a taxi." His voice sank to a hoarse whisper. "Can I come over tonight? You'll break my heart if you say no." He walked a short distance away, greedily gathering the phone to his mouth.

Irwin, who was at least ten years younger, represented the youth Daly fervently hoped he had left behind. The regular texts he received and his hushed mobile calls suggested an unruly love life. Daly liked his eagerness and the intense pitch at which he appeared to be living, even if most of his working week was caught up with routine investigations into criminal damage and house burglaries. However, there was a clumsy lack of caution about Irwin's detective work and Daly feared that on some days his mind strayed from the scenery of the crime to inhabit romantic plots of his own making.

Irwin returned, snapping his mobile shut.

"You look like crap," he said appraising Daly's face. "All those lonely weekends are making you as irritable as a monk. That's your problem you know, you don't get out enough."

Daly's separation was common knowledge amongst his colleagues. It was hard to hide that kind of thing in the police force. Only the sorted and settled rushed home on a Friday night with smiles on their faces. He nodded at Irwin's comments as though they had provided a crumb of comfort.

"There's no such thing as fidelity anymore," Irwin continued, winking. "Everyone's either just getting on or off the relationship bus. All of us are single, the married ones just a little less so."

Daly turned away, feeling the discomfort of his marital status encumber him like a broken wing. The breakdown of his relationship with Anna had made her the focus of overwhelming emotions, just as she had been at the start of their courtship. He hoped these were transitional feelings before he adapted to the easy, glamorous life of bachelorhood that Irwin aimed to personify.

However, watching the younger detective saunter up the drive, his hand rolling through his thick hair as he half-garbled, half-sang the words of some pop song, Daly wondered what indignities he would have to suffer along the way.

A young police officer with a nervous expression on his face lifted the tape aside to allow them into the cottage. Daly felt the same way about entering the house of a murder victim as some people feel about breaking into a church. Something to do with disrupting the sense of solitude and peace contained within four walls designed to hold the violent world at bay.

"Devine must have stepped on someone's corns, someone well connected with a paramilitary outfit," said Irwin, his enthusiasm returning. "Who do you think it was? The real IRA, the continuity IRA, the INLA, or the truly, madly, deeply IRA?"

"Republican paramilitaries aren't the only pack of dogs about," replied Daly. "But I guess that's where the smart money lies."

There were no signs of forced entry or a struggle at the front door, or in the cottage's cramped rooms. Devine had left so suddenly he hadn't bothered closing the back door behind him. Perhaps he had wanted to give himself a running start. The phone was off the hook, and in the scullery kitchen a pot of congealed porridge sat on the hob.

"Every house tells its own story," said Daly.

Irwin stuck his finger into the porridge and tasted it. "This one must be 'Goldilocks and the Three Bears.'"

The two detectives walked into a living room with an interior design that could have been delivered complete from the 1950s: On a long shelf, an ancient radio propped up a religious calendar and a dirty bottle of Knock holy water, nostalgic souvenirs of Catholic Ireland. On a table, a portrait of the former pope was winning the equal-rights war with a dusty statue of the Virgin Mary. Even the swathe of sunshine cutting across the room from the tiny window seemed to be frozen in time. Daly noted the picture of the pope was free of dust.

He picked up the statue of Mary and blew off a cobweb. Her eyes were hollow, and her features more harrowed than those of the icons he remembered, as if the Virgin had been having too many sleepless nights. Perhaps it was his imagination. Or maybe it was the effect of all those lost souls keeping vigil and mindlessly chanting their devotions a hundred times a day and night.

Devine had been no better than most at bachelor housekeeping. In the kitchen, empty bottles of stout spilled out of a box under a dirty table. While in the spare room, the sagging cushions of a battered sofa were covered in an old blanket, and another chair was upholstered in cracked black leather. The floor surface throughout the cottage was linoleum patterned with green tiles but the effect was marred by too many years of hard wear.

The only element that did not give the impression of a life in transit was the collection of ducks filling a Welsh dresser and the deep windowsill in the kitchen. Daly did not breathe, believing, at first, they might be real. They were carved from wood and looked to be hand-painted. As he moved closer, the room shone with the sporadic glitter of their glass-beaded eyes.

"Duck decoys," remarked Daly. "People who live alone can allow themselves eccentric interests."

"They look like antiques. I bet they're worth a few quid," said Irwin, casually handling one. He almost dropped it in surprise when the head nodded up and down in imitation of a feeding bird.

"At least they help explain why a duck whistle was lodged in his throat."

"How come?"

"A moment of inspiration from his murderers. Warped, but at least it fits in with Devine's personality. They must have known about his interest in duck hunting."

Daly recalled that the missing man, Hughes, also had a passion for duck hunting. He saw a theme developing.

"Perverse," said Irwin with distaste. "And there was me thinking Republican paramilitaries had all taken up flower arranging and human-rights campaigning."

A doorbell rang and they both turned in unison.

Irwin walked off and returned a little later, scowling.

"No one there. One of the men must have nothing better to do than play pranks."

The house had been dusted for fingerprints, every door handle, glass, drawer, and windowpane. Unusually, only one set of fingerprints had been found. Daly had already surmised that Devine had been the reclusive type.

"According to his nearest neighbor, Devine moved to this hovel at the start of last year," said Irwin.

"Why do you think he did that?"

For an answer, Irwin opened the back door. A gust of wind blew a swirling nest of old leaves and dried sycamore keys across the threshold. Daly stepped out to a secluded view of Lough Neagh and its labyrinth of tree-lined coves. He could see but not identify a number of headlands stretching away into wind-tossed oblivion. It was the ultimate poacher's perch, hidden from sight, untouched by the life of roads, fields, or villages. The short walk to the shore, bounded by deep thorn bushes, was like a stroll to the edge of humanity. A line of geese honked overhead, their long necks urgently outstretched. Daly followed their flight and let his gaze wander to the horizon, as this was where nature's signposts were pointing. He allowed himself a moment of introspection before turning back into the cottage.

The sound of the doorbell buzzing broke the solemn air again.

Irwin's face was flat and hard as he made his way back down the corridor. This time he was gone for longer.

"I don't know what type of jokers the force is employing these days," he said on his return. "They're all denying it was them."

"It's not the doorbell," said Daly, pacing through the rooms, listening carefully. He looked into the dark hallway and into the silent living room. There was no movement from the holy statue or the picture of the pope, or among the glittering decoy ducks in the kitchen. He watched the dust fall through a ray of sunlight. A thin, fine layer of ancient dust suspended in the air.

The cottage buzzed again, discreet but insistent, calling their attention. "I know you're there. Why don't you answer me?" it seemed to be saying. The hairs on Daly's neck stood on end.

"Do you believe in ghosts?" asked Irwin from behind.

"There are nights when I don't even believe in myself," replied Daly. "However, there must be a rational explanation for this. Perhaps Devine has some sort of alarm that keeps being tripped."

He checked the phone and put it back on the receiver. The line was dead.

They walked up a narrow set of stairs to an attic bedroom. There was a sheaf of papers on a chest of drawers. It consisted of bills and brochures on duck decoys and other hunting paraphernalia. The two of them went through the drawers, searching in the pockets of trousers and shirts. At the bottom of one of the drawers was an envelope, already opened. Daly took out a photograph and a handwritten invitation card. It was for a duck-hunting club reunion that had taken place a year previously. *After lunch and music there will be a lecture given by our president, David Hughes*, it said. The photograph showed a group of old men posing in front of a duck hide with a collection of dead ducks. Daly, who had already examined Devine's passport and driving license, spotted the deceased in the front row of the photo, his unsmiling face, wary and sad, like that of a man kneeling at his own grave.

Daly had just time enough to register that the postmark on the envelope was local when the buzzing sounded from downstairs again, as though something deep inside the walls of the cottage was vibrating.

"It's coming every ten minutes," he said.

Daly opened the hot press and tapped the water pipes. In the kitchen, he checked the small refrigerator and the immersion heater, both switched off. He positioned himself in the living room and waited. Irwin paced restlessly about the house, twitching at imaginary sounds. The house seemed to fret too, creaking and shifting on its foundations.

On the stroke of ten minutes, the picture of the pope began to vibrate, and another ripple of dust formed on the shelf. The buzzing was louder this time—remonstrating, urgent. Daly lifted the picture frame. Wedged behind it was a round black device, vibrating as it moved along the shelf. Daly scooped it up before it scuttled back into darkness. It was a pager, the ring tone switched off. Daly pressed Receive and a message flashed up: EYES ON TARGET A TO C3 HEDGE FROM BLD 1. TALKING TO POSS UKM. METAL OBJECT IN HAND. It had been sent two days previously, but never answered.

Irwin looked at the message and gave Daly a searching glance. "Whose eyes are they talking about?"

"A duck hunter's? I don't know."

Irwin squinted his eyes in concentration, making his face look like a schoolboy's. "Perhaps the target was Devine. If that's the case, the eyes got their man."

Daly searched through the pager's memory. There was a series of further messages, equally cryptic. Two had arrived in the past week and were written in a kind of code—one that had been carefully devised. They ostensibly referred to the movements of one man around a building, probably his home. EYES ON TARGET A FROM C4 STATIC AT GABLE END, and then A CARRYING PAPERS TO C3 HEDGE. UNSIGHTED. REAPPEARS STATIC AT C2. THEN BACK TO BLD 1.

Daly wondered why they had been sent. To caress Devine's sense of paranoia, or warn him he was being watched? He stared through the small window at the fringe of trees bounding the garden, their leafless branches swaying together in the wind. He thought of Eliza Hughes and her wandering brother, shadowy movements in the night and of a pair of eyes that never seemed to rest in this mysterious landscape.

Before they left the cottage, an expensive-looking Mercedes swung into the drive and an elderly man, small and silver-haired, slipped out of the driver's seat. He had the air of comfort and complacency that accompanies the rich like the smell of cigar smoke and the swish of golf clubs.

"Inspector Daly," he announced, "once again we are victims of circumstance. It's rarely a good morning when our paths cross."

The driver was the solicitor Malachy O'Hare, a big shot in the local legal field.

"What are you doing here?" asked Daly.

"Curiosity. I wanted to see where Joseph had holed himself up." The solicitor's voice, musical and rich, was more accustomed these days to buying rounds of drinks than saving the hides of criminals. He also appeared to be out of touch with police procedure.

"This is a crime scene, Mr. O'Hare." Daly pointed to the yellow tape. "That's as far as you can go."

"One of your officers called me this morning. Joseph was an ex-employee, a legal clerk who worked forty years for the firm." O'Hare's eyes were playful and engaging. "We suspect he may have had some belongings of ours." His tone was light but insistent.

"Well, that's exactly the kind of information I'm interested in," said Daly with a sudden professional smile. "What kind of belongings?"

"Oh, just a few folders belonging to some old cases. Nothing legally active, but we have the confidentiality of our clients to worry about."

"Follow me," said Daly. "While we're walking you can tell me what you remember about Mr. Devine."

"What can I say apart from the fact that he was a good legal clerk? He never revealed much about his private life."

"But you believe he removed some important files."

O'Hare wiped his expensive-looking shoes on the threadbare doormat before entering the cottage. "Let's say some concerns had been raised."

Even in the gloom of the cottage, Daly could see a distracted look cloud the solicitor's eyes. He waited patiently, hoping the rhythm of their exchange would reveal why the solicitor had taken the unusual step of rushing to a crime scene.

O'Hare frowned and surveyed the collection of duck decoys. He raised an eyebrow at them as though they were a jury hovering on a verdict.

"It's extraordinary what a colleague can conceal over the years. I never knew he had an interest in ducks. Perhaps he did have an obsessive streak. It's not nice to speak ill of the dead, but I always thought he was a dull, venal man."

"We're not here to judge his personality," replied Daly.

O'Hare glanced up at the detective, scanning his face, looking for what might be hidden between his words.

"Devine was employed as a paralegal almost as long as I've been a solicitor," he continued, with the unhurried meticulousness of a prosecutor laying out the case against the accused. "And believe me, he was a dull man. Those decoys haven't budged a muscle since we came in, but there was more life in any one of them than in that man, God rest his soul. I'd have rather shaved my head than get caught in a conversation with him. He was like a true bogeyman about the office. But then a tedious nature is probably a strength in the legal profession. No one with an aversion to boredom ever survived working in law."

"Can you think of anyone who might have wanted him killed? A disgruntled client, perhaps."

"Our firm is almost exclusively concerned with the ordinary affairs of humanity: contracts, conveyance, leaving a will…. I can't see a client getting sufficiently enraged to kill Joseph. Though there was an occasion when he served a writ at a funeral. The coffin containing the man's father was being lowered when Joseph handed him the papers. I don't think he was aware of the emotional ramifications. But that was a long time ago, back in the '70s. Apart from that, I can't think of any reason that would drive someone to kill him."

O'Hare gave in to his curiosity and lifted one of the decoys.

"We should get an expert in to value these," he said, but he was no longer looking at the ducks. Instead, his eyes roved hungrily around the room.

"Perhaps I should send a man 'round for a few hours to go through Joseph's belongings. Some of these decoys are antiques and collector's items. His estate needs drawn up. You can lock our man in; even search him when he comes out. Just an hour or two is all he'll need to document anything of value."

"And have him rummage through possible evidence? You should know better than to suggest that."

"Yes, yes, of course, you're right."

O'Hare glanced again at Daly and took measure of the solid air of suspicion that was forming between them. He tried to change tack.

"Have you formally identified the body as Joseph's?" He leaned toward Daly, groping for a more cordial footing to their conversation.

"If not, then you're trespassing in the home of a missing man, and we have two crimes to solve instead of one. You think it was impossible that he was killed in such a way?"

"It does strike me as strange."

"What I find strange is that when a police officer calls you this morning you drop everything and hightail it out here. That's strange. Devine was a minor staff member who left your office a good while ago."

"Oh dear," sighed O'Hare. "Everything about this setup—the surroundings, the decrepit state of the place—strikes me as highly unusual. I can't imagine why he came here in the first place."

"Anyone who moves to a place like this is trying to escape something. Traffic jams, the rat race, boredom, the past," suggested Daly. "It wasn't just for the long rainy afternoons and the occasional sunset."

O'Hare's face turned grave. "I fear we are in for a few unpleasant surprises. You must tell me if any sensitive documents turn up. This could be very bad for the firm's reputation." A crude grimace distorted his mouth, and he whispered, almost to himself, "the past is an overflowing shit-pot of trouble and Devine has stirred it all up with a big stick."

"This man's murder is the only unpleasant surprise I care about. We'll be working hard to catch his killers. If anything comes up, we'll let you know."

O'Hare took a final anxious glance about the living room. Devine's death had tightened a coil of fear around him. His nervousness reminded Daly that, as a solicitor working during the Troubles, O'Hare had probably carried a gun in self-defense. They were violent times, and solicitors were the least likely group of people to attract new friends.

"You don't look well," said Daly.

O'Hare kneaded his arm. "High blood pressure. The doctor says I should spend more time on the golf course. If it wasn't for Devine ringing me on Thursday I'd be there now."

"That would explain your anxiety," said Daly. "What did he ring you for?"

"It was a strange conversation." O'Hare's face was pale and grim as he spoke. "He said he wanted to talk, but not on the phone. When I asked where, all he said was 'You'll see.' He said he wanted some information about an old case. He also admitted to removing some important files. But he wouldn't be drawn any further. I tried to chat to him about general things, the weather, his health, where he was living. He told me he had found a wonderful location on the lough. 'A good place to die,' were his words. I began to suspect his mind was losing its footing."

Just then, a shout from Irwin drew their attention outside. Some of the officers had found the remains of a fire at the bottom of the garden. The solicitor followed Daly out.

Amid the fine gray ashes was a box of partially burnt papers. O'Hare recognized the box and began beaming like the sun. His self-confidence returned and he reached for the charred files with a sense of triumph.

"Hang on. Nothing can be removed from the fire," warned Daly. "Not even by our officers. We have to follow our procedures."

"Why?"

"There's building waste among the ashes. We can't rule out that it's asbestos. The burnt fibers are harmful if released in the air. No one can touch the ashes until a team with protective gear arrives. And at this moment I have no idea how long that will take."

"These files might be a ticking time bomb, who knows what confidential information they might contain," said O'Hare, his voice rising.

"Lung cancer is a horrible disease. I've never seen anyone die of it myself, but I hear the sufferer finally drowns in a froth of blood and phlegm."

O'Hare raised a voluminous handkerchief from his pocket and placed it over his mouth. For a moment, he and the detective stared at the ticking time bomb. A look of frustration burned within the solicitor's eyes before his charming equilibrium restored itself.

"Very well, Inspector. Thank you for your assistance. I would like to be notified when the contents of the fire are examined. Those files are still the property of the firm."

When O'Hare had left, Daly returned to the fire. The solicitor's instinct for survival had proved a solid enough foundation on which to base a minor deception, he thought to himself as he sifted through the ashes and retrieved the file. One misled solicitor would hardly upset the scales of justice.

7

Oliver Jordan. The name still meant nothing to Celcius Daly, but it was the only one he could decipher as he scanned the scorched legal notes. It was written several times in a pedantic hand so minute as to be practically illegible, added almost as a footnote to what appeared to be police custody notes. It was the same name inscribed on one of the crosses in Hughes's makeshift cemetery. The only other detail that jumped out at him was the date of the notes, taken between August and November 1989.

He decided the file would have to wait for a more detailed examination. It was early afternoon, and he was late for a meeting with a local politician. He placed the papers into an evidence bag along with Devine's pager and tossed them onto his passenger seat. He told Irwin he was leaving and drove back to the station.

He had yet to drink his first coffee of the day, and he craved its cerebral buzz. Concerned that he might nod off to sleep, he rolled the window down a chink. The drip-drop of birdsong from the tree-lined shore threaded into the car. The forest was alive with the bubbling sounds of blackbirds and thrushes.

Daly was on his way to meet Owen Sweeney, a Republican politician. He had known Owen as a boy, given him lifts to school on the back of his bike while he did his morning paper round, in fact, but their paths had diverged many years ago. Sweeney had rung him in a fury over the helicopter search for David Hughes. The helicopter was equipped with a PA loud-hailer system. At one point, on Sunday afternoon, it had hovered over a crowd returning from a GAA match, requesting them to assist in the search for the missing man. A panic had ensued because the football fans thought a dangerous maniac was on the loose. Sweeney claimed the helicopter pilot had targeted the fans on purpose, to harass them on their way home.

The press will have a field day on this one, he had warned Daly. The detective imagined the headline: ALZHEIMER'S PATIENT IN PAJAMAS AND SLIPPERS TERRORIZES GANG OF FOOTBALL FANS. Daly loathed the melodrama and political blackmail that accompanied community liaison work in post-cease-fire Northern Ireland.

At a bridge, he passed a mud-spattered transit van, which appeared to have broken down. He slowed and observed the driver—a skinny, pasty-faced youth standing at the side of the vehicle with a mobile phone pressed to his ear.

The van had a flat tire, and even though he was in a hurry, Daly braked and pulled up with his warning lights flashing. He had a feeling that something else was wrong.

As soon as the youth saw Daly, he sprinted off, disappearing up a lane overgrown with brambles and bushes. The back door of the abandoned van lay open. Approaching it, Daly sniffed the heady, acrid bouquet of diesel. He peered inside at its illicit cargo: a double row of fuel containers, half covered in oily blankets. He had happened upon a botched fuel smuggling run.

Daly had been involved in a few deadly games of high-speed cat-and-mouse with such vehicles as they flashed down the M1 motorway and disappeared up country lanes. The drivers were always young men who ten years ago would have happily toiled on a tractor all day in a muddy field. Now they could earn thousands of pounds for the dash from the border to the ferries at Larne, or to loyalist paramilitary gangs in Belfast. Smuggling, as old as the border itself, was breaking a range of political boundaries. Agricultural diesel, originally from the Irish

Republic, was smuggled across the border by former IRA men, treated in secret sheds, and then driven to loyalist heartlands in the city. For sworn enemies pounds had become more important than politics or the pope. There was no religion on a ten-pound note, after all.

But it wasn't just illegal. It was highly dangerous. The back of a van was an unsafe place to store thousands of liters of combustible fuel. Daly felt the bonnet of the vehicle to see if it was still warm. The engine was cold. As a makeshift fuel tanker, the van was a ticking bomb.

His eyes caught the flash of the youth's tracksuit, slowing down as he found cover amid the shrubbery. Afterward Daly realized this was the point when he should have let the youth escape and radio in for help. He had a van full of evidence, and an important meeting to get to. Instead, he took off in pursuit. Not out of fearlessness but because the person who was running away from him was still only a flash of tracksuit, a shadow flying away, a page torn from a book he had yet to read.

About a hundred yards up the lane the youth stopped, apparently convinced the middle-aged passerby would not give chase. When Daly saw him at the end of a tunnel of leaves, his face was as expressionless as a sheet of ice. The only thing that moved was the vapor of his breath trailing into the shadows. Then the boy darted off again, his gait quicker, more fluid, his body weaving around sprawling shrubs, jumping over crumbling walls, disappearing into whorls of leafy shadow. Daly lumbered behind, crashing through the outstretched branches.

The lane ran roughly parallel to the main road and a gleaming line of new bungalows. It burrowed through overarching thorn trees and alders, twisting by the oddly angled walls of dilapidated cottages and outhouses. Nobody knocked down buildings in this part of the country. They just built bigger ones, deposing the previous generation's homes to overgrown lanes such as these. The Armagh countryside was becoming a maze of dark, forgotten little lanes, as dark and crooked as the past.

The shrubbery thickened, reducing Daly's visibility to a few yards. He stood still, listening to the rain ping on leaves and the branches swaying in the wind. Up ahead he saw a patch of the youth's shiny tracksuit hanging motionlessly as though snagged on a branch. Had he stopped to let the detective catch sight of him again? Daly felt an equal measure of fear and curiosity as he approached. He wondered whether the youth felt the same. After all, they were two of the most primitive emotions, shared by all species, even criminals and policemen.

He shouted out, "I'm a police officer. I want you to come back with me to the van."

Through the undergrowth, he caught a better view of the youth's face. Thin and white, with a wet fringe of hair. The apparition of a truant schoolboy. His face looked empty of fear, empty of curiosity. In the Republican strongholds of Armagh, they taught children from an early age not to show any emotion to enforcers of the law. Daly could sense the boy was not ready to cooperate with him. Fuel smugglers were like border Republicanism itself. Self-reliant and cunning, but too easily seduced by the powerful forces of money and politics.

Any hope Daly might have had for a successful arrest was ended by the metallic rip of a quad bike blasting along the lane toward them. The youth gave Daly a cheeky wave before hopping onto the back of the bike. Then the driver fishtailed the machine and accelerated toward Daly. A wooden stick appeared in the passenger's hand and hung low as the bike careened past. Daly felt a blow to his knees and fell to the ground as if shot.

"Up the hoods!" shouted the boy with the stick raised in the air. The length of wood disappeared from view, along with the bike, but Daly had seen enough to recognize it was a hurley stick. It ought to have been a comfort that the youth was into Gaelic sport rather than guns or knives. Although the stick might not be classified as an offensive weapon, the young man had wielded it with the precision of a marksman.

By the time Daly made it back to the broken-down van, it was raining heavily. He was soaked through and hobbling. He examined the back of the vehicle as a lorry passed, its headlights sweeping over him. In the flood of light, he saw that the containers were empty. Slowly he closed the doors. Why had the boy run off when there was no contraband to incriminate him? He got his answer when he saw the smashed glass of his own passenger window. He looked for the bag containing the legal files and the pager but it was gone. The wet black hull of another lorry thundered by, wipers lashing in the heavy downpour. Daly felt its cold wind pass through him as if he weren't there.

It was getting dark. Too late to ring Sweeney and apologize for missing the appointment. The day was almost over and two important pieces of evidence had been stolen from him in what appeared to have been a planned ambush. He had accomplished more as a boy on his morning paper round.

8

Daly worried that, as the winter drew on, he and the office walls were beginning to share the same coloring—a dull matte gray. He suspected neither his face nor the walls flattered each other very much. The light of the frosty morning came in through the windows of the police station but did little to relieve the gloom inside or out.

His last holiday had been a weekend break to Paris in spring. It was also the last time he and Anna had gotten drunk together. The last time they had enjoyed each other's company. Pity all he remembered now was the expensively priced champagne and wine, and a view of the Eiffel Tower drowning in the rain-spattered window of a taxi. He supposed it had been romance of a sort.

He surreptitiously eased his shoes off under the table. Leaning back in his chair, he thought of Devine working in a busy solicitor's office, sitting bent and sun-starved, surrounded by legal papers, day in, day out, for more than forty years. An office that probably looked very like Daly's own room. Four walls filled with a grayness that fought its way into every living cell of the body. Had Devine ever wondered if he was missing out on life? If so, his killers had robbed him of any chance of making up for lost time.

The murder barely made sense to Daly. It contradicted the dull order of the legal profession and threw Devine's whole life out of focus. Perhaps there had been something in the half-burnt files that provided a link to his horrific death. If so, why had it taken so long to come to light?

Solicitors, like priests and doctors, were bound by an oath of confidentiality. It dawned on Daly that Devine had been privy to a horde of secrets. Maybe in his retirement, an act of recollection had floated up some detail from an old case. He had been unable to speak out at the time, but things had changed when he left the firm. Secrets had that effect as the years passed, mused Daly; they rose up with a force that could capsize lives.

After a while, he slipped on his shoes and got to his feet. It was too soon to draw conclusions but he felt he was on the right track. He went out to the coffee room where Irwin and Harland were trying to persuade a female officer to share her bag of crisps.

A look, smooth as steel, slid across Irwin's charming face when he saw Daly. He got up and made four cups of black coffee. Everyone at the station was used to taking it that way, since the milk in the fridge was usually well past its sell-by date.

"I'm not disturbing you?" asked Daly, glancing at the retreating figure of the young female officer. Deep down, he wondered if he were alive at all.

"No. And so what even if you were?" replied Irwin.

The detective told Daly he'd been unable to get through to Father Jack Fee. "The day after he found Devine's body he left on some sort of a retreat," he said. "Apparently, he'll be gone for several weeks."

"What's a retreat?" asked Harland.

"They're like second honeymoons for Catholic clergymen," explained Irwin, winking at Daly. "Reinvigorates them when they get bored with the pope and all that Roman diktat. The priests go off somewhere nice and peaceful to spend a little quality time with God."

Daly smiled thinly. "What's that funny smell, like pears?" he asked.

"Perfume," replied Irwin. "Not mine, I might add."

"Of course."

Irwin handed him a mug of black coffee and yawned.

Daly sipped at the mug and eyed the younger detective over the rim.

"Anything come through on the broken-down van?" asked Irwin.

"It was stolen from a house at Mullenakill yesterday afternoon. The owner said two masked men broke into the house and demanded the keys."

"You think they knew what was in your car?"

Daly shrugged. "Too early to say. If it was an ambush, they were quick off the mark."

"Maybe it was just a coincidence."

Daly's raised eyebrow suggested he was a man who did not believe in coincidences.

They moved on to discussing Devine's career at the solicitors', and what links it might have with his murder.

"You still think a former client murdered Devine?" asked Irwin.

"Not necessarily. But we need access to all the cases he was involved in to rule out the possibility. All we can do at this stage is scrape away the layers of paint to find what's hidden beneath."

Irwin put down his coffee. "It won't be easy extracting that kind of information from O'Hare's firm."

Daly almost missed the question mark left hanging by the comment.

"What do you mean?"

"You don't remember the senior partner, Brian Cavanagh? He died of a heart attack a few years ago. But back in the '80s, he was a self-styled human-rights lawyer with an interesting client list. Let's just say he wasn't the type to spend his spare time rehearsing the Queen's Oath."

An image went off in Daly's mind like a flashgun. A shiny-eyed, shrewd firebrand of a solicitor reading an angry statement outside a courthouse. A series of high-profile cases involving IRA men had brought Brian Cavanagh media notoriety. To his critics, the solicitor's interest in human rights extended only as far as the Republican prisoners he represented.

In fact, within the security forces, there were unfounded rumors that he provided a constant stream of messages between prisoners and the IRA leadership. As a Catholic, Daly tended to believe the unofficial version: that Cavanagh, like many solicitors working for Republican clients, wasn't politically motivated, his only interest was getting at the truth. Either way, the missing file began to take on a more menacing significance.

"There's something Mr. O'Hare's not letting us in on," said Daly.

"He seemed preoccupied at Devine's cottage."

"Any connection between Devine's death and his firm will arouse a lot of public interest. We'll let him sweat it out for now. See if the press comes up with anything interesting."

"By the way, Butler has sent a preliminary report on the forensics. He left you this."

He handed Daly a brief handwritten note that began with Butler's characteristically sardonic humor: *Cleaning up is always the hardest thing to do after a party. However, Devine's murderers were professionals. So far we haven't found a scrap of DNA that doesn't belong to the victim.*

Five minutes later Daly was sitting in his car, the engine running.

The case had to be linked to terrorism and Northern Ireland's bloody past. He had suspected it the moment he saw the body on the island. The lack of a prime suspect in Devine's life helped confirm his instinct. He released the clutch, and soon he was driving by the empty orchards on the road out of town, wondering what grim forces the legal clerk had entangled himself in.

A fine drizzle began to fall, and in the grayness, the low, arching branches of the apple trees took on the solemnity of a great funeral procession. This part of the Armagh countryside had earned itself the nickname of the Murder Triangle during the height of the Troubles, a series of tit-for-tat killings devastating both the Protestant and Catholic communities. The roads he was driving through had to be some of the most ghost-run in the country.

He pulled the car to a stop at a narrow crossroads. A ribbonlike stream of water twisted and turned its way down the road from the summit of a hill. He was of two minds. When another car drew up behind him and flashed its headlights, he decided to follow the lead that had first caught his attention inside Devine's cottage.

It took him half an hour to find his way back to the farmhouse where David Hughes had gone missing. In daylight, the farmyard looked more desolate. The wind sniffed at a fence of broken wire. Rainwater filled a line of empty post holes, and an ancient tractor with a rusted seat stood in a lane of mud. The farm seemed to have sunken into a forlorn state of waiting.

However, in the garden, a full washing line flapped in the cold breeze, suggesting that Eliza Hughes was not the type of woman to neglect her household routine. This time the door was locked with a series of bolts. Eliza spoke to him first from behind a pane of frosted glass. Her eyes were wide with fear when she pulled open the door.

"I'm sorry," she said. "I don't like opening the door to strangers."

"We've no news of your brother, yet," said Daly hurriedly. "I just have a few questions to ask you, that's all. It won't take much of your time."

She put away a scrubbing brush and bucket, and led Daly down a corridor lined with miniature gilt picture frames of hunting scenes. They stepped into a kitchen where a dishwasher and washing machine were busy twins of suds and noise. An oppressive cleanliness reigned throughout, in spite of the emotional upheaval the woman had endured.

"I used to tell David every day that everything was fine because I didn't want him to worry," said Eliza, her words sounding dull and hopeless. "Now I have to keep telling myself the same. Things aren't fine, though. I'm falling to pieces behind a wall that I built brick by brick around David and myself."

Daly felt a note of sympathy with her sense of abandonment. In a way, it mirrored his predicament with Anna: not knowing the whereabouts or motivation of a loved one.

He nodded and suggested she should accept any help that was available. Then he groaned inwardly at the clumsy way he was expressing himself.

"Are there any family members that can stay with you?"

Her breath caught as she said no.

Daly took out the photograph of the duck hunters and the lecture invite, and showed them to Eliza. Her fingers shook slightly as she looked at them.

"This was before David took ill. I thought he would have continued into healthy old age long after any of the others."

She pondered the group of faces. "A dwindling band of brothers," was all that she remarked.

"Do you recognize Joseph Devine?"

"Yes, I do. Bottom left." Her face went blank. "I read in the paper he was found dead on Coney Island. Is that why you've come here?"

"Unfortunately, yes. I have to ask these questions whenever a murder has been committed." Daly paused. "How well did David know Mr. Devine?"

There was an awkward silence. A crow began to scrabble on the roof, its caws echoing down the chimney. It was clear to Daly that he ought to have delayed visiting Ms. Hughes. He did not know how important the link was between her brother and the dead man. He wasn't sure of what he was trying to uncover, and he had no way of providing the reassurance the woman so clearly craved.

However, Eliza's answer was firm and unhesitating. "Apart from the odd meeting of the duck-hunters' club they hadn't seen each other in years. They weren't really on speaking terms."

"What about the other men in the photo?"

"I only know them by their first names, and even they might just be nicknames."

Then without warning, she burst into tears.

Daly turned his back and filled a kettle. While he rummaged for cups, Eliza composed herself.

"Have you no theory at all about who took my brother?" she demanded.

"You've told me there was no evidence of any trouble in his life apart from his illness. You said that David lived an ordinary existence with simple, regular habits. Went to church on Sundays, tended to his orchard and garden, and went duck hunting in the winter. Is that all you're giving me to work on?"

"Yes."

Almost imperceptibly, Daly shook his head. He tried to keep the impatience out of his voice. "There has to be something more to his life. I have to know everything about him, the people he was in touch with, what was on his mind, who he would be likely to visit, before I can come up with any theories."

He paused and handed her a mug of tea. "Meanwhile I also have to devote my attention to an important murder investigation. Any information you might have about Joseph Devine would be very helpful. And I need it as soon as possible."

She nodded. "I'll supply you with anything I can think of. In the meantime, you should talk to Ginger Gormley. His father organized duck hunts on some land they owned. He kept a logbook with all the details of the duck-hunting club."

According to Eliza, Gormley lived in a farmhouse in a wooded cove along the lough. Daly dialed his number from Eliza's hall, letting it ring without getting an answer. The house was hard to find, so Daly had her draw a map. She was certain Gormley would be at home.

He was struck by the impression that Eliza's emotions began to buoy up as he left. She stood at the door watching his car pull away with a look of relief on her face. He tapped the steering wheel with his fingers, wondering what items of interest still lay inside the cottage waiting to be discovered.

He had little difficulty following the map, and after twenty minutes or so found himself driving up a lane toward a large square farmhouse that had been divided into a number of different homes. He guessed that Gormley's parents and siblings lived in separate quarters within the building. The house resembled a latter-day fort, guarding the extended family's privacy even though their only neighbor was the lough. Daly looked up at the large windows, which were like reflective shields filled with the light of the sky. An upstairs window closed and a shadow disappeared from view.

The landscape of the lough shore with its coves and hidden bays lent itself to withdrawal and refuge, thought Daly. And this was the home of the archetypal lough-shore family.

A battleground of shovels and hoes, rakes and scythes lay in the overgrown grass that ran right up to the front door. Somewhere a dog started barking.

Daly rang the doorbell. Fortunately, he did not have to wait long. A man carrying a spade appeared from behind the house and stopped dead in his tracks when he saw his visitor.

"I'm sorry for disturbing you," said Daly. "My name is Inspector Celcius Daly. I rang, but I got no answer. I'm looking for Ginger Gormley."

"That's me," said the man. He had a shock of wild ginger hair, fleshy lips, and bright, suspicious eyes. Daly could see he was on his guard.

"I want to ask you a few questions about David Hughes. He's missing and his sister is very worried."

Gormley appeared to relax. He shouted at the dog to stop barking, and led Daly through a front door into the farmhouse.

"Celcius. That's a strange name. For a policeman."

"My mother named me after Brother Celcius, a monk at the Christian Brothers in Dungannon," explained Daly. He paused. It was his experience that an early enquiry about his name usually indicated a difficult interviewee. "I'm glad my mother was into religion and not art. Otherwise she might have christened me Salvador."

Gormley responded to the joke with a brief grunt and no eye contact. He had perfected the art of abruptness. Daly feared the interview was going to be long and fruitless.

"Hughes owes me money. I doubt if I'll see any of it now," he grumbled.

They walked into a large room, a combination kitchen–living room and, judging from the blankets covering the worn-out sofa, a bedroom, too.

"I've been suffering from the flu. Today's the first day I've stepped outside," said Gormley.

He cleared a pile of underwear from a seat for Daly, who thought to himself that at least it was an attempt at hospitality. Unfortunately, the underwear had been hiding some scraps of leftover food, the provenance of which was obscured by a thatch of blue mold.

A bland vacancy fell over Gormley's face as he dropped into an armchair. Daly had seen that look before. The expression said he'd seen nothing interesting and there was nothing interesting to be said. Of course, there was a way of penetrating such defenses, but it usually entailed a trip to the police station and a spell in an interrogation suite.

"I heard this morning there was a search for him. How's it going?"

"Not so good, at the moment."

"Good. I hope it stays that way. David was a prisoner in that house. It was a rescue party he needed, not a search party."

"The man is suffering from Alzheimer's," said Daly sharply. "According to his sister, he requires round-the-clock supervision."

"If he was that ill, he was bloody good at hiding it."

A look of tension furrowed Gormley's freckled brow with the realization that he had probably said too much. Daly sensed he was not a natural talker, a lough-shore boy unused to small chat or evasion. Whatever was on his mind bolted straight out of his mouth and rolled on the ground like a playful puppy.

"You've seen Mr. Hughes recently?"

Gormley said nothing, hoping Daly would come to his rescue and ask another question. He flashed Daly a contorted smile, and Daly smiled back. He waited, and slowly Gormley relaxed his guard. Sometimes you had to give people time to open up. He was prepared to give people like Gormley all the time in the world.

"He woke me up well after midnight on Saturday," Gormley said with a sigh. "I heard a rapping at the door and found him standing on my porch. I didn't know he wasn't supposed to be out. When he saw me, he danced a little jig, as he always did when going on a duck-shooting trip. He was wearing an old hunting jacket and it was dripping with the rain."

"Did he say anything to you?"

"Only to hurry up because we were going on a hunting expedition."

Daly watched as Gormley's face took on a look of boyish amusement.

"It was news to me," he continued. "None of the duck flocks were in. Just a trickle of birds on the southern shore. I'd been watching every night from the marsh at Derryinver. All I'd caught up to that night was the flu." He grinned at Daly. "But I took him in and made him a cup of tea. I just played along and made up a bed with some old blankets right on that sofa there. He seemed in a funny mood, and I thought he could do with a good night's sleep."

Daly wondered how any guest could enjoy a restful night on that sofa.

Gormley leaned forward, his eyes shining. "David was a real article. He was the oldest member of the club, and the most respected. He called here most nights before his sister started locking him up. We'd sit discussing the usual topics—religion, politics, and, of course, duck hunting. He was no blood relation, but I called him Grandda, although I never said it to his face. I'm not sure how he would have taken it. I could listen to his stories for hours, but that night I could see his memory was beginning to let him down."

"Did he tell you what was on his mind?"

"He seemed worried about something. Before I went to bed, he wanted to check my collection of duck decoys. To see if any were missing. We counted all six of them. He seemed upset and said everyone knows you ought to have an odd number. Thirteen was luckier than having an even number like six, he warned me."

Daly looked puzzled.

"I think he believed ducks would be more attracted by an odd number of decoys. One without a mate, you see." He flashed another grin. "That's duck hunting for you."

"What happened in the morning?"

"He told me he was going to see a friend. I gave him some money for a taxi because he was short. But he said he was going to walk it. The last I saw of him, he was brushing down his thick white hair with his palm. He had an old hunting gun tied across his back and he was chuckling. He told me, 'I'm away to hunt down an old friend, Ginger.'"

"Who was the friend?"

"He didn't tell. And I had no reason to ask."

"Have you a list of the members of the duck club? I'm going to need their addresses."

"I don't keep records like that. Dad used to organize shoots on the marsh out the back. It's about ten acres of reed beds and forest. For lack of a better term, Dad was organizationally challenged. He had a logbook, which sounds good, but the only information it held was the number of men gunning and how much was owed. That was all the information he ever needed."

"What about addresses?"

"Dad didn't need any addresses. If someone wanted to hunt, all they had to do was tell him."

Daly showed him the photograph of the duck-hunter's club.

"Recognize the man on the bottom left?"

"Sure, that's Joseph Devine, the man who they found on Coney Island. He worked in a solicitor's firm. Hughes used to always joke that he'd come in useful if they shot anyone by accident."

Gormley gave him the names of the other men in the photo, which Daly noted.

"I'm investigating the murder of Joseph Devine. Is there anything you can tell me that might be of use to the investigation?"

"I read the newspapers," said Gormley, trying to avoid the question. "I guessed you were here to talk about more than a missing man."

"How well did you know Mr. Devine?"

"Not much at all. He was a very quiet man, very discreet about everything he did."

"When did you last see him?"

"I'm not sure. Might have been a few days ago. Or could have been months back."

"What do you mean?"

"Devine was very protective about his privacy. He used to come and go on the lough and visit the hides here as he pleased. I think he was here a few days ago. At least, someone was. I saw his boat at the pier and assumed it was him. He didn't like to be bothered."

Daly considered what Gormley had said for a moment. "In other words, you're not sure whether he was here or not. Interesting, but not much help to this murder investigation."

"You're right. But that was Devine. He was never a showy hunter. Didn't have any nervous tics or any need for company. Nor did he leave much trace of himself behind. He was very careful. That's all I remember about him. He could sit and wait in a hide for as long as it took."

Daly thanked Gormley for his time and handed him a card with his details. "If you remember anything, please call me," he urged.

He drove off down the lane. The trees closed around the house, shutting off a view of Gormley standing in his garden, a cloud of midges revolving above him in a patch of evening sunlight.

Daly felt a measure of satisfaction with the interview. It struck him that the starting point in his search for Hughes had been found. The old man was not completely confused. Instead, he had left his cottage with a purpose, a search for someone or something. Whatever it was, Daly suspected he had not found it at the Gormley homestead.

9

The lough-shore fields and hedgerows were slipping back to fog and water. The mist crept ashore while the old man watched, wandering on the road behind him. Listening carefully, he could hear the muffled flight of each water droplet, the soft implosion that marked the disappearance of another tree, another house, another landmark as the fog sneaked up and enclosed him in walls of whiteness.

It was early morning and David Hughes was walking alone past sleeping farmhouses and shrouded thickets of birch and elder. His feet were wet and the muddy bottoms of his pajamas trailed from under his waterproof trousers. The cold had gotten under his thick overcoat, making his body tremble. He had eaten his last cooked meal the previous day, and even his belly felt cold. However, his eyes were bright with exhilaration. It was a victory to be on the road at all. Away from the ghosts and shadows that had scared the wits out of him during the long winter.

Even though he was in a hurry, he could manage only the small, mouselike steps of an ill man not fully anchored in reality. His body felt like a massive bulk to be coaxed awkwardly through the gaps in the fog. The harder he tried, the slower his progress became. Little by little, he advanced along the road.

He worried that his illness was going to betray him. All the shadows needed to know was which direction he had taken. They would follow his tracks and wait until he tired himself out. He had to keep moving, keep making decisions. He knew with certainty he had taken the correct course of action. When he discovered that Joseph Devine was dead, his first instinct had been to hide in the gloomy cottage and barricade himself behind a locked door. But that was what they wanted, he realized. To have him imprisoned by fear. If he turned back to the cottage, they would be there, gathering at that sinister gap in the thorn hedge, ready to trap him with their terrible stories of the past.

His shuffling steps stopped. He stood impatiently, wanting to reach down and grab hold of each resistant limb. The fog thickened, spreading white wings of atomized water over him, and he tottered as if brought to a dangerous brink.

Where was this unfathomable hesitation coming from? It was his illness. Alzheimer's seemed to have a direction and will all of its own, a destructive force he had no control over. He concentrated on lifting his feet from the mud that seemed to suck at them, but they refused to move.

As he stood there his thoughts and memories vanished one by one, swallowed up by the mist inside him. He was reduced to an inner silence, a trance, breathing in the damp morning air.

For a while, he forgot about his flight from the cottage, the stumbling in the dark, the flashes of light, the sharp pain whenever he tripped and fell, and the frantic throbbing of birds escaping into the night sky.

It was early morning and he was on a road he had known all his life. But he had reached the end of himself. The point where the rest of the earth tips over into oblivion.

He smiled, feeling the skin on his face tighten and then go numb. The moments ticked by as the mist seeped deeper into his clothes.

A dog barked at a nearby farmhouse. His legs began moving again, and his sense of urgency returned. By now his clothes were wet through, their heaviness tugging at him as he continued his shuffling progress. The fog had soaked him as thoroughly as a heavy downpour, droplet by droplet, without him realizing. There was no need to hurry, to make haste, after all, he thought. Small steps like small drops had a cumulative effect; they achieved their goal in the end.

He looked up and gave a start. In the distance, the watery air took on a radiance, intensified and divided into two glowing halos. A car with its headlights blazing appeared out of the fog. The visitor, my guardian angel, has come at last, he thought.

Over the last year, he had retreated too deeply into the care of his sister. He realized that now. Not since childhood had he felt himself so completely in the power of another. Although he had found the grim courage of his sister endearing, she had behaved more badly than a prison warden. He had done a good job managing to escape the cottage without waking her. He had risen when honest souls were sound asleep, and slipped into the night. There was work to do, another mission to complete with the visitor's help. In his mind he was determined there would be no boundaries he would not traverse, no challenges he would not endure in order to reveal the identity of the person who had murdered Devine.

The car pulled alongside him. He grasped at the passenger door handle before the vehicle had even stopped.

But the driver wasn't the man he had been expecting. His face was sharper, more cunning, like a wild animal's, registering and analyzing the vulnerable condition of its prey.

"You!" said Hughes in recognition.

"Get in, David," ordered the driver. "I'm taking you on the road to salvation."

He climbed in without protest. He had reached that stage in his illness when even a face from an old nightmare had a reassuring effect.

10

Daly drove slowly along the dilapidated terrace of council homes looking for the right house number. His car slid unnoticed through a street full of children, boys running and jumping after a football, a row of girls shouting from the edge of the pavement, their sharp, disdainful cries ringing in the winter air. Broken toys cluttered the tiny front lawns. Even the grass looked made of plastic.

Daly got the impression of cramped houses so overburdened with children that childhood itself had been shoved outside into the gardens and onto the street. This was what passed for parenthood these days, he thought, children driven to the edge, to make room and time for all-night parties and days spent watching chat shows on wide-screen TVs. The only thing that broke the air of deprivation was a sleek black BMW parked at the bottom of the street.

He was looking for the house of Oliver Jordan's widow, Tessa. A search through old police files revealed that Jordan had been an informer shot by Republicans in 1989. He was one of a number of IRA men killed at the time over fears that different cells of the organization had been infiltrated by moles. Six months before his abduction, Jordan had been arrested by police after his fingerprints were found on an IRA bomb that failed to detonate.

The street had one of the highest crime rates in Armagh, and during the Troubles was nicknamed the Ponderosa. After the cease-fire, the name somehow stuck, and well-meaning officials still came out with clipboards looking for directions to a cowboy ranch in the Wild West. When he got out of the car, the children disappeared like rabbits down a warren. A watchful silence surrounded him. It was wariness and silence that distinguished Republican estates after the cease-fire. Not petrol bombs or riots, but silence.

An attractive-looking woman in her late thirties answered the door at Number 14. Her face was jagged but fresh, with a smattering of youthful freckles but also the ache of loss ripening in her eyes.

"If you're the police, you're bloody quick. My son called you only five minutes ago."

She stepped back into the shadows. Daly wasn't sure if she was angry or relieved. In the hallway he smelled the acrid whiff of smoke and caught sight of a child with dark, empty eyes, her face like a doll's that had been left out too long in the rain. He followed the flowing figure of the woman through the back door to a concrete yard at the back, where a burnt-out wheelie bin lay on its side, still smoldering. The smell of petrol colored the air.

"This is what I woke up to this morning," said the woman, grim-faced. The winter pallor of her skin made her look like an overanimated ghost. "Last weekend they broke the living-room window and set light to the letterbox. I'm a child minder. How can you look after other people's kids with that sort of intimidation going on?"

Daly listened to the details of the attack, following the glint of her green eyes and the bounce of her dark hair against her neck before introducing himself. He held out his hand, but she refused to shake it.

"Mrs. Jordan, the reason I'm here is to ask you some questions about your husband and his disappearance."

"What's that got to do with the burnt bin?"

Her anger flashed like a spark about to ignite the petrol-laden air.

"We have reason to believe Oliver's death may be connected to a recent murder. This new case might throw light on who abducted your husband."

"I already know who killed Oliver. It was his so-called comrades in the IRA. But they'll never be brought to justice. Not by the likes of you, anyway."

Under the staircase, he thought he saw another child lurking in a shadow. Silence and shadows, he thought, the legacy of the Troubles. He followed her into a room that was even darker than the hall. For a moment, the shadows reminded him of a childhood game in which he and his friends would dare one another to crawl into an old river tunnel.

Tessa Jordan self-consciously pulled the curtains back a little. He saw that the room was decorated with photographs of a dead man. There were shots of Oliver Jordan at school as a teenager playing Gaelic football on a Sunday afternoon, and on his wedding day with his sad-eyed bride. As a reminder that Mrs. Jordan was a devout Catholic, a picture of the Sacred Heart of Jesus also kept watch from the wall. Out of childhood habit, Daly flinched from the all-knowing, all-seeing gaze.

"I know this is hard for you, but I wanted you to know before you read about it in the papers," he said. "There might be more stories printed about Oliver's abduction."

She barely reacted. Daly realized they were on territory that had been trespassed a thousand times by the press.

"So you're a detective from our new police service, the PSNI," she said, measuring him up. "Let's see your identification."

Daly obliged and waited as she studied his card.

"New badge, new name, same old police force, though." She sniffed skeptically, as though the story of Northern Ireland's new inclusive police force was a transparent fiction.

She leaned back, crossing her legs, taking a deeper measure of Daly. The detective felt her eyes searching him out, a sense of danger resonating in the air, as though they were two people considering a secret tryst.

"Oliver's murder left me the single mother of a very young child," she told him, her voice weak but cold. "I hardly had any time to grieve. All I want now is his body returned for a proper burial."

She regarded Daly for a second. "Don't worry; I'm not going to cry.

I never did. I was the heroic wife of an IRA man. But when I heard what they were saying about Oliver, that he had been an informer, it was as if I had been stabbed. I didn't think I'd be able to take it, the accusation that he was a traitor."

Daly relaxed a little as she kept talking, feeling like an intruder who had temporarily broken through enemy lines.

"But eventually the pain sharpens you, and you begin to see things clearly. You have no idea how dull real life is until you feel that sort of anger boil inside you. We found out from our solicitor that Special Branch knew who was responsible for Oliver's abduction not long after it happened, but no charges were ever brought. When we asked to see the police reports of the investigation, they told us they'd been lost. The authorities have behaved dishonestly. They have lied to us and misled us at every turn. What made the IRA kidnappers so special that the police had to protect their identities?"

"Perhaps it's time for a new investigation," said Daly. "New clues have a habit of turning up, and witnesses can be jolted into remembering vital clues even years later."

"What hope is there of solving the case now, seventeen years after the event?" Her voice was more despairing than angry. "Since the cease-fire, we've been campaigning to have a public inquiry into Oliver's abduction, but the British government keeps refusing. I'm quite used to it by now, this burning sense of rage rising from within. The anger isn't just bearable, it's electrifying. We Catholics must be hardwired to feel injustice, don't you think, Inspector Daly?"

Inwardly, he had to agree. He recalled the thrill of anger he had felt as a new recruit in Glasgow dealing with sectarianism, especially when it was meted out by colleagues. On one occasion, a senior detective had forgotten he was still in the room and remarked to his officers: "That's the trouble with Fenians, you can never trust them." Daly had watched the muscles on the inspector's face tighten with anger and humiliation when he realized his mistake. He had felt his own blood thicken with anger. Of course, the comment was the tiniest of slights compared to the ordeal Tessa Jordan had described.

"Sometimes personal injustice shapes us and brings out our better qualities," he suggested.

She snorted. "For months after Oliver's disappearance, I used to sit up in the middle of the night with the baby in my arms and listen to the wind. The baby might be crying at the top of its lungs but all I heard was the wind howling over the roof. It was so loud I used to think it was boiling up from inside me."

She paused again, and the silence felt so empty that Daly struggled to find words to fill it. "They say anger is the first stage in the grieving process."

"What are you trying to do, Inspector Daly?" she asked. "Turn this into a counseling session? Is that how you get your probes into people?"

When Daly failed to respond, she talked on. "I'm just like any another woman trying to get on with raising her family. Oliver's mother spent her whole life campaigning to prove he wasn't an informer. It was a vicious lie that hurt her deeply. She raised her son in the fear of God, to be obedient and respectful. And that's the way Oliver was. The campaign to have his body returned wore her out. Now she's in a nursing home. It's only right I take up the fight. Branding Oliver an informer has blighted my own son's life. All I want is the truth and for his body to be returned. I don't care about punishment or justice, just the truth."

Daly admired the simplicity of her request. For a moment, he sensed surrender in her eyes, a serenity in her soul. The living room was like a shrine to Oliver Jordan, but if a transcendence had occurred it was in his widow. Tessa Jordan was a very different woman from the sad-eyed girl of the wedding photograph. It was not just age that had changed her. She had tasted the powerful emotions of grief and anger, and they had transformed her, filling every vein in her body and brimming up in her shining green eyes. Her fight for justice was like a slow-burning martyrdom. He found himself wondering if there had been a lover in her life in the intervening years. Somehow, he suspected that loneliness had never driven her into another man's arms. He cleared his throat. The time for making silences in their conversation was over. Time for more pushing, less listening.

"I have some questions to ask."

"Fire away."

"I understand your husband was on remand for bomb-making charges. Who represented him?"

"O'Hare solicitors."

"I mean who specifically?"

"Malachy O'Hare himself. He sent me a condolence card when Oliver disappeared."

"Why did the IRA believe your husband was an informer?"

"There was a bomb left on Thomas Street. It was meant for an army foot patrol, but someone had removed the battery from the detonator. Oliver was the last person to have handled it so the suspicion fell on him. His fingerprints were all over the device. He was arrested but then released without charge. That signed his death warrant. When the IRA found out, they claimed he had cut a deal with Special Branch."

"And you believe he didn't?"

She stared at Daly. "Why are you here, Inspector?"

"Because evidence relating to your husband's disappearance was found at the house of a murdered man."

"Are you talking about Joseph Devine? The man they found on the island?"

"You knew him?"

"I had a visit from him a few weeks ago. Dermot, my son, answered the door. When I saw Devine, he was looking at Dermot as though he'd seen a ghost. He was hardly able to speak. I felt sorry for him, took him in, and made him a cup of tea. He wanted to talk about the evidence we had gathered on Oliver's murder and the search for his grave. He was doing some sort of research project on the disappeared. He claimed he'd narrowed the search for their bodies. But I didn't trust him. There was something secretive about him. It made me uncomfortable, and I couldn't understand what he was getting out of it." Her eyes narrowed. "Did the IRA kill him too?"

"That's what we're trying to determine."

"He probably had it coming to him."

Her harshness surprised him. "Why do you think that?"

"He shouldn't have been intruding on other people's grief. When you try that, things blow up in your face...."

Before she could continue, a teenage boy barged into the room. When he saw Daly, he stopped dead in his tracks and fumbled with something in his coat pocket, a look of fear filling his face. Daly watched him maneuver closer to his mother, his hand still grappling with the object in his pocket. The detective had levered himself to a half-standing position when the boy finally pulled out a purse and handed it to his mother.

Daly swallowed and lowered himself back into the armchair. He studied the boy's face, struck by the resemblance to his dead father. It was as if time had gone into reverse and a ragged, more youthful version of Oliver Jordan had untied his hands, removed the tape from his eyes and made his way back from the shadowy wood, where a gun had just shattered the dawn silence.

"This is my son, Dermot," said Tessa. "I was pregnant with him when they took Oliver. He never saw his dad."

Daly introduced himself. The fear discharged itself from the boy's face, but something about his awkward stance and the effort that showed as he forced himself to meet Daly's gaze piqued the detective's curiosity.

The boy's body arched away from Daly as he backed out of the room. Perhaps his odd behavior was due to the invisible shadow cast by the father labeled an informer, thought Daly, the sense of shame the boy had carried into the world from the moment of his birth, as contaminating as original sin.

Daly was beginning to suspect that Devine had been murdered because of his investigations into the past. Somehow his death was linked to the abduction of Oliver Jordan and a possible cover-up by Special Branch. Daly wondered to himself why the police had botched the original investigation if the victim was a suspected mole. Surely if Jordan had been an informer, the police would have been keen to find out how their man was discovered and who had killed him. He began to think that Tessa Jordan might be right, that whatever her husband had been guilty of, it was not spying for the security forces. He felt wary, interested. He was following the tracks left by Joseph Devine, but the two of them were circling above a deeper mystery, one shrouded in a darkness to which his eyes had still to adjust.

He had no more questions to ask Tessa Jordan. Before he left, he promised to keep her up to date with any developments in the case.

"What about the burnt-out bin?" she asked.

"I'll send an arson team 'round to examine it, see if any clues were left behind. I'll also put a patrol car on the street to keep watch. It might deter any further attacks."

This time at the door, Tessa Jordan shook hands with him. Daly glanced up the staircase, but the shadowy children had gone. The street was still quiet when he got into his car. He glanced in the rear-view mirror and saw the teenage boy standing on the doorstep with his mother. Together, they looked like two survivors just crawled out from the crater of a bomb.

11

Chief Inspector Ivan Donaldson pointed to the reinforced security gates at Derrylee Police and chewed vigorously at his thick mustache. A black panic still hung around the watchtower and gates, even though it had been a decade since a mortar bomb last rattled the cups and saucers in the police canteen.

"Those gates survived countless bomb attacks, but now they're to fall before the gaze of architects and planners," he complained. "Do you know the local rag has branded this station the ugliest building in Northern Ireland?"

Daly noticed that Donaldson's mustache chewing was a little noisier than usual and that the chief appeared perturbed.

"Looks like we're under attack from the forces of good taste, sir," said Daly, staring at the scorch marks and dents that covered the metal gates. For years they had acted as a magnet for grenades, rockets, and all sorts of homemade incendiary devices. Now as part of the demilitarization process, they were to be pulled down and sent to the scrap heap.

Earlier, Daly had walked into his office to find the chief poring over his notes into Devine's murder. The detective had felt an instinctive uneasiness, a reflex he could no more control than that resulting from a struck knee.

At Donaldson's suggestion, they made their way across the car park toward his large gold Audi.

The chief inspector clicked his keys and checked beneath the car. Inside, he started the engine and switched on the heater.

"Sometimes I wonder if we're any safer than we were during the Troubles," he remarked.

Daly stared at the windscreen and waited for Donaldson to continue. The leather seat was comfortable, and he began to turn over images in his mind from his interview with Tessa Jordan. The car was a good place for a briefing. It allowed them both the opportunity to avoid eye contact. The engine ticked idly, and for a moment Daly thought the chief's voice might prove to be a pleasing soundtrack as he drifted toward the gates of sleep. Then the tone of Donaldson's voice changed abruptly.

"There's one thing I want to make clear, Inspector," he said. "Special Branch isn't involved in the investigation into Devine's murder. But they have been advising me on the bigger picture. It's important you should be discreet."

"About what?"

"Talking to anyone about what the case throws up. Full stop." His voice had stiffened.

Daly shifted his body toward the passenger door.

"Especially about any link to the abduction of Oliver Jordan," the chief continued. "In their opinion, that avenue would complicate things."

Donaldson turned to look at Daly. His face was blank, but his concentration was like that of a gambler at a roulette table, waiting for the spinning ball to find its slot.

A long silence filled the car.

"I think Devine's death complicated things in the first place, sir," replied Daly.

Donaldson was undeterred. He returned to gazing out the windscreen. "For your information, Special Branch has told me they think it unlikely Republican paramilitaries were involved in Devine's murder. Too frenzied an attack, and the body was left at the scene of the murder. Typically, the IRA did their killing across the border and dumped the body in the North. Separates the forensics and complicates the investigation."

"That's very helpful of Special Branch. But I hear they haven't been as forthcoming with theories about Jordan's abduction." Daly's voice did not have to adopt a belligerent edge; the air was already awash with it. "What's the official line they gave his widow, Tessa? That he disappeared off the face of the earth on his way to work one morning?"

He watched Donaldson carefully for his reaction. His use of Mrs. Jordan's first name would have indicated he had already met the woman.

The chief had been well briefed. "As I understand it, a series of detectives from the branch were assigned to investigate the abduction, but, for one reason or another, they all left. One retired, another moved to a different division, one detective died, and the final one was seriously injured in a bomb explosion. By itself that's not unusual. There has always been lots of turnover in Special Branch. However, somewhere along the transfers some important files went missing. The Jordan family maintained it was a cover-up, and the press have run with that angle. If they get a whiff of his case being investigated again, they'll be all over us."

"I've a question for Special Branch. Don't you think the Jordan family deserve more justice than they've been given?"

Donaldson was overcome by a fit of coughing, the legacy of a career spent smoking two packs of Benson & Hedges a day. When the fit had settled, he placed his hand across his chest. A look of condescension strutted across his features.

"Inspector Daly, you're new to this police force, but I'm sure you're a competent detective and well intentioned. I've been a police officer for more than forty years and I find it hard to renounce the things I have always believed in. One of the things I am certain about is that we won the war, and not the IRA. It was a violent time. I'm not denying that. You must understand that it was Special Branch's ring of informers and spies that made the IRA realize the pointlessness of the armed struggle. Oliver Jordan was unlike the countless innocents on both sides who lost their lives. He was an IRA man. Never forget that."

"Is that meant to absolve Special Branch from any responsibility in

79

bringing his killers to justice? What if Jordan's killers also murdered Devine because he was about to expose them? If they turn up on my doorstep, am I meant to shelter them too and help them evade justice?"

"They didn't do it," said Donaldson coldly. "All the suspects involved in Jordan's murder are dead. If they did turn up on your doorstep, Inspector Daly, I'd be very worried indeed."

He started the car and indicated to Daly that it was time to leave. "My loyalty is to the peaceful society we created, Inspector. What we achieved wasn't easy. There were many dark days when officers had to go out on the streets in the afternoon after burying a murdered colleague that morning. Sometimes the rules got lost in translation. It's a regret, of course...." He trailed off. The tone of his voice, however, suggested something less than bottomless regret.

"Stay in touch, Daly, and I'll let you know if anything crops up from Special Branch. And remember, you're in a very fortunate position. You only need worry about loyalty to your commanding officers."

Let me know what? wondered Daly. He doubted if Special Branch was going to help shine any light on the investigation. And what did he mean by loyalty to his commanding officers? Of course, as a policeman he had to obey commands. But wasn't there a higher authority, another moral code to be obeyed? If a plot to protect a Special Branch spy lay at the heart of the investigation, he would expose it and make sure the scumbags involved in the cover-up would be brought to justice.

His meeting with Donaldson had been uncomfortable, perplexing even, but oddly, he found himself looking forward to a future encounter with Special Branch. He wondered whether that revealed a capacity for masochism he never realized he had, a desire to pit himself against disproportionate forces when any reasonable person might just walk away.

Perhaps Tessa Jordan had been right in a sense, and Irish Catholics were hardwired to react with rage to injustice, even when it might bring about their own downfall.

12

Five days had passed since Devine's murder, and the brutal news had been splashed across the front pages of the national and local newspapers. The police meeting scheduled at nine a.m. was their first as a team during the investigation. Daly licked his lips and was surprised at their dryness. He could feel sweat forming on his forehead and wondered if he was coming down with something. He began to speak, hoping that the calm of experience would carry through in his voice, but for some reason it did not. He checked the faces of the other officers to see if they noted the anxiety in his hesitant opening. Irwin looked groggy, while Harland tried to stifle a yawn. O'Neill was busy tapping a pen against her teeth. Daly guessed that for some of his officers the meeting was like dozing in front of a TV screen. It didn't matter if the sound was faulty, just as long as there was a picture to look at.

"Let's look at the search for David Hughes first," he said before a tickle in his throat developed into a coughing fit.

The fact that he had led murder investigations countless times before provided no assurance he could do it again. He knew he would have to face the depths of himself once again, and he worried that he had changed. Working long hours on tough cases in Glasgow had forced him to develop a hard-boiled emotional privacy when on the job that was like a bunker in no-man's-land. Its defenses had been considerably weakened by his separation from Anna, and the last few months spent investigating vandalism and car crime in the rural back-waters of County Armagh.

"I think our missing man is going to stay missing," announced Irwin.

He and Harland had traced the remaining members of the duck-hunting club, but there was no evidence any of them might be shelter-ing Hughes. They had also checked with hotels, bed and breakfasts, even nursing homes in the area.

Daly suggested they issue another press release to enlist the pub-lic's help in the search.

"Is there not a good possibility the poor bugger is dead?" asked Constable Harland.

"Somehow, I doubt it," replied Daly. "I believe he's staying with a friend of sorts. At least we can be fairly sure he hasn't been kidnapped. Or being held against his will."

"If no offense has been committed and he left of his own free will, why are we getting involved? Is it our business if a man wants to take himself off and get his head showered for a while?"

"The circumstances of his disappearance are still suspicious enough to warrant our interest," said Daly. "Never mind the fact that a confused old man is at large, probably armed with an untrustworthy hunting gun."

They moved on to the murder enquiry.

"We're going to have to dig deeper into Devine's life," said Daly.

The team decided to move on two fronts. Daly would make a start on reinvestigating the circumstances of Oliver Jordan's abduction while Irwin and Harland would examine the cases Devine had worked on while employed by O'Hare solicitors.

Before the meeting broke up, Daly handed Irwin the remnants of the newspaper clippings he had found in the hedge at Hughes's cottage.

"You should show these to Devine's former colleagues. I believe they might have a connection with his past, and possibly his murder, too."

When he returned home, the scolding cluck of a flock of hens greeted him. They were a brood of leghorns, which his father had kept for company and the odd egg. He had forgotten to feed them that morning, and they sounded angry. They fluttered into the air as he walked up to the front door, their feathers wild and wet from the hedgerows. Black clouds had gathered in the sky and large drops of rain fell on his head. He paid no heed to the birds and plunged into the damp darkness of the cottage.

The wheel of detective work had begun to bear him away from the confines of his father's cottage, and he wondered if it was time to clear out the house, put the place up for sale, and free himself of its burden. The impatient cries of the fowl echoed with the voices inside him, equally plaintive and imperative—Oliver Jordan and Joseph Devine seeking deliverance from beyond their graves, and David Hughes, confused and frightened, gathered up in a net of secret memories.

He made himself something to eat. Then he lit a turf fire, and sat down, idly flicking through a manual on chicken rearing he lifted from a pile of old farming journals.

He woke with a start a few hours later. He found himself sitting slumped over the gray grate like a man waiting for his lover to turn up for dinner. The fire had gone out, and he could feel the thin threads of cold creeping through chinks in the window frames. The clock on the mantelpiece showed almost midnight. He knew from experience this was not the place or time to get drunk, and he resisted the temptation to switch on the radio to catch the late news bulletin. Newsreaders were too obsessed with crime, doling out the accounts of random violence to their audience like bedside stories. He craved a cigarette and wondered if he would sleep tonight.

The ashes settled into the grate. Crows creaked from the chimney top. He detected a ghostly whisper in the air—the sound of his father reciting the intricate prayers that were his nightly routine. Even after six months, he still expected to see his father sitting beside him by the fire, wreathed in pipe smoke. Soon the ashes of the turf the old man had dug last spring would be swept up and scattered among the potato ridges. He shivered in the armchair. There was the past, and there was sleep, but in neither could his mind find rest.

He put on his overcoat and picked up the car keys. In spite of the weight of tiredness tugging at him, he decided to return to the station and examine Devine's files.

Outside, the moon was shining. The feathery weight of the frost burdened the trees and crumpled the thick grass in the front garden. The sound of the lawn crunching underfoot was more tangible than the memories in his head. The soft wing-beat of a bird, probably an owl wheeling for prey, circled in the branches above. Living in Glasgow, night was a time to lock the doors and huddle inside, but out here, in the deep Armagh countryside, it was hard to imagine evil or peril simmering in the dark. Unless, of course, you listened to the honeyed voices of the newsreaders.

The hens were roosting in their coop. Before he locked them up for the night, he threw them some chicken meal. They gawked and scratched about, looking dirty and down-at-heel, their clucking hoarse and timid. The countryside was full of foxes and the night air probably carried the whiff of danger. Daly hoped the coop was secure. He didn't want to wake up some morning to a bloodbath.

He got into the car and drove along the lough shore through Clonmakate and Maghery. A lone taxi sat by a forest plantation at the Birches, its engine ticking over. He crawled along country roads. The shapes of trees shining in the frost were like the nerves and arteries of a dissected corpse. On a whim he turned south at the motorway roundabout and made his way to Portadown and the house of Tessa Jordan.

At Dalriada Terrace, he could see behind the curtained windows the ghostly blue margins of TV screens, but at number 14, the lights were yellow and orange. The Jordans must be the sole watchers of another channel, he thought. He got out and looked up and down the street. Bulky toys still lay abandoned in the front gardens. There was no sign of the patrol car he had requested. He felt a twinge of annoyance. A door opened somewhere, and a harsh voice greeted the arrival home of a drunk. The street felt like a dingy holiday resort inhabited by the inmates of a concentration camp.

He was just about to get back into his car when he noticed the yellow and orange colors intensify in the Jordans' front room. Then he heard a boom and the crash of glass breaking. He felt the heat before he saw the flames escape from the broken window. Very quickly, they engulfed the entire front of the house. He crouched against the garden fence, feeling a heavy blanket of heat roll over him. He tried to move but felt pinned down. The sounds of wood splintering and glass breaking erupted from within the building. He listened intently to the trapped sounds of the fire, hoping to detect a human shout or cry, but heard none.

Fumbling for his phone, he tried to ring the fire brigade.

It felt as though the heat had hurled his voice to the back of his throat. He struggled to give directions to the operator. Above the spitting sounds of the blaze, he could barely hear the woman's voice.

Fearing he had wasted too much time already, he ran toward the door. More by luck than brute strength, he managed to break it down, stumbling into the smoke-filled darkness of the hall. He hung back at first, like a timid bather, listening for any sounds that might lead him to Tessa and her son. The house seemed empty of human life. The flames had taken hold of the living room, the furniture, and the walls. A jagged light lit up the staircase. He shouted out Tessa's name against the condensed roar of the fire, but got no reply. It was like confronting a trapped violence, the compacted heat forcing him backward.

He took a running leap up the stairs. The flames had yet to reach the first floor, but the smoke was rising up the stairs in black plumes. He could hear a thick sigh as it spread along the landing floor.

He burst into a bedroom, shouting, "Get up! Get up!" But the beds within were empty. He checked the smoke alarm on the landing ceiling and saw the battery had been ripped out. Holding his breath, he groped toward the main bedroom and rolled himself through the door.

Someone was lying on the double bed. Daly shouted, but the body remained lifeless. He fumbled his way toward it. The body was a solid, unmoving mass. For a moment, he feared Tessa Jordan had suffocated in her sleep.

Then he realized it was only a set of pillows. His head was pounding and he could barely breathe. The stairs behind him were no longer intact, so he took a chair and broke the windowpane. In the garden below, a woman and a boy, huddling together, stared up at him in surprise. They watched as he lowered himself onto the outside ledge, slipped on the crumbling plaster, and pitched backward toward the ground.

His arm was in pain when he awoke. Tessa Jordan leaned over him.

"Can you hear me?"

"Yes," he said.

"Is that you, Inspector Daly?"

He tried to turn to one side. "I'm the one meant to be rescuing you. What happened?"

"A group of men dressed in black come to the front door with a can of petrol. Dermot raised the alarm. We had to leg it out of the house and hide in the garden."

Daly could make out the boy's anxious face in the light of the fire.

He sat up and gasped with the ache in his shoulder.

"You're injured," said Tessa. "The ambulance will be here soon."

"I don't need any help," he said, picking himself up.

"That's the second time you've appeared as soon as I rang for help."

"Bloody telepathy." He winced. "I'll have to do something about that."

Within minutes, the lights of the ambulance and fire brigade were bathing the street in a reassuring blue. The fire roared with a sickening glee as the firefighters fought to control it.

A paramedic rushed toward Daly, but he brushed him away.

He walked on, and a group of firefighters surrounded him like members of an opposing football team.

"I thought you were a detective, not a bloody firefighter," said Martin O'Hanlon, the chief fire officer. He looked Daly up and down, taking in his scorched clothes.

"I was answering a call nearby and saw the fire start," said Daly vaguely.

He wanted to ask O'Hanlon an important question. A detail inside the house had struck him as unusual, but the force of the fall had dislodged it from his memory.

"The fire started in the living room," Daly told him. "I could smell petrol. The family has been attacked before. We'll have to put a patrol car down here every night."

"You won't need to," said O'Hanlon. "The house is ruined. They won't be staying here for a while."

"Of course," said Daly.

"There's no need for you to stay here. You look as if you should go home."

For a family burnt out of their home, the Jordans looked remarkably relaxed. Daly found them tucked in the shadow of the fire engine, sheltering from the cold. Tessa gave Daly a look as though she were personally responsible for his grim appearance.

"How's the investigation going?" she asked.

"It's not going anywhere."

"Too busy trying to save people from fires, I suppose." There was a hint of a smile on her pale face.

She shivered slightly as he put his jacket around her shoulders. From his brief contact, she felt like a woman who had escaped the clutches of an icy river rather than a blazing fire.

"No one ever makes progress," she said. "That's the nature of Oliver's case. You'll never hunt down clues that have vanished off the face of the earth. Just as you'll never be able to charge people who are protected by the state. Every Catholic knows that."

"Thanks for the tip."

"We never had an armed struggle. The whole thing was a horrible game run by secret agents and psychopaths."

Even though his shoulder hurt and his clothes smelled of smoke, Daly tried to maintain a professional air.

"What are you going to do tonight? Is there anywhere you can stay?"

"My sister lives out in the country. We can stay in a caravan she has on the farm."

"I'll give you a lift, if you like?"

Under his jacket, she was wearing a dark green dressing robe. The fabric parted as she slipped into the backseat of the car. The pale skin of her thighs was dappled with the light of the emergency services. The movement of her legs ignited a subtler fire within him.

Dermot got into the front of the car, his mouth set in a frown, his hands clenched in his lap.

As he drove, Daly began to feel revitalized. Not exactly happy, but the blaze had fueled his sense of determination. He also felt he had earned the right to ask Tessa more questions about Oliver's disappearance.

"Has it ever occurred to you the arson attacks might be linked to your campaign to find Oliver's body?" he asked.

"No," she said. "Why should I think that?"

She stared into his rearview mirror with evident unease. He thought it was strange she should deny a link between the intimidation and her fight for justice. Surely she must suspect somebody out there had something to hide and might go to any lengths to avoid detection.

"This time I'll make sure a car watches your sister's house. Hopefully the arsonists won't know where she lives."

He glanced into the rearview mirror again and saw she had fallen asleep. The boy sitting in the passenger seat beside him was still awake. Daly could feel an intense concentration from him.

His imperative was to ensure their safety, but as for a larger strategy, he had none. He had no doubt that but for the boy's watchfulness, the latest fire could have been fatal. From his car phone he put out an alert for the arsonists based upon the boy's description.

Then he turned the heater on and relaxed into his seat. The boy beside him sat like a ghost stranded from a bad dream.

"Are you still at school, Dermot?" asked Daly.

"I'm doing A-levels. One of them's criminology."

Daly didn't say anything. He could understand why the boy wanted to study crime. It probably helped create a mental distance from terror. Analyzing it was a way of preventing fear from paralyzing oneself.

They drove several miles without exchanging a word.

"Doing criminology was a mistake," announced Dermot. "The more I read about the study of crime the more it seems a waste of time. My teacher talks about poverty and inequality, but really some people are so evil they're beyond human understanding."

Daly nodded and tried to change the subject, but the boy appeared not to hear him.

"Law and order are no comfort to people like my mum. I've watched her. Her life is a tightrope walk on a wire tied at one end to the police and people like you, and at the other to the IRA and the so-called protectors of Catholics. She doesn't trust any of you."

"That can't be healthy."

"Look at where we're forced to live. It's a hole. I can't wait to get out. I wish they'd burn the whole place down. Even then my mother would still want to stay there."

"That's where her roots are?"

"No. She's just set in her ways."

"Mothers can be like that."

The boy gave him directions that led them up a deep lane lined with ragged fuchsia bushes.

Before they pulled up at the farmhouse, he turned to Daly. "Can you do me a favor?"

"I'm listening."

"I've work experience to do as part of my criminology course. Just a day or two. I was wondering if I could follow you around?"

Daly paused for a moment. He glanced at the sleeping form of Tessa in the backseat. Her face was a pale blur hidden behind her dark hair.

"I can't see it being a problem," he said. "We're meant to be an accessible police force these days. Headquarters is always encouraging us to let people see how professional we've become."

The car swung up to the front door of the farmhouse. Tessa's sister was ready to greet them, framed against a neat porch filled with over-wintering geraniums. She looked older and softer than Tessa.

Daly got out to introduce himself, but the sister, who had stepped closer to the car to inspect them, backed away. He knew he didn't look good. Judging from his reflection in the car window, he would have scared most people away.

The woman looked relieved when Tessa climbed out of the car. She half-scolded, half-reassured her, and they embraced.

"You won't back out of your promise?" asked Dermot.

"I never back out of anything."

Before going into the house, Tessa turned and walked back to Daly. Her hand stroked her hair back from her flushed cheeks. Her eyes, however, were level and calm.

"You're a good man," she said. "Don't waste your time investigating what happened tonight. The people who set my house alight were just drunk vandals. Tomorrow night, it'll be someone else's home."

Daly nodded. Either she could not understand that Oliver's killers might also want her dead, or she wanted to protect them in some way. Perhaps her lack of suspicion was no bad thing. It might help scale down his sense of mistrust and paranoia. When he got into the car, he felt so exhausted he wanted to lie down and sleep. He drove straight home, his mind a blank.

13

When Daly walked into the main office in the police station, Irwin was already sitting there, yawning, and O'Neill was on the phone with an open magazine on her lap. She replaced the receiver and pulled a face. Harland, Robertson, and O'Brien were gathered around a computer screen. Judging from the tight grins on their faces, they weren't writing crime reports.

"How's it going?"

"Like shit." Irwin spoke for the rest of the team. "Thank God I'm off duty at one."

Daly could feel a weariness in the room like a physical weight. Bouts of lethargy in difficult murder cases were not unusual. He hoped it was no more than a periodic fit and that his team would not miss an important clue or lead.

For his part, he felt energized by the events of the night before. Among the many imperatives thrown up by the investigation was the safety of Tessa Jordan and her son. It had a power that seemed to him not just instinctive but also moral. He worried that it might establish itself as the major motivation in the case and weaken his decision-making.

"Who was meant to be watching the Jordan house?" he demanded.

"Harland and Robertson," said Irwin. "They were called to a break-in at a petrol station. A digger was driven into the cash machine. Some idiot must have forgotten his PIN number."

Daly grunted.

"Sightings of Hughes have started coming in," said O'Neill. "Nothing of any worth, though. A woman called to say she saw him at Malaga airport last Friday. The day before he disappeared."

"Eliza Hughes also phoned," said Irwin. "She wants you to call out to the cottage. It sounded urgent, but she wouldn't say why."

Irwin and Daly pored over a preliminary report the fire service had drawn up on the blaze. Traces of fire accelerant had been found splashed in the living room. The smoke alarm wasn't working, which was a serious oversight by Tessa Jordan considering the history of arson attacks.

"What's that smell?" asked Irwin.

Daly shrugged and got up to leave.

"It's perfume. I can smell it from your jacket." Irwin smirked. "You've been behaving strangely, Celcius. All those late nights and not a lot to show for it. How come you were out at the Jordan house after midnight?"

Daly left the room before Irwin could ask one question too many.

Outside he saw that it was going to be a fine day. He relished the trip back to the lough shore. A fine southwesterly breeze was blowing and he filled his lungs before getting into the car. Thirty minutes later, he caught sight of the blue wedge of Lough Neagh between rows of pine trees. The sky above the water was filled with slow-moving clouds carrying their freight of winter visitors, geese from Siberia, whooper swans from Canada.

Hughes's cottage held two surprises for him. When he arrived, the door opened before he could ring the bell. Eliza Hughes was wearing a pair of Marigold gloves and her sleeves were rolled up to the elbows. Her face looked tired and her eyes were wide. Daly had seen that look before in people whose loved ones had been missing for several days or more. They were the eyes of a woman whose gaze was beginning to fasten on the nightmare from which she was trying to awake. The nightmare that was rising like a flood of water around her feet. She blinked in the bright daylight and led Daly into the kitchen where she had been scrubbing pots in the sink.

"Every time I see you I keep expecting David to be at your side."

Daly did not know what to say. Eliza's gaze swung around the kitchen from object to object, as though the room were immersed in an element that made her distrust her eyes.

"Would you like a cup of tea?" she asked. A pot was already brewing on the hob. Daly gingerly took a cup from her and began filling her in with the details of his visit to Ginger Gormley's.

However, before he could finish, she interrupted him.

"You had better take a look at this." She handed him a postcard. "It arrived this morning. It's from my brother."

Daly stared at the card in surprise. The picture showed a hunter wading out into murky water to release a flock of duck decoys. The message on the back was written in an unsteady hand. It said:

Dear Elira,

    I've gone for good. Please don't think of following me. Don't worry, my kind hosts are taking good care of all my needs. If only they would stop talking about God and salvation.

                                     Love, David

P.S. If only that old bird would talk, imagine the stories it would tell.

The message was more confusing than reassuring. Daly guessed it was the product of a mind sinking into senility. He glanced at Eliza and saw a hopeful smile creep across her face.

"I'm sure it's from him. He misspelled my name. 'Elira.' It was his pet name for me when we were growing up."

Daly examined the postmark. The card appeared to have been posted from Portadown.

"At least we know he's alive," she added.

"Do you have any idea where's he at?"

"No. I can only guess he's with friends. Perhaps they don't even know he's ill."

"Do you think the postcard's meant to be a clue? Is he trying to tell us what he's up to or who he's staying with?"

"I don't think he knows himself."

"We'll keep an open mind. He may still be a danger to himself. Then again he might be out with friends shooting ducks as we speak and having a great time."

"It's possible," said Eliza, nodding. "He'd been looking forward to the hunting season, but I was too frightened to let him near a gun, even during his lucid periods."

The postcard lay on the table between them. A note from a mind on the edge of oblivion.

"Patience," said Daly eventually. "We'll establish where he is sooner or later."

He asked permission to walk around the house. He wanted to get a sense of the type of person David Hughes was. Eliza agreed and went back to scrubbing her pots.

Hughes's bedroom looked barer than it had been on the night of his disappearance. The smell of fresh disinfectant hung in the air. The bed had been stripped of its blankets and sheets. All traces of the old man had been scrubbed away. He got the impression that for Eliza Hughes the greater part of looking after her brother involved an arduous amount of cleaning. Even in the depths of his illness, Hughes must have felt suppressed by her relentless routine. A scrubbing so fierce it threatened to wipe all trace of him from the face of the earth.

It was only when Daly turned to leave the room that he remembered. Something else had been in the room that night. Something that had not been cleared away. For several moments he didn't move, afraid the fragment of memory might slip away.

The candle with ashes and paper piled around it. It had sat on the cabinet next to the bed. On the night of Hughes's disappearance, it had struck him as odd. Now he knew why. It had been the one blot of untidiness in the room.

When he asked Eliza about the ashes, she was uncertain at first.

"David might have burnt some paper after he went to bed," she suggested.

"Did you see him with anything earlier?"

She thought for a moment. "I remember he was reading the local newspaper, the *Armagh News*. It was when I brought him his cup of tea. He had his back to me and was poring over one of the pages. When I tapped him on the shoulder, he looked up at me as if he'd seen a ghost. Then he folded the newspaper sheet and put it in his pocket. It was the obituary page. I left him alone and we didn't speak. That was the last time I looked into his eyes."

"Had you read the newspaper?"

"No, but I had my own copy of it so I didn't mind."

"Did you notice any change in him afterwards?"

"He did seem a little preoccupied, but then I thought he was having one of his moods. He went to bed early and I called in at about ten p.m. When I went into the room to put on the pressure mat he was fast asleep, snoring away."

Daly was silent while Eliza's eyes widened in alarm.

"You think there was something in the obituary page that made him decide to run away?"

"That's what I'm trying to determine," he replied. "David reads the newspaper and for some reason gets rid of it before anyone else can read it. Later that night, it appears he faked a burglary and then fled the house. Something in the newspaper might have alarmed him. Did he say anything that evening which seemed out of place?"

Eliza blushed. "He didn't say anything at all. But then he had days like that. I was his carer, but in many ways we had a distant relationship. It was ridiculous. Some weeks he refused to speak to me at all. I had no idea what was going on in his head, apart from the clues he left in his messages."

"Don't worry. That sounds quite normal to me. I refused to speak to my father from the age of fifteen."

"David could be lucid at times. And he had always been very bright. The illness didn't seem to affect his confidence. He believed he could manage anything he had done before. Just a bit slower. Which made it more difficult to care for him. To keep him safe."

"He needed your help about the house?"

She laughed lightly. "David was beyond helping. He did his own thing. Whether it was right or wrong, he didn't care."

Daly let the air clear for a moment.

"I've asked you this before, but can you think of any reason David might have feared for his safety?"

"I can't imagine any." She gazed down, off-center, then back up at Daly.

There it was again, thought Daly. Something evasive and not quite straightforward. Why don't I believe you?

"Have you still got your copy of the *Armagh News*?" he asked.

"Yes." She retrieved the paper from a pile ready to go into the recycling bin.

Daly spotted the death notice immediately. It was bordered in black, and unusually worded. However, that wasn't the strangest thing about it. The obituary was for Joseph Devine, and the date at the top of the paper read February 19, the day before Devine was murdered. The final line read: *His spirit that could never take flight in life, has finally taken wing. For further arrangements contact Bill.*

14

Armagh News reporter Owen Murphy was a slight, fidgety young man with curly black hair. Daly remembered meeting him at the station's weekly press briefings. The first time Murphy had attended one, Daly asked a senior journalist from a rival paper to vouch for the young reporter. Something about the nervousness of his smile and his casual clothes had sparked Daly's suspicions.

The newspaper shared a building with a Chinese restaurant and an Indian takeaway. Murphy took Daly and Irwin up a back staircase covered in greasy carpet. A primitive-looking vent from the Chinese restaurant dripped curry stains down the wall. The patch of carpet beneath had rotted away. Inside the newsroom, a sense of agitation filled the air. The rattle of journalists' keyboards blended with the sounds of the busy kitchen across the corridor, food being chopped, pots boiling, and the clink of knives and forks.

Fast food, fast journalism, thought Daly. Both working to deadlines, both serving up what the public desired, only to leave everyone with a queasy feeling afterward.

"We need to know who placed Joseph Devine's obituary in last week's paper," Daly told Murphy.

"Simple," replied the reporter. "A man came in and handed me the copy. He told me he was a brother of Devine's. He paid the fee and we put it in the paper."

"Devine didn't have a brother."

"So it was someone posing as his brother. It's the first time I've heard of a bogus relative. We get lots of reports of bogus callers. But never a joker pretending to be the brother of a dead man. I had no reason to doubt him."

The journalist rifled through some files on his desk and booted up his computer. "What's the big deal, anyway?"

"Policemen have an aversion to lies," said Daly. "Perhaps it's because everything we do ends up going before a judge and they loathe fiction in their courts. We need to find out who this person was and why he placed an obituary before Devine was killed."

"Before he was killed?" Murphy raised an eyebrow. He tested one of the cups of coffee sitting on the desk and looked thoughtful.

"OK," said the reporter. "It's just dawned on me. Devine's body was found on the Sunday. But we had the obituary in the Saturday edition." He gulped down a mouthful of coffee. "I see your point now."

"We need a description of the man who claimed to be Devine's brother," said Irwin.

The journalist held back. "What crime has he committed?"

"That's exactly the question going through my mind at the moment."

Murphy leaned back, weighing up what bargaining power he might have with the policeman.

"Devine's murder was very violent. What leads are you working on? Republicans, perhaps? Or do you think they're subcontracting work these days?" His eyes gleamed at the prospect of a scoop.

"This is a murder investigation," warned Daly, "not fair game for a reporter sniffing out a story. Holding back information is obstruction. If you like, I can ask you to come down to the station where we can discuss this further."

Murphy flashed a quick smile and held up his hands. "No problem, Inspector. Always glad to help the local constabulary. Wink-wink, nudge-nudge, and all that. We've a good working relationship with you guys these days." He paused for thought. "I didn't really get a good look at him, unfortunately. Old. Early sixties, I'd say. Gray stubble. He looked like a tramp, to be honest, as though he hadn't been taking care of himself."

Daly produced a photograph of the duck-hunting club.

"Can you pick him out in this group?"

Murphy barely paused. "Sure. That's him right there."

The two detectives stiffened in surprise. The man Murphy had identified was the last person they expected.

Irwin leaned over Murphy's desk, his bulk solidifying, shoulders hunched. He slapped his two hands upon the paper-strewn desk. Pages flew up like fluffed feathers around Murphy's frightened face.

"Try again. And this time take it seriously. This is a murder investigation, remember."

Murphy spoke slowly and carefully.

"The man who gave me the obituary is the gentleman kneeling down. Second from left." He looked up, clearly hoping that Irwin would back off, but the detective loomed closer, his face splashed with patches of red.

"You're lying. That's the victim. Joseph Devine."

"What I'm telling you is the truth." Murphy's eyes turned hard and bright, his teeth set in a mocking grin. "Do the brainwork. You already know the obituary came in before he was murdered."

Irwin straightened up, perplexed. "That suggests something very elaborate and"—he searched for the right word—"deranged."

"Hard to believe, I know," said Murphy.

His attention was deflected by a phone call. He covered the mouthpiece and turned to the two detectives.

"Look. I'm sorry I can't be of more help. If I think of anything else, I'll let you know."

Daly spoke, half to himself: "No need to apologize. You've told us what you think is the truth, which makes a pleasant change, for a reporter."

As they walked back down the stairs, they could hear the vigorous rattle of Murphy's keyboard start up again.

"Bet you he's typing up his next big headline. Murder victim predicts own death," remarked Irwin.

"Let's hope not." Daly's voice was thoughtful. "Somehow Devine must have known he was about to be killed."

"Sounds like he was unhinged. If I suspected I was about to be murdered I wouldn't waste time and money writing my own obituary. That's something only a madman would do."

"Or a spy. Perhaps it was a message to someone. Devine would have been paranoid about being watched. His telephone calls and letters might have been intercepted. Writing that obituary was something he did with a lot of careful thought."

Irwin studied Daly's face. "I'm beginning to see a motive now," he said. He licked his lips before continuing. "Devine wanted to fake his own death. He submitted the obituary and then planned to make his escape. He wanted to be clear of his enemies. To live the life he always dreamed of. Somewhere sunny with a view of the sea, perhaps. While everyone back home thinks he's been killed or abducted." Irwin grinned. "This is good. Working together. This is a breakthrough. Right?"

"Except that he never got clear of his enemies," said Daly. His words chased all the liveliness from Irwin's hopeful face.

15

Overnight, workmen had begun dismantling the steel fence surrounding Derrylee Police Station. It was the first stage in removing the building's military-style fortifications and presenting the new face of civilian policing. Like stripping a soldier of his weapons, right down to his flak jacket and helmet, thought Daly as he surveyed the builders' mess.

He found the old steel gates blocked by a pile of building material. When he tried the intercom at the new public-friendly entrance there was no answer. He felt a mood of frustration overtake him as he toured the perimeter. He contemplated negotiating the scaffolding and wire screening erected by the builders. Instead, he retraced his steps and tried the intercom again. Still no answer. He banged the metal door and shouted out the names of the officers who should have been on duty. He was furious. "What the hell is going on?" he snarled, looking up at the security camera.

Eventually the electronic door swung open at a snail's pace, and he was greeted by a grinning Officer Harland putting out a cigarette with his boot. Daly was about to deliver a lecture, convinced that a breach of security had occurred but then he stopped himself. More a case of an excess of security, he realized.

"I thought we were supposed to be a more accessible police force these days," he grumbled.

As soon as he walked into the building, there was a call for him at reception. He picked up the phone. The voice was low and furtive. At first, he didn't recognize who it was

"I'm not catching you in the middle of something?"

"No, not at all."

"I've been thinking. I want to give you something on Devine that might help you."

It was Ginger Gormley. Daly waited, but nothing was forthcoming.

"Can you remember anything in particular?"

"Not really. I don't think anyone really knew Devine. He was a very private person, and secretive. He was always looking over his shoulder."

Daly hunched over the phone, trying to keep the hungry impatience out of his voice. "Did he ever tell you why he behaved that way?"

"No. But one memory does stand out. It's not much, though."

"Tell me."

"It was about ten years ago. A few of us had been at a hide near Oxford Island. The wind was high that day, and the ducks were nervous. We managed to shoot nothing. It was dark and we were heading back to our cars at the marina. Someone came running up to Hughes and made him jump out of his skin. It was Bosco Devlin, a local boy, and a bit of a simpleton. 'Mr. Devine,' he said, 'Mr. Devine, the Searcher sent me....' Joseph turned 'round and his face was white with anger. 'Piss off!' he shouted at the boy. But Bosco didn't budge. Devine was shaking with rage at this point. 'Screw the Searcher!' he roared, spitting at the ground. Then he lifted his hand to hit the boy. A few of us had to hold him back while the boy ran off as fast as his legs could carry him. There wasn't a word out of Devine afterwards, he just scowled the rest of the trip home."

"Tell me more about the boy."

"Not much to add. A few months afterwards, Bosco stumbled upon a group of IRA men in a hedge, preparing a gun attack on the RUC. He was supposed to have shouted at them, 'I'm going to tell on you.' Shortly after that, he disappeared. His body was never found."

"I appreciate your help."

"So what are you going to do now?"

"That depends. Maybe we can figure out what your story means." Then, as an afterthought, he asked, "Is there anything more you can tell me about Devine's collection of decoys?"

Gormley gave a soft laugh. "Those decoys were retired. They were too valuable to be put out on the lough. But Devine still used them for hunting. On the Internet, that is. He posted photos of them on a website to lure in decoy collectors. Americans mostly, excited about finding the next treasure. Some of the decoys were real works of art. Antique shops couldn't get enough of them. The good ones fetched as much as a thousand dollars. Devine had this saying: If only this old bird could talk, imagine the stories it would tell."

Daly's grip on the phone tightened. It was the same saying Hughes had quoted on his postcard. For a moment he had a clear sense of Devine outmaneuvering everyone completely, even in death, his enemies condemned to floundering in his wake. Like ducks that cannot fly. A line from the obituary chimed in his memory. *His spirit that could never take flight in life, has finally taken wing.* A decoy was a bird that could never take flight. It was also a snare, a thing used to lure someone into a trap. He tried to hold on to the sense of clarity, that he was staring at a vital clue, but the feeling deserted him. His mind returned to the phone call.

"Have you heard anything about David Hughes?"

Gormley snorted with amusement. "Grandda still giving you the runaround?"

Daly heard himself sigh. "I'm glad you called, Mr. Gormley. Ring again if you think of anything else."

But the line was already dead.

He had a lot to think and talk about as he walked through the station. He tried without success to find Irwin. O'Neill wasn't in either. He leafed through his messages and saw with surprise a meeting with the chief inspector was penciled in for ten a.m.

"Any word of what that's about?" he asked the officer who had taken the call.

"Some restructuring to the investigation team. That's all I've heard." He sat back at his desk and waited, going over in his head what

Gormley had said. No concrete information had been supplied, but Daly was beginning to develop a clearer sense of the type of man Joseph Devine had been. O'Hare had led him to believe there was nothing remarkable about Devine, that he had led a very dull life. However, that was barely the beginning of the story. The deeper he dug, the more he realized there was nothing dull about Devine. It was just that he had allowed very few people the chance to know him.

Then there were the connections to Hughes. They had known each other and hunted together. Both led isolated lives and were preoccupied with the past. In the background of their lives was the tragic story of Oliver Jordan. However, as far as the investigation was concerned, there was still a chasm between the two men's lives. What else did they have in common? An image kept working its way to the forefront of Daly's mind. Hughes's postcard of an old man wading out as far as possible to set a dozen duck decoys floating into dark waters.

He got up and looked for Irwin's report on the firm of solicitors but found nothing. All the time he was listening for the sound of his colleagues' footsteps in the corridor. It irritated him that Irwin wasn't there. His annoyance turned to wariness when he saw Donaldson's gold Audi pull up outside with Irwin sitting in the passenger seat. He realized he was going to be the last to find out what changes were in store for the investigation team.

His fears were confirmed when Irwin sauntered in and flashed Daly a knowing smile. As if he was a confidant to some private conspiracy. The detective began packing items from his desk into a brown box.

Daly got up to make himself toast and a cup of coffee. He had just sat down when Donaldson walked into the room. The chief inspector reached out to shake Daly's hand with a perplexed expression on his face.

"Just wanted a quick word with you," he said. "I've recommended Detective Irwin for a transfer to Special Branch. A vacancy has arisen there that needs to be filled immediately."

Daly did not feel like finishing his toast. "What about the murder investigation?" he asked. He had a sensation of being wrenched off course. Like a ship that had hit a rock.

"He's still assigned to the case. But he'll be reporting to Special

Branch from now on. You won't need to keep tabs on him. It's a joint investigation now."

Donaldson looked at Daly. The chief's expression froze, and Irwin stopped packing. His body seemed to freeze too. The way people freeze when they think someone might jump from a ledge.

"I expect your full cooperation, of course," said Donaldson. "This will give us extra manpower and the special expertise of Special Branch. They have a historical interest in the case, after all."

Daly paused, trying to work out what Special Branch was up to.

"What about the report on O'Hare's firm?"

The chief cleared his throat. He was the quintessential old-time RUC commander, displaying an iron resolve to ignore what shenanigans were going on around him. "As far as I understand, that report is now in the remit of Special Branch."

Daly found a string of curses in his mouth. Fortunately, they came out under his breath. His face reddened, and he felt the moorings of his self-control begin to loosen.

"This is purely an operational matter," Donaldson explained. "I had to let Irwin go."

He pretended to be oblivious to the emotions working through on Daly's face. He turned to Irwin and then shot a glance back at Daly. "Everyone happy?" he snapped, more in the form of a command than a question. Then he left the room.

Daly watched Irwin continue to pack his things. Donaldson's shadow still hung in the room. His departure had been so abrupt it had been left behind, caught between the door hinges.

"Off to the collusion factory, then," said Daly, unable to keep the goading out of his voice. His toast was cold but he still bit a lump out of it. He was anxious to convey an attitude of cheerful cynicism.

"There's nothing I hate more," he continued, chewing with relish, "than a detective who prefers to pay criminals and recruit them as informers rather than catch them."

Irwin turned his back to Daly and began rummaging through his drawers. The skin on the back of his neck was mottled red like a goose plucked for cooking. Daly wondered, Had he managed to annoy him?

"Donaldson's right, of course," said Daly, opting for a different tack.

"This is a complex case. Your appointment might help us move the investigation on."

"How so?" Irwin turned. The liveliness was gone from his eyes, his face a blank. Special Branch had taken his soul already.

"Now that you're working for Special Branch, you can get me the contact details of the detectives who worked on Jordan's abduction. And find out why no one was ever charged."

Irwin said nothing. Daly's requests were withered by his steel-blue eyes and the volume of cold air that now flowed between the two of them.

"Do you know what the first criteria for forging a career in the police force is?" asked Irwin. "Loyalty. A concept that seems to have bypassed you. You think that one dead informer is more important than the future of policing in this country. People like Oliver Jordan were the lowest of the low, double-crossing everyone and taking the queen's shilling. That's the way you have to treat them, Daly. Not like you do. Digging into their pasts like they're a long lost part of your family tree." He folded the lid of the box. "By the way, an Inspector Fealty in Special Branch asked me to keep an eye on you. I told him you were getting nowhere."

Daly leaned back in his chair while Irwin remained standing.

"In every police force there are those with a blind faith in the system, and then there are the suspicious ones," said Daly. "I belong to the latter. I believe there's more to Jordan's abduction. I want to reexamine the investigation, go over the statements taken by the detectives at the time, and whatever leads they followed."

"It's too late. From what I've been told, the investigation was a complete dog's dinner."

"How's that?"

"I told you. A dog's dinner." Irwin's face was deadpan. "A pair of police dogs tore up all the evidence one night. The *Kennel News* carried a story on it. The animals had to be relocated to Kent for fear of reprisals."

Daly blinked. "Well then you can tell Inspector Fealty I want the contact details of the detectives who were so careless with the evidence in the first place."

"You'll have trouble finding them. By the way, if you've such a suspicious nature why are you babysitting Jordan's son on Monday? Or don't your suspicions extend to Catholics and the sons of informers?"

Daly felt his temper begin to smolder.

"Getting emotionally involved with a victim. I thought policemen weren't supposed to do that," continued Irwin. "I should warn you there's more to Tessa Jordan than meets the eye. She'll want more from you than a comforting shoulder. You'd better watch yourself."

"Is that a tip-off?"

Irwin smirked. "It's the only one you're going to get from Special Branch."

16

The man with the gun in his jacket was instantly aware of any departure from the harmony of the expected. He had been trained to spot any deviation from the normal, and already a string of peculiarities about the hastily arranged rendezvous point was causing him concern. It was not just the heavy mists. From a safety point of view, he disliked this part of the lough shore, the solitude of the forest reaching down to the water's edge, and the road lost to view, and with it any signs of civilization. Pleasant enough for tourists and fishermen, but a treacherous location to meet David Hughes and his kidnappers.

Special Branch Inspector Ian Fealty had followed the directions set out in the postcard. They had wanted him to come alone to the isolated headland. Neither was he supposed to be carrying a weapon. They had told him they wanted to talk, to share information. They wanted to discuss different courses of action before deciding what to do with Hughes. Other than that, he had no idea what to expect.

If they were looking for privacy, they had chosen the right location. It was late afternoon, and already the mist was beginning to swill in from the lough, sprawling over the rocks and tangled branches of the storm beach, distorting and dismembering everything that lay within its reach. God only knew what submerged horrors might have been washed ashore. He remembered that he was supposed to look as though he was out on a stroll. Moving as quietly as he could, he picked his way over the debris of winter gales. The honking of a flock of geese out on the water sounded muted, ghostly. The air grew uncannily still. Somewhere out there, across the mist-shrouded membrane of the lough, the kidnappers were probably watching him.

Special Branch had been in a stir since Hughes's disappearance. They had discussed what needed to be done for days and nights. But no one could reach agreement, except that they all agreed they were possibly facing a doomsday scenario. It was only when the strange postcard arrived out of the blue that they were able to put a plan into action. The details of which were passed onto the special committee, which had given the green light and assigned him his current mission.

Fealty tried to reduce the rising tension by doing deep-breathing exercises. However, they didn't work. His instinct was to turn back and wait for a further message from the kidnappers. Let them sweat a little, he thought. He consoled himself by feeling the dead weight of the Browning in his pocket. The kidnappers had promised to bring Hughes along to the meeting as proof the old man was still alive. They would not be expecting a Special Branch operative to endanger his life.

Unfortunately for Hughes, the committee had decided that drastic action had to be taken if Special Branch were to prevent its whole network of spies and informers from collapsing.

The mist thickened and grew oppressive. Fealty reached out with his gun and pointed it at the fragments of dark rock and trees revealed fleetingly. He did not like his situation. In the dwindling light, the lough's surface looked as black and thick as tar. He kept imagining the prow of a boat twirling out of the mist, or pale faces materializing at an arm's length away. Even the most highly trained operatives made mistakes when they could not see clearly, the unruly brew of imagination tricking them into misreading what they did see. He had only studied photographs of Hughes, never having met the man. The committee had warned he might be deranged or suffering from some sort of memory loss. It struck him that the location suited the old man the most. He had lived all his life along the lough shore and would know the place like the veins and knuckles on the back of his hand.

Fealty tried to keep his bearings and checked his watch. If the mist remained much longer he would call off the meeting, pretend he had gotten lost and missed the rendezvous point. He was about to quit and head back into the forest when he heard the rattle of a boat drifting onto the stony shore. He stepped toward the sound. There was a heavy grinding noise as the boat ran aground, and then a crisscross pattern of tiny waves broke upon the shore at Fealty's feet.

"Is anyone there?" he shouted into the blanket of whiteness.

"Who is it?" sounded a man's voice, deep and firm.

"The decoy has come," said Fealty, using the agreed phrase.

"I'm waiting for you," replied the voice.

"I need to see you. I've been sent to talk to David Hughes."

"I'm here. Come right ahead."

He pushed into the whiteness, unable to distinguish anything. A gust of wind dissolved some of the mist, and an old man's face with an unkempt beard materialized into view. He was sitting at the prow of a boat. His hair and beard were wet through. Fealty was surprised. Hughes appeared to be by himself.

"Wouldn't it be better if we went for a walk together?" he suggested.

"I don't want to leave the boat. This is not a good place to be marooned. Too damn cold. If you could get hold of some whiskey, though, that would be a different matter."

Fealty was momentarily confused. There was no sign of the kidnappers and the old man sounded off his rocker.

"It's a hell of a place, I agree," replied Fealty.

The mist swung back, leaving Fealty groping as the boat drifted away and disappeared. When the mist cleared again he found himself farther along the shore, the boat gone. Fealty decided he needed to feed Hughes a line, anything to rein him back out of the mist.

"You'll catch a cold out in this weather," he shouted.

"That only happens to townies like you," came the reply. "I wash in cold water, every day. Even in winter."

The boat was nearby. He could hear the slapping of oars in the water. He realized that Hughes must have someone with him.

"What information are you looking for?" shouted Fealty.

This time the voice was different, younger and edgier, more in control. "We need the names of the detectives who investigated Oliver Jordan's disappearance."

Fealty found himself staring into the blank face of the fog. The weather was making things impossible, and the question left him puzzled.

"What has Oliver Jordan got to do with you?" he asked.

"I'm the one asking you. You don't need to ask me anything." The voice grew faint.

Fealty shouted out a name.

"I'm not interested in him. He's dead."

Fealty shouted out several more, but wondered if they had heard him. He waded into the water, but the fog immediately closed around him. It was like trying to push your way clear of a slippery monster that lashed this way and that. The sound of the oars returned, farther up and then down the shore. The boat passed to his left and then to his right. Somehow, it was circling him, trying to make him lose his bearings. He stumbled back to the shore and climbed over the gnarled roots of an upended tree. The fog lifted again, and he felt disoriented, as though his sense of direction had been reversed. His destination had become his point of departure.

He wheeled around just in time to see the prow of the boat appear out of the mist, advancing toward him like a spear. The old man bore down upon him, his arm pointing out as if to signal a warning. For the first time Fealty saw the other person, a slack shape hunched in the back of the boat. As Fealty peered at him, the figure unwrapped a scarf from his face. It was the face of a man Fealty did not expect to see, not out here with Hughes. This fog is leaving me confused, he thought. A tangled mess of memories floated up before his eyes. The Searcher had produced so many potential recruits the authorities couldn't vet them quickly enough. They had been forced to turn people away. So many different faces. But he was sure he had seen the man in the boat before. He began to suspect there were no kidnappers, and that Hughes was working with some kind of accomplice.

"Over there," spat Hughes at Fealty, pointing into the trees. The

Special Branch officer turned around. A feeling of unease gripped him. Who might be hiding among the trees? A bunch of armed men? It was the perfect location for an ambush. Then he saw, through a gap in the undergrowth, two black-crested birds. He relaxed and adjusted his position, but he was still startled when their wings broke into flight, shattering the silence.

"Crested terns," explained Hughes. The old man was close, almost within touching distance. He examined Fealty intensely. "I need to see your ID."

Fealty put his hand into his inside pocket and fumbled, unable to hide the fact that there was a gun there. He repositioned it with his damp hand and pulled out his police identification. As he handed it to Hughes, an oar swung up from the boat, knocking him into the water.

"We need the names of the other detectives," said Hughes again.

"Why?" spluttered Fealty as he hauled himself out of the water.

"The answer to that should be as plain to Special Branch as the sash on an Orangeman," said Hughes. "I need the names because there are loose ends from the past that need tied up." His voice turned hoarse, savage. "You should fear growing old. When your time is near, you find yourself looking down into the whole of your soul as if you are on the peak of a mountain. You see everything, even the secrets hidden in the darkest corners. Your mistakes can't be concealed forever."

Fealty now realized the old man was deranged. He needed to play for time. He gave Hughes the names he wanted and dragged himself onto a rock, removing the gun at the same time. Ideally, he would have liked Hughes and his accomplice's death to look like a hunting accident, but that might prove too tricky. Two clean shots were all he required.

The mist congealed again, swallowing up the boat and the two men. Fealty thought he could hear the splash of an oar nearby but couldn't determine in which direction, or whether he had really heard it. All he could make out was the knocking of his heart in his chest.

"I have a message for you from headquarters," he shouted. "You can have whatever you want. Resettlement. A new identity. The last thing they want is for you to be out wandering in this no-man's-land."

"I'm OK," came Hughes's voice, faintly, across the water. "Nobody knows where I'm staying. It's the perfect place for me. I'm like a rain-drop hiding in a waterfall."

"There isn't any perfect place for you anymore. Your photo has been plastered across the papers all week."

"I've seen it. Even *I* didn't recognize myself. It was just another photo of an elderly man with an illness. People just see old age and blot out the rest. It won't help you find me."

Fealty worried he was losing them. "We can give you security and money, anything you want."

"Whatever you have for me in that jacket pocket I don't want it. I'm finished with you all." Hughes's voice was almost beyond hearing.

"Don't you want to know why Devine was killed?" Fealty waded out into the water. "He was in contact with us in the weeks before he was killed. He was a very frightened man."

However, all the Special Branch officer saw was the dense black waters of the lough undulating beneath the fog's anxious face.

17

On Monday morning, Daly went out of his way to pick up Dermot Jordan from the bottom of the lane at his aunt's farmhouse. Daly watched the boy cringe and go rigid at the sight of his mother rushing toward him at the last minute with a lunchbox. Tessa Jordan hugged him and her eyes crinkled sadly on feeling the resistance in his body. She had splashed on some makeup, and she flashed a smear of a smile at Daly. Her red lips heightened the paleness of her skin.

Dermot climbed in with a shy, grateful nod to Daly. The detective pressed the accelerator and the boy closed his eyes, almost in thanks, and relaxed into the purring motion of the car.

"How are you bearing up, Dermot, living on a farm?"

"Apart from the constant smell of manure, it's OK."

After a while, he turned to Daly. "I found something. You might be interested in it if you're opening the case into Dad's abduction." He reached into his pocket and pulled out a card.

"We can look at it when we get to the station," said Daly.

For the rest of the journey, Dermot sat staring straight ahead. Daly kept glancing at him. He was turning the card repeatedly in his hands. Daly could feel his tension. He wondered what the boy had to show him.

When they entered the station there was a commotion of shouting and swearing at the front desk. An elderly man with clenched fists was being bundled toward the front door by two police officers.

"I'm a retired police officer, and I'm not drunk, if that's what you think. Let me speak to someone before I get really angry."

"Piss off," said the desk sergeant, within earshot of Daly. "Before I arrest you for breaching the peace."

Daly intervened and helped the old man regain his composure. He took out a battered RUC identity card, which Daly inspected closely.

"I really was a police officer, and I'm not drunk," the old man told the detective. In spite of his protestations, his jaw appeared to be loose and his words were slurred.

The ID card showed that he had once been Constable Noel Bingham of the RUC. Daly examined a photo of a smartly dressed policeman with neat hair and a confident face. However, in the intervening years time had doodled all over Bingham's features. A set of thick eyebrows now fluttered above a pair of eyes that were like two watery holes of darkness. Broken veins ran along the sides of his nose, and his mouth had soured and slipped closer to his chin, caved in with the weight of a lifetime's worth of grievances.

"You understand we have to be careful," said Daly, dismissing the two officers. He made Dermot sit down in the waiting room before returning to Bingham.

The retired policeman's alcohol-heavy breath hung in the air.

"Now, what is the purpose of your visit?" demanded Daly.

He looked at Bingham's face and tried his best to picture him as an RUC officer. He failed. It was like seeing one's reflection in a distorting mirror at a fairground.

"I have some information on David Hughes," said Bingham, peering around Daly. His cheekbones were gaunt peaks at either side of his haunted eyes. "Where's McKinley and what's-his-name, the fair-haired man from Ballymena? They used to be in charge of this place. Christ, I can't even remember his name."

"They were before my time," said Daly. "Just tell me what you have on David Hughes."

Bingham straightened up. "David was a first-class Special Branch officer. I was with him and O'Brien. We were undercover men. Our team still exists, somewhere in here," he said, pointing to his heart. "There was Dodds and Ferguson, too. They were OK. What was Dodds's partner called? He got caught in too many bombs. That was his trouble. Lost one limb after another. Adair. That was his name. You don't lose many men, these days."

"Are you telling me David Hughes was a former Special Branch police officer?" Daly wanted to grab his arms and shake him to attention.

Bingham regarded him with a sullen face. "That's what I said. We used to think we were invincible. It was our destiny to serve this wee country and the queen. I never thought I would be manhandled in this very police station."

"This is something I'll have to check up on," said Daly. The search for a missing man threw up many cranks with crackpot notions. As his eyes met Bingham's, the old man winked and grinned. A string of credibility snapped in Daly's mind.

Bingham glanced with contempt toward the desk sergeant. His voice turned loud and patriotic, an Orange Order–schooled voice, carrying the booming tone of Lambeg drums. "That's the problem these days; too many Fenians in the force." He paused, struggling to shape his next thought. "I'd like to see them lying in a ditch manning a border checkpoint in the bad old days. And for fifty quid a week, too. These young officers are so smug. Look at them. Does it ever cross their minds that police officers once had to pay the ultimate price for this country? For Christ's sake, they don't even take the Queen's Oath anymore."

Daly checked his patience. Bingham was a wall he had to batter against because he still suspected there was something there, something that might be of importance to the investigation.

"Have you seen David Hughes recently?"

"I picked him up on Saturday morning on the Derryinver Road." Bingham stuck out his chin defensively. "He was walking towards the motorway. He was like someone who had escaped from a nursing home. I didn't ask him where he was going. I just made sure he got in. I told him I'd give him a ride back to his house, where Eliza would make him a good cup of tea. He seemed confused and frightened."

"Did he tell you where he was heading?"

"I should have found that out." Bingham sounded repentant. "He told me he wanted to buy a bus ticket, but he didn't have enough money. I figured he just wanted to get to Armagh or Dungannon."

"You could be right," said Daly.

"Maybe." Bingham's head swung around in a wary arc. He seemed worried that someone might be listening. "David was frightened. I think I told you that."

"Did he tell you why?"

"I don't think he knew himself. I could hardly get a word out of him. Not like the David I knew. But then he had Alzheimer's, didn't he?"

Silence was an option he would have chosen himself, thought Daly, if he was stuck in a car with Bingham. He had stopped thinking of Hughes as a man with an illness. Not many Alzheimer's patients were able to leave behind their network of support and survive on their own for several days.

"What happened when he got into the car?"

"I pulled into a garage and told him to wait while I phoned Eliza. I waited and waited, but no one answered. When I got back to the car, David was gone. I drove up and down the road but there was no sign of him. I thought someone else must have given him a lift."

Bingham's sunken black eyes fastened onto Daly's. He looked weakened, frail, as though the effort of recounting the story had drained him.

"Why did it take you so long to contact us?"

Bingham's tongue moved heavily in his mouth. He licked his lips and his eyes flicked away. He was not quite drunk enough to be completely confessional.

"I don't read the papers. Seeing David like that was a hard blow. I never thought he would get so ill. In the end he was only trying to escape the past like the rest of us." He glanced at Daly and then looked away. "That's what I've been trying to do this past week. Fight my own battles."

His eyes locked onto Daly's again. Then he waved his hand. "Ah, I've wasted enough of your time already. Good luck with your search. I'd like to offer you my services, but then I'm retired from a police force that no longer exists except in graveyards up and down the country."

Daly wanted to fire a series of questions at him, but Bingham insisted on leaving.

He walked unsteadily out of the station, muttering to himself. His voice was almost inaudible. "All the old fool wanted to know was where the bloody duck decoys were."

Daly was still coming to terms with what Bingham had told him when Dermot appeared from the waiting room. He showed Daly the card he had been holding.

"When Joseph Devine called at our house he left behind his jacket," explained Dermot. "My mother kept it, meaning to return it. But then we found out he had been killed. She thought it best to donate the jacket to St. Vincent de Paul. When she went through the pockets she found a card with a detective's name and address on it. Kenneth Mitchell. She remembered he was one of the detectives at the early stages of the investigation into Dad's abduction. She wanted to throw the card away, but I held on to it. I suppose I thought it would come in useful at some stage."

"We'll make a detective out of you yet," said Daly, taking the card from him with a grin.

"I wasn't wrong, was I?"

The card looked to be from an old-fashioned address system. It had Mitchell's name, address, and even a telephone number. It also mentioned that the detective had been badly maimed in an IRA explosion. Scribbled on the back were the words *Senior Investigating Officer, Oliver Jordan abduction.*

"I wonder where Devine got it," said Daly. He felt an increased momentum tug at the investigation, a sustaining pull that was leading him in the direction of Jordan's abduction.

He looked at Dermot, square in the face. For the first time he saw beyond the withdrawn pose of the boy's profile, the long black hair that hung in two protective wings, the awkward hunch of the head sinking into a set of narrow teenage shoulders. The boy's hair half-hid a face that was as innocent-looking as a choirboy's. However, his body was leaning forward with a dangerous intensity, and his eyes burned as though he were welding himself to Daly.

18

The days passed according to plan, and, bit by bit, a picture pieced itself together. David Hughes waited in the house where the wind was always moaning under the eaves. He could come and go as he pleased, but he chose to remain in the room that was as bare as a monk's cell. He sat on the edge of his bed and recited his prayers, his lips moving slowly like a young child learning to read. Through the window, he watched the other inmates of the house, mostly elderly men and women, wander across the expansive lawns.

Afterward he walked over to the sink and ran himself a glass of cold water. The reflection in the small mirror surprised him. He saw the nose, lips, and beard of a grizzled old man. He looked more than his seventy-odd years. However, it reassured him to see the firmness of his chin had not been forgotten, or the falconlike glare of his gray eyes. His tight mouth and pursed lips still exuded determination.

His face had once struck terror in the hearts of weaker men, the informers he had groomed and slowly brought into the fold. Frightened men caught up in sectarian intrigues with no idea whom to trust. Even now, his flared nostrils and the corners of his mouth registered contempt at the thought of them.

His work for Special Branch had left him with an eternal look of scorn, he realized. He examined the features of his face in concern, as if a mask had grown there like skin and flesh. Would he ever be able to cast it off? The mask was a projection of his own spirit, the persona he had adopted to deal with all those years of terror. He would never be able to wipe away that look of cold contempt.

His hand shook slightly as he brushed back his hair. Over the last twelve months, his illness had tamed him. Infirmity, when it came, was not in the form he had expected. He had always believed he would succumb to a heart attack, or some abrupt physical catastrophe. Not Alzheimer's disease. Not this long, drawn-out wait, with chaos slowly seeping around him like a poison gas. Even now, sitting in this room, waiting for his visitor, he did not fully understand what was happening.

His mind was like a house that had been repeatedly burgled by a memory thief. It was a brutal and chaotic crime. Some of the most personal objects were gone forever, drawers plundered, furniture upturned and broken, while other valuable items were left strangely intact.

The sparseness of his new accommodation was a comfort. It was reassuring to be surrounded by objects he could identify and understand. The bed and sink, and the mirror above. The bedside cabinet with a well-thumbed Bible, the brown leather file and a radio.

However, a flat, circular object suspended from the wall was causing him some confusion. He knew it had a connection with the arrival of his visitor, a clue lying waiting for him to decipher or calculate. The numbers one to twelve were organized in a circle, and he stared intently at them. He could not figure out why anyone would put numbers in a shape like that, making it so difficult to add or subtract them.

At least the visitor knew what he was doing. He nodded contentedly to himself. He had chosen the right man for the job. His recruitment skills were still sharp in spite of his illness. If it hadn't been for the visitor, he would be a dead man now. He was sure of that.

Their first meeting had been a happy accident. Out of habit, the old man had not revealed his real name. The visitor might easily have been one of those shadowy men from the past, still bent on revenge. He might even have been a journalist, or a legal researcher, poking his nose where it didn't belong. However, the visitor had been none of those.

He had told the old man the catastrophe that had befallen his family, a story that, to Hughes's surprise, prompted tears. They had sat together afterward, sipping tea and watching the sun set over Lough Neagh. They arranged to meet again, and soon it became the norm for them to sit late into the evening, the visitor with a notebook and pen, the old man talking at length. The kind woman who brought them tea joked that he was having his biography written. You must be famous, she remarked.

He turned to the bedside cabinet and lifted the leather file. He opened it carefully and lifted out the thick bundle of handwritten notes and maps. Through the walls, he heard his neighbor begin to snore. He replaced the notes within the file, turned on the radio, and lay back on his bed. The visitor is like me, he thought. He likes everything clear-cut and well planned. If only his mind was as good as when he handled his circle of informers. This illness has betrayed me, he thought with bitterness. His impatience intensified, rose up, and enveloped the whole room—the dark walls, the sink and mirror, the strange object on the wall, and all the other accouterments of his carefully organized surroundings.

At the appointed time of four p.m., the visitor opened the door and entered the room. The old man had tried to resist sleep, fearing that his dreams would force their way out and fill the room like a fog. However, in the end he had succumbed, lying on his back, his arms loosely folded across his chest, a deep rasping breath dragging his rib cage up and down.

The visitor stood for a while in the middle of the room and listened carefully. A thin rain fell outside with occasional drops pecking the window.

The visitor said nothing and waited, not wishing to break the impression that the old man and all his secret knowledge lay within his power. He had gotten over the instinctive recoil he felt on first learning of the old man's past, the shock at each spilled reminiscence that was like a jab in the guts.

As the old man had rambled on during their first meeting, the visitor realized he might know the answers to questions that had haunted him for years. He had almost given up hope of finding an explanation for the tragedy that had darkened his life. The Troubles were over, and the truth was being whitewashed by politicians. That was the horror of the cease-fire, that your perceptions could be so blurred you no longer recognized the terrorist. The threads of causality linking paramilitaries with their atrocities had been broken. Three decades of bombs and shootings now drifted away from the rational ordering of things like terrible acts of a vengeful God, with murderer after murderer floating free from their crimes. What was required to bring them together again was the simple act of recollection.

However, Alzheimer's had clogged up the old man's memories with obvious inaccuracies and meaningless references to his childhood. The story's traces had been scattered by the illness. But now the visitor was determined to pick them up one by one.

The rain fell heavier against the windowpane, blurring the view, numbing the mood in the unlit room. Everything will go as planned, the visitor reassured himself. Before the old man's memories poured irretrievably away, he would have his moment of revenge.

The sound of his own breathing rose, became hard and dry. Hughes sat up in bed suddenly, his eyes full of light and urgency.

"Where am I?" he asked.

He took in the figure of the visitor, and a look of recognition passed across his face.

"I was afraid."

"What do you mean?"

"I thought they had moved the beds around while I was sleeping."

"The beds don't move." The visitor's voice was reassuring. "They are here to stay. Just like you."

He helped the old man to his feet and sat him at a table by the window. Hughes turned to him, his face sharpening.

"You smell like the IRA."

"What do you mean?"

"I smell the whiff of diesel and sweat. The aroma of terror. You've been running from someone."

The visitor ignored the comment, producing a set of photographs and more maps, and laying them on the table. The old man gazed up at him with a look of worry.

"You must tell me if they move the beds around. Otherwise, I'll be completely lost. We'll work out a warning sign. Promise me that."

"I promise you."

Carefully the visitor guided the old man's attention back to the maps.

Sighing, he lifted them to the light. The features of his face hardened into a mask. He stifled a groan as he tried to make his brain function. A series of grotesque images flashed into his mind, a man hanging upside down in a cow shed, cigarette burns on the back of his hands, clumps of torn-out hair lying on the manure-decorated floor. Torture was part of Hughes's business, and he had come across it many times in his career. The secret, he had instructed his men, was to find the victim's weak point.

When he lifted his head up, the visitor's eyes were hard. They were like fingers reaching into his mind.

"How did you get away?" the old man asked. "There were three IRA men there that night and they had you tied and gagged."

"How do you know that? Were you there too?"

"I was in the vicinity," the old man replied evasively, rubbing his hands as though washing himself of any responsibility. He spoke very slowly. "How did you manage to survive?"

"I survived because death is not the end."

19

Given the seriousness of Kenneth Mitchell's injuries Daly had expected him to be living in some sort of sheltered accommodation, so he was surprised to find the directions taking him to a farm close to the border at Aughnacloy. It was a windy day. The border roads were tortuous, a tangled web of former cart tracks and winding lanes that led everywhere and nowhere. Perfect for smuggling diesel or, in his father's day, a horde of fattened pigs, mused Daly.

The weather seemed unable to settle into one particular mood. A desolate sky alternated with views of a low, sharp sun. After a squall of rain, the clouds cleared and the wind dropped completely.

On the approach to the house, Daly glimpsed a tranquil lake flashing through trees, disturbingly still through the black branches, like a view of a dream or another dimension. A neat, stone-built house overlooked the lake. The reflections of the trees, some thickly branched, some sparse, added to the stillness of the scene.

He noticed a look of anxiety pass across the boy's face. Daly wondered if he was handling this right. The difficulty was he didn't know what exactly he was trying to achieve by coming here. By itself, rubbing Special Branch's nose in it was hardly a good enough reason.

"You know, you can sit this out and stay in the car," Daly told him.

"It's OK. I know the details of the investigation as well as the furniture in my bedroom. The amount of hours I've sat in bed going over it all in my head..." He looked at the lake. "It's the stillness that makes me feel anxious. I want to drop a huge stone into that water."

It was too quiet for Daly's taste too. The backdrop of the forest enclosed the house and guarded the icy stillness in the air. He watched the transfixed trees, waiting for some form of movement, the shadow of a bird, or the tremble of a leaf, but none came.

"I want you to ask him where Dad's body is," said Dermot. His face was as motionless as a photograph.

"You think he might know?"

"Mum thinks he's capable of remembering some clue or lead that might help the search."

How can you forget something like that in the first place? wondered Daly. How long can you keep details like that hidden? He looked at the boy. If Mitchell did know the story behind Oliver Jordan's disappearance, it was about to come back and haunt him with a vengeance.

A brand-new jeep filled the small garage next to the house. The grounds looked as though an expert gardener regularly tended them. The gravel paths were free of weeds, and juniper trees in pots sat at the front door. The vines of some creeping plant covered the walls.

Mitchell's pension must have included a generous compensation package for his injuries, thought Daly. Either that or Tessa Jordan had given Dermot the wrong address. Perhaps he should have phoned first before allowing the suspense to build. He rapped the front door.

After a while, an elderly man walked stiffly from around the side of the house.

"I don't use the front door," he said, reaching out to shake Daly's hand. "As you can see, I have a problem with steps."

His hand grip was bone-cracking. Daly felt as though the energy of the man's entire body and personality had been transmitted through the handshake.

"Detective Kenneth Mitchell?" asked Daly.

A look of concern flashed across Mitchell's face. He reached out a hand to hold on to the steel bar that ran around the house. He looked Daly and Dermot up and down, his eyes narrowing to two flecks of flint.

"Haven't been called that in a long time."

Daly introduced himself and fished in his pocket for his ID, but the old man was already walking away.

"I don't want to be bothered. The past is the past. Better left that way."

"Oliver Jordan. What about him?"

Mitchell turned around. His features were compact, unyielding. There was a light in his eyes, but no warmth. The same cold light that filled the lake and outlined the groping branches of the trees. The muscles began to move on his forehead and jaw.

"What do I care about a dead informer?"

"I'm investigating the murder of Joseph Devine and the disappearance of David Hughes. If I could just talk to you for a while."

Mitchell studied the ground for a moment. "Not much harm in talking, I suppose," he said. "I served as an RUC officer for more than thirty years, and in that time I was stalked, hunted, and had my body torn apart by Republican terrorists. One morning as I drove to work, a bomb went off under my car. It was attached to the ignition. The force of it blew the clothes off me. The first thing I saw when I came to was the tattoo of the Ulster flag on my bare arm. I reached down, but couldn't find my left leg. They found my boots twenty yards away in a ditch. I should have saved the IRA the bother and left the force when the Troubles started."

He glared at Daly, his eyes icy and still.

"I just need some background information." Daly tried to be as honest as possible. "I don't really know why I'm here, only that I have a feeling there is something unexplained about Oliver Jordan's disappearance. There are those who say the police never wanted to find his kidnappers. I don't know if that's true or false. I hope it's not true. This is his son with me."

For the first time Mitchell looked genuinely unsettled. As though he were the observer of two worlds jarring together: a pair of unexpected visitors on a winter's morning, and the memories of seventeen years earlier. Both worlds were full of pitfalls. He glanced at Daly and managed to squeeze out a smile.

"You can come inside as my guest. If only for the pleasure of watching a PSNI officer flounder when confronted by the past." He glanced at Dermot with curiosity. "You can come in too. I thought you were too young to be a new recruit."

They entered the house around the back. Through a half-opened door, Daly glimpsed a spare room full of artificial legs.

"For the past ten years I've searched a replacement for the real one the IRA blew away," said Mitchell, sitting down and removing his left leg. "The problem with prosthetics is their weight. You don't notice how heavy your legs are because they seem to move by themselves. This one's light, but after a few hours it's like having a pair of forceps pinching you. Better that than being too loose, though. Those ones tend to chafe and buckle underneath. Then there's the stump." He lifted up what remained of his left leg. It was gray and misshapen with loose folds of skin. "It changes shape over the years. So they keep having to change the socket. The last time I was fitted, they scanned my leg with lasers. My consultant told me, without a trace of irony, that it was a giant step forward."

He lifted a walking stick and hobbled over to the kettle, showing a brisk indifference to his disability.

"My mother used to say that nine-tenths of a person was willpower. The IRA could never blow those nine-tenths away."

Mitchell looked at his two guests. "But then, you haven't come to listen to stories about my leg." He shifted his amputated limb. "You know, I can still feel the tendons throbbing in my missing foot. It's been following me all these years." He stared at Dermot. "Like a bad memory."

"Can we talk about Oliver Jordan?" asked Daly.

"I told you I don't like talking of the past. I worked on countless murder investigations like Oliver Jordan's; many of them involved informers and the intelligence agencies. It was a dirty little war that had to be fought. But you can't expect me to remember every case after all these years."

His eyes sank into their sockets.

"There's a good reason why you should be able to remember more about my dad's case," said Dermot.

"What's that?" Mitchell's response was as quick as the crack of a whip.

"It was the last one you ever worked upon. You retired on health grounds a month after being assigned to the investigation. March 20, 1990."

Mitchell sat silently. The corners of his mouth dropped into an appraising scowl.

"Now do you remember?"

"Listen, son. The past is the past. You've got to leave it behind. Nothing you can do will bring your father back. You ought to be studying at college, or partying, or learning how to hang-glide or something. Not here in this room with me."

"I just want the cover-up to end. I want the facts. Facts don't lie or deceive."

"Nor do they forgive." Mitchell sighed. He paused, his eyes darting back and forth. Something quick and dark had caught their attention. A reel of images from the past flitted through his mind.

"All I can give you is my opinion. Your father was a very interesting man."

He returned to his tea and gave no indication of expanding upon his observation.

"Interesting to the IRA? Or to Special Branch?" asked Daly.

"Interesting to me. I watched many men unravel during the Troubles. Men in the security forces, neighbors, on both sides. I saw there was a void in them where there should have been pity and respect for life. Oliver Jordan was different. At least, I like to believe so."

"How come?" said Daly.

"I think he managed to figure out something for himself. He lived in a Republican heartland, and the natural thing for him would have been to support the IRA in whatever they did. Oliver was a true child of the Troubles. He was only a toddler when the Civil Rights movement started. His parents were unemployed; their housing was poor. The Troubles ended any hope he would have had for a normal life for his family. Riots flared up right on his doorstep. Oliver lived and breathed in the company of Republicans. They also killed him. But Oliver was a man of courage in spite of the terrible pressure that was brought to bear upon him."

"What do you mean?" asked Dermot.

"Your father was asked to fit out a bomb by his boss, an IRA man. It was not uncommon for this boss to put pressure on his staff to do little jobs for the Republican cause. He gave Jordan the job of fixing the electronics for the detonator. For some reason Jordan left out the battery, and in so doing signed his death warrant. The bomb was meant to go off at a Remembrance Day parade, but it never detonated. Special Branch investigated the incident and arrested several IRA men. When the IRA discovered that Oliver had sabotaged the operation, suspicion immediately fell on him that he was an informer."

"How did the IRA find out there was no battery in the device?" asked Daly.

"A legal slip-up, supposedly. Somehow sensitive details of the Special Branch investigation found their way into documents requested by the IRA men while they were on remand."

"Who were their solicitors?"

"O'Hare and Co."

"Who also represented Oliver," said Daly.

Daly glanced at the boy. Dermot was pale and silent, peering through the window at the branches of a wintry tree, and then at the shadows in the room, his eyes as piercing as a knife. Every now and again, he would glance back furtively at Mitchell and digest what he was saying. The story came to him in pieces. Some psychological defense mechanism was cutting up the truth of his father's death into morsels he could bear.

Daly's stomach tightened. He felt a protective yearning toward the boy. He worried that he was exposing him too harshly to the past. But he had insisted on coming, and it was he who had supplied the address of the retired detective.

"It was Devine who slipped in the information about the battery. Wasn't it?" said Daly.

"If it was, I never found any evidence."

"But that suggests Oliver was framed."

"An army intelligence officer told me the IRA had been tricked by Special Branch into thinking Oliver was the informer. It was the branch's theory that few tears would be shed over his death. He had worked for the IRA, after all. It also diverted attention away from the person who was really touting. The detail of the missing battery was deliberately slipped in."

"What role did Devine play in this?"

"It was obvious to me that Special Branch had not only a window into O'Hare's firm and their Republican clients but also the means to pull levers within it and eliminate opponents."

Daly thought of Joseph Devine, the dull clerk sitting sun-starved in the legal dungeon of O'Hare's practice, secretly working all those years for Special Branch. Given the number of Republican clients the firm represented, Devine could have caused all sorts of problems.

"I had a sneaking admiration for Devine," admitted Mitchell. "If he was a spy, he was a clever one. Agents like him were the tools of the security forces. Survival meant walking a tightrope all the way to eternity. There was no hopping off. The more successful the spy became, the greater the risk of discovery. Once an informer has passed the first piece of information to the police, he is trapped—open to blackmail from his handlers if he withdraws cooperation, facing certain death if the IRA finds out. Republicans have only one sentence for touts—execution. Everyone knows that."

Mitchell sank back into his chair and closed his eyes.

Daly looked at Dermot. Oliver Jordan would have known that too. The IRA had probably extracted some sort of confession from him. Most victims eventually tell their captors exactly what they want to hear, and beg for their lives.

"You're suggesting Oliver was sacrificed by Devine and Special Branch to protect an important informer within the IRA?"

"I'm not suggesting anything, Inspector Daly. I'm only bringing these suspicions to your attention."

"What did the IRA do with Dad's body?"

Mitchell sighed heavily. "Understand this. When it comes to finding out how a group of IRA men got rid of a dead body, everybody in this country is suddenly deaf and blind. The closest I got to the truth was from an old farmer who told me he was buried in bog land. That was the only lead I ever got."

"Sounds like this farmer might be a reliable witness. What was his name?" asked Daly.

"I don't remember."

"What do you mean you don't remember?"

Mitchell shifted in his chair but said nothing.

"Why are you being evasive?" asked Dermot.

"I told you I don't remember his name. Has it become a crime in this country to forget?" He stared at the two of them, eyes full of vehemence. "If you don't mind seeing yourselves out, now. My leg hurts when I'm stressed."

He stood up shakily, and the boy rushed to steady him.

The stump of his leg flailed in the air, and he fell back heavily. Daly rushed to help the two of them. He was afraid that Mitchell would miss the seat completely and end up sprawled across the floor.

"Thank you." Mitchell grimaced and held on tightly to Daly's arm. Again, he felt the compact energy of the man transmitted through his fingers.

"I don't want a bad fall in my condition. One silly mistake and I'll end up drooling in a dark corner of some nursing home."

"Surely not," said Daly.

They helped heave Mitchell's body into the chair. With a grunt, he readjusted himself as though his body needed reining in and subduing like a surge of uncontrollable emotion. He squeezed Daly's arm.

"If Devine was murdered because he was an informer, you'll have a job drawing up the list of the people he double-crossed."

Daly looked into the retired detective's eyes and saw a fresh pain take shape there, one unconnected to any limb or part of his body.

"Be careful," warned Mitchell. "A person like Devine doesn't go to his grave without dragging a few more along with him." He sank back in his seat. "That's all I can tell you. I'm tired now." He looked at Dermot. "Your hunt in the shadows for the truth will never end."

When they were outside, Dermot turned to look back at the windows of the farmhouse.

"They're running scared."

"Who?"

"Special Branch. The IRA. And the every second one of them that was an informer for the British."

They drove past the black trees that fed on the icy stillness of the lake.

"Why are you helping us?" asked Dermot.

"I don't know. Because it's my job. Maybe we'll never solve why your father was taken away. But it's a mystery that I've stumbled upon, and I can't stand mysteries."

In the silence between himself and the boy, Daly felt an equal measure of hostility and ease, with the ease just about coming to the fore. He hoped that Dermot and his mother might realize that as a detective he was motivated by more than just maintaining the status quo and protecting the reputation of the police force. A raw desire for justice was beginning to shape his thinking.

They had not come away with any concrete leads, but at least the pattern was becoming clearer, he thought. Not complete. There were still many gaps, but at least he could guess why Oliver Jordan's disappearance had haunted Devine.

They drove in silence. The trees thinned out and the shadows disappeared. They sped by muddy fields and untamed hedgerows. Mitchell had one thing in common with Devine, thought Daly. He, too, was trying to escape the past by going into the woods. But the creatures of the forest had their troubles as well. The past might be less relevant to their survival but they still had predators to worry about.

Daly switched on the radio and flicked through the stations until he found a Smiths song playing. He turned up the volume.

"I am the son and the heir of nothing in particular…" sang Morrissey.

The guitars released a shuddering wave of adolescent angst that filled the car. Daly glanced at the boy, but his profile was still and composed.

The detective's mind wandered along the tortuous paths of his own teenage years. A memory floated up from the aftermath of a late-night party—the sudden privacy of an empty sofa, a shared bottle of cheap cider, licorice sweets, and the long black hair of a girl he had never kissed. There had been something about how her hair lay curved upon her slender shoulders, her green eyes shining with a secretive, submerged light, and the lips of her mouth pursed in wanton silence. He had talked and talked. He remembered how her eyes swam up to meet his while her body remained detached and distant. He had waited but missed the opportunity to kiss her, reluctant to shrug away the solitary nonchalance of adolescence. It alarmed him to realize that all the women he had loved since were a composite image of this girl with the shining black hair.

"This is like a movie," interrupted Dermot.

Rain was falling, pounding the tarmac, drenching the windscreen. Daly gulped like a drowning man coming up for air. The windscreen wipers thrashed back and forth at monsoon setting, but he had no recollection of switching them on.

"What's that?"

"I mean, I've never seen anything like this happen, except in a film."

His voice had changed. There was an edge of tension there, and something else, amazement. He was leaning forward and watching the left-wing mirror intently.

Daly glanced in his rearview mirror. Through the rain, he could see a car some way behind.

"That car's been following us," said Dermot.

Daly's reaction was to say nothing, show nothing.

The rear window was obscured by a glistening screen of raindrops, making it difficult to determine the car's registration. Daly's foot found the accelerator, and the car rode forward with a deliberate burst of speed.

"What makes you think that?"

"Easy. It's been behind us since we left Mitchell's place."

Daly switched off the radio and glanced doubtfully at the boy. He slowed and watched the car behind loom closer. A black BMW. Where had he seen one like it before? A lorry overtook them, thundering by in a wash of water. The car crept closer, but not near enough to show the number plate.

He turned left at the next junction and glanced repeatedly at the deserted road behind him. They drove under a row of trees, fat drops plopping onto the car roof. The BMW swung into view again, its bulk taking up most of the narrow road.

"What are they going to do?" asked Dermot.

They swung right at a crossroads, crossed a bridge. The BMW lagged behind and switched on its headlights as the rain fell heavier.

Daly wished he were on his own. Dermot was a civilian, and a schoolboy at that. It was wrong to involve him in a murder enquiry. When he glanced over at the boy, he saw that he was trying to scribble down a description of the vehicle.

"You're enjoying this," he remarked with surprise.

"Yes," replied Dermot after a moment's hesitation.

"Don't you find it worrying?"

"I don't know. I can't say."

"I'm turning back," said Daly grimly, but when he looked in the mirror the car had gone. As if it had suddenly unfolded a pair of wings and flown away, bored with its prey.

"I'm taking you straight home, Dermot."

"I don't want to go back. Not yet."

But Daly was adamant.

By the time they arrived at the farm, his suspicions were starting to ease. The boy must have been mistaken, he reassured himself.

"Who do you think was following us?" asked Dermot, determined not to give up.

"I don't know. Maybe the car was lost and following us because they thought we knew the way."

"They were going 'round in circles if they were relying on you."

Daly grinned. Perhaps he was making some progress after all. Yesterday he thought he was going in reverse, knowing less all the time, rather than more.

There didn't appear to be anyone at home when they pulled up at the rambling farmhouse. Dermot went to the caravan while Daly took a walk around the outhouses. He did not want to leave the boy on his own, though he was sure he was capable of looking after himself.

"Is anyone there?" he shouted. A goat with a bell looked up from a hedgerow and made a wild regurgitating noise. It twitched and rolled its eyeballs at Daly. He remembered a saying of his father's: a horse only thinks once in its lifetime about killing a human, but a goat does so countless times.

He called out a few times and eventually got a lighthearted cry in response, and slow footsteps. Tessa Jordan appeared in Wellington boots and a floral skirt, a large bundle of stalks and dead flower heads tucked under her arm. Daly thought he detected a bashful glow in her cheeks when she recognized him. Perhaps it was the flush of physical exertion.

"I was clearing the vegetable garden."

"Looks like hard work."

"It is, just a touch." She stood still. The sun came out and brightened the edges of her dark hair. "Yesterday I planted some cabbage seedlings but the goat came along and ate them. I had to beat it with a stick."

"You look just at home."

"Not really," she said, smiling. "But I'm getting there."

Not for the first time, it struck Daly that Tessa Jordan was an attractive woman. He noted the slender curves of her body as she leaned the bundle of cuttings against her hip, and the luster of her hair and skin in the wash of weak spring sunlight.

In spite of the sun, the air was cold with the sharp, empty feel of winter. When Daly looked at Tessa's eyes, he saw a vague sense of loss take shape there. She suspected he had some news about her husband.

Despite himself, he felt a reflex of desire. Then he saw her wedding ring glinting in the sun and, rather selfishly, he felt depressed. How could he compete with the memory of a dead man?

"Don't tell me about the investigation," she urged him. "I don't want to hear anything. Not yet."

"What else shall I talk about?"

"Anything."

Daly was at a loss for words in spite of the forcefulness of her entreaty. The investigation was starting to consume all his thoughts.

"Your goat is making a strange noise."

"I'm listening."

"To me or the goat?"

"To you. Tell me a story."

But his mind was a blank. Her anxious, dark eyes peered up at him. He was struck by the expression of worried tenderness in her face, and made no resistance when she suddenly buried her face against his shirt. A list of endearments passed through his mind but his mouth opened and closed silently. He had always told himself it was impossible to love two women at the same time—too many contradictions to resolve in the heart. She pressed her head deeper against him, and he felt an unraveling inside, a sense of things flowering at the wrong time. He was a police officer and she was a widow, but the real interplay was between two lonely people. So much tension was mixed up with the pleasure of feeling her cheek brush against his chest.

She breathed in deeply, seeking out his scent, and looked up. "You look exhausted," she said.

"I have to go," he replied gently. "Dermot's back at the caravan."

"Stay a little longer. Tell me what Mitchell said."

"Dermot was there too. Perhaps it's better coming from him."

He extricated himself, feeling a tingling of embarrassment in his cheeks, and made his way back to the car.

It was still light when he arrived home. The sun had bored through the blanket of grayness and was sprinkling the waters of the lough with a dappled light. He stretched his cramped limbs and took off with a spurt of energy across the patchwork of fields to the shoreline.

The breeze was soft, and he soon found a sheltered spot under an oak tree to rest. The evening felt like a comparative heaven to the purgatory of dark winter nights he had endured in the cottage. He watched the smoke start to rise from the chimneys on the western shore of the lough.

Even though the sun was setting, Daly sensed by a hundred little signals that light was beginning to win over darkness above and below. A sharp volley of swallows shot over a row of trees and swooped overhead, a traveling kink against the edge of winter. He reassured himself that he no longer lived at the brutal front edge of history, that he was beyond the reach of the bullets and bombs that had blighted the careers and lives of policemen like Mitchell. The evening air was thick with the promise of spring.

Soon the daffodils his father planted would be bursting out of the hedge banks. He would take pleasure in their appearance this year, a simple, enclosed contentment that had much to do with the sense of failure that had overshadowed his personal life for the past six months.

When he got back to the house, he found an envelope pinned to the door. Written inside was a series of places and times. It took him a moment to realize the list described every single journey he had made that day, with all the times indicated accurately.

He opened the door of the house and locked it behind him. He felt uneasy. He stood in the hallway and looked into the rooms, listening as if a burglary might be in progress. The distant sound of crows settling down to roost formed an unruly backdrop to the silence of the house. He went into the kitchen and stared at the sink, where a tap was slowly dripping. Instead of cooking something to eat, he took down a bottle of whiskey and poured himself a generous measure. He sipped it, facing the door in a strange state of expectancy.

If he had developed an instinct for the practicalities of survival, he did not show much evidence of it that evening. By the time the moon rose, he was already asleep in an armchair facing the back door, an empty bottle of whiskey cradled in his lap.

20

The clear skies overnight meant a sharp frost. Daly drove to work through an icy landscape as faultless in its construction as an underwater kingdom of coral. To his hungover brain, the merciless morning was crammed with burning crystal. He blinked in the jagged light, his eyes swimming with the strain of focus. He was late and the car steered with a mind of its own, skidding along the frozen lough-shore roads. He dipped in and out of the vehicle's grinding bag of gears, cursing to himself as he fought for control.

By the time he reached Derrylee Police Station, it was after nine thirty a.m. He walked into the building, flashes of light firing behind his eyeballs. The desk sergeant eyed him with curiosity and handed him a report sheet.

There had been a hit-and-run in the early hours of the morning. When Daly saw the name, his cheeks puffed out in a smothered explosion of surprise.

"Inspector Irwin said he'd deal with that one," the sergeant told him. "Apparently the victim was a drunk. A taxi driver saw him stumble onto the road trying to wave down traffic just before he was knocked down."

"Only one kind of journey he's going on now, and that's the final one," murmured Daly, casting his mind back to the last time he saw the victim.

"Any details of the vehicle?"

"None so far."

Daly postponed the coffee he needed to jolt his brain into action, and drove out immediately to the scene. He found Irwin standing with the police photographer. The detective was nonchalantly chewing gum, evidently undisturbed by the sight that lay before him. In the field nearby, newborn lambs were bleating their woes and jumping about, as though their hooves were entangled in the roadside annihilation.

Irwin took in Daly's disheveled state. "Inspector, what a pleasant surprise."

"Really?" Daly blinked.

"Of course. Usually I'm taking orders from you. But not today. Special Branch is handling this case. It must be quiet down at Derrylee this morning for you to rush out here."

"Why is Special Branch so interested in a hit-and-run?"

Irwin turned to the body on the road.

"Because he's one of ours. An alcoholic. Retired, of course. The front bonnet of the vehicle must have come as a nasty surprise. He still had a cigarette butt in his mouth. Clenched between his teeth. A smoker to the end."

The body of former Special Branch RUC officer Noel Bingham lay spread-eagled on the road like that of a wild animal caught in full flight. His head was set at a contradictory angle to the rest of his body, his bulging eyeballs twisting out of their sockets. His final moments might have been spent trying to outstare an approaching predator, thought Daly. A trail of blood, thin as a rat's tail, stretched from the back of his head.

Daly looked closely and saw the cigarette butt wedged in the dead man's mouth, the teeth locked like a trap against the cold of the morning.

"At least he avoided a hangover," said Irwin, flashing a look back at Daly. "A passing taxi driver identified him. Apparently, he spent the evening getting drunk at the Four in Hand, his usual haunt. He was making his way home and trying to flag down a lift when someone forgot to stop. On another night he might have been lucky enough to stumble into a ditch and sleep it off."

"Makes your report nice and neat then," muttered Daly.

Irwin nodded. "No one's touched the body yet. Forensics will compile a report and see if we can find any scraps of evidence that might identify the vehicle. We'll give out a press release asking the public for eyewitnesses. Other than that, the case is more or less wrapped up."

Daly surveyed the roadside for a moment, thinking how Irwin's early arrival at the scene had affected the investigation. For a start, he would have wanted to cross-examine anybody who had seen Bingham along the road. He had a string of questions lined up like an ammunition belt. Surely someone had seen the vehicle that knocked him over. And if they hadn't, that would tell him something too. Unfortunately, it was too late. Irwin had let them go without taking their contact details.

The forensic examiner arrived. It was not Butler but a locum called Carberry—a pale, plump man, with a shirt collar too tight for his neck, and a face that lacked confidence and authority. He introduced himself with a sweaty hand. In comparison to the nervous Carberry, Daly suddenly felt clearheaded, coordinated, invincible.

"How long are you going to take?" he asked a little brutally.

Carberry put down his case. "I can't tell you right now. You must know that."

Irwin smirked. Carberry looked from him to Daly and back again as if the two detectives were ganging up against him. For a moment, they had.

The examiner's unease spread from his eyes like a stain. He nodded quickly and bent down to the body. His hands shook slightly as he lifted out his instruments. Irwin grew bored, stuck another stick of gum in his mouth, and strolled away.

As Daly waited, a dazed-looking farmer appeared in the field of sheep and lambs. He was carrying a bale of hay, his face a blank as he tried to fit the sight of the police officers, the white tape, and the dead body into his usual morning routine. Frozen breath hung above his mouth. Daly watched as a look of slow realization dawned on his ruddy features.

Carberry removed the dead man's jacket, letting a wallet slip and splay its contents onto the road. Something caught Daly's attention. He bent forward with an evidence bag and closed it around the item.

Carberry watched him out of the corner of his eye.

"An old RUC ID card," he remarked, "they'll be collectors' items soon."

Later, in the privacy of his office, Daly examined the card with a magnifying glass. The smudged mark at the top of the photo was indeed a bloody finger mark, as he had first thought. Unfortunately, it was smooth and featureless, most probably the imprint of a gloved hand. As such, it raised a series of questions. Why had someone with bloody gloves bothered to check the victim's identity? It was hardly the natural reaction of a hit-and-run driver. A disappearing act was what interested them, rather than the name of their victim. Bingham's accidental death suddenly took on a sinister possibility.

Daly realized he needed a chronology of Bingham's last days, right from the morning he had given a lift to David Hughes to the moment he inhaled his last drag of nicotine. He wanted to know everyone the former RUC man had spoken to. If necessary he would take his photo and call at the Four in Hand and every other pub in the area.

He bumped into Irwin as he was leaving the building.

"Still not settled into your new headquarters?" asked Daly.

"Just wanted to see how the builders were getting on. You're in the thick of a lot of rubble and dust here. Reminds me of a bomb site." He grinned at Daly. "Just like the old days, eh?"

"I'd like to see the report on the hit-and-run before you send it to Donaldson."

Color suddenly flared in Irwin's cheeks. "Are you taking over this investigation, or are you just being nosy?"

"I talked to Noel Bingham two days ago about Hughes's disappearance. Let's just say his sudden death has aroused my curiosity."

"That's very vigilant of you."

"Just doing my job," said Daly with emphasis. "I want my own version of how he met his death."

"Your suspicious mind at work again? Let me drop you a hint about how Bingham was killed. The fatal combination of too much alcohol, a dark roadside, and the internal combustion engine."

When Irwin left, Daly felt the effect of their conversation buoy his mood. He spent the rest of the day trying to trace Bingham's movements in the hours before his death. It seemed, however, that Bingham had been overlooked by all, ignored like the relic from the past he had become. Drinkers in the Four in Hand had other things preying on their minds, and Bingham had streamed through their midst like an invisible shadow. Until the front bumper of a vehicle speeding into the night gave him a one-way ticket to join his dead companions. By the end of the day, Daly was no closer to determining whether the hit-and-run had been deliberate.

As Daly approached his father's cottage that evening, a row of double-parked cars blocked the road. He slammed on the brakes. Two marshals in fluorescent jackets were directing traffic in and out of Brendan Sweeney's house, the father of the Republican politician Owen Sweeney. The old man had once been a friend of his father's, and had been seriously ill for several months. Daly assumed that he had died and the crowds were mourners descending upon his wake. He reversed and made his way back around the lough shore. It was getting late, and he was hungry. Tattered rainclouds made the twilight sky look punctured with holes. He made slow progress in an anticlockwise direction, inching along narrow, barely remembered roads, reversing out of dead ends, losing a mudguard against an upended telephone post. He passed huddles of derelict cottages among stony knolls, and small fields that were little more than nests of nettles and briars. Spatters of rain gleamed on his windscreen with the last surge of evening light. Eventually the roads arranged themselves into a more familiar pattern and he found himself back at Sweeney's lane, caught in the traffic, his wheels slithering in the mud. There was no question of getting home for several hours at least. The rain was falling heavily and the marshals had run for cover.

21

There were clean sheets on the bed in the room with pale green wall-paper. A low window framed with lace curtains looked out into the heart of a rainstorm, its heavy clouds pulsing over a vague terrain of murky bog and thorny fields. Somehow, the single pane of glass kept the ramming wind and cavorting raindrops at bay. It was a neat, homely room, a room that Daly would have relaxed in with great comfort had it not been for the two men dressed in paramilitary uniforms standing to attention beside an open coffin.

Daly did not know if the IRA men, whose faces were hidden behind sunglasses and low black berets, knew he was a detective, but they saluted him as he entered the room like any other mourner come to pay his respects. Something about their leather-gloved hands and pistol-bearing holsters told him their presence was more than the usual military sideshow that accompanied the funerals of Republican sympathizers.

Equally serious was the group of old women sitting on the white-sheeted bed, reciting the rosary, their faces a set of masks too—wrinkled, absorbed, pious. Daly felt the room vibrate with their deep concentration.

The women made some space for him, moving by intuition, without breaking the stream of their prayers. Their fingers slaved over black, clicking rosary beads, stacking up the Hail Marys and Our Fathers. He sat among them and briefly closed his eyes, his mind letting the detail of their words blur and slip out of hearing, their voices a variation of the voices that had filled his childhood. As a boy, he had been enraptured by the fervent sounds of the rosary and in private moments lately, he found himself drawn nostalgically back like a recovering patient to the whiff of hospital anesthetic.

There was a pause in the prayers, and he looked up. Through the window, he saw several sheep trying to wriggle through a southward streaming hedge of blackthorn and crooked gorse. From the downstairs kitchen came the private murmur of conversation and more prayers.

The door opened and several mourners entered the room with bowed heads. A few greeted Daly, but the others ignored him. Their voices were low, preoccupied. Oddly, he had yet to detect the slow outpouring of grief that normally filled the air at an Irish wake. People passed one another in the corridor outside the room, their conversations hushed and inhibited.

As if possessing one throat, the old women started praying again, their devout voices trickling through another set of sorrowful mysteries. Daly felt one of the IRA men eyeball him and flex his muscles, inviting him to follow the ripple of his waist down to the heavy black pistol sitting in its holster. If this were a church, Daly thought, all the statues of the Virgin Mary would have fainted to the floor.

The IRA men performed a salute and moved to the side to allow the new batch of mourners a glimpse of the coffin. Daly's eyes were drawn to the gnarled face of the dead man lying there, gaping out of a creamy white shroud. For a moment, he felt the room dissolve into a series of shifting masks, the anonymous faces of the IRA men merging with those of the old women, and the frozen features of the dead man. The click of the rosary beads combined with the snap of the paramilitaries' heels as more mourners crowded into the room and pressed against the walls. Religion and violence all mixed up, like mixing drinks, thought Daly, dangerous and intoxicating.

Brendan Sweeney was survived by his son, but the feted politician was nowhere to be seen. Although Brendan had been a friend and neighbor of Daly's father, the two men had not spoken to each other since Daly was a boy.

The old man looked smaller than he remembered. Irrationally, Daly had been expecting the corpse to look the same as the living man, but the vigorous, full-blooded farmer of his memories had shrunk, the features of his face contracting inward to a miniature waxwork of the man who would have given his life for a united Ireland.

"Time to leave," said one of the IRA men, putting his hand roughly on Daly's shoulder.

"I'm still saying my prayers," said Daly, looking up in surprise.

"Save them for yourself." The IRA man refused to move.

Daly sidled by and crept downstairs into the living room, which was filled with people chatting in small groups. He tried to plan an escape route to slink through the crowd, but the IRA man had followed him downstairs and was blocking the only exit. Instead, he sat down and stared at the empty TV screen—anything to avert his gaze from the curious glances he was attracting.

The woman next to him turned around and smiled, revealing a nicotine-stained set of teeth. His confidence returned and the feeling of crossing a dangerous frontier receded.

He had only been sitting a moment or two when the atmosphere in the room suddenly changed. Somehow, he had missed the word or glance that had interrupted the muttering conversation and brought the room to silence.

"Why is no one talking about Brendan?" asked a mourner who had taken center stage. People looked at one another balefully, as if appalled at their failure to rekindle the memory of the dead man.

The silence in the room grew heavier.

"What difference will it make? He's past caring now," the man added.

A man on the other side of Daly stood up and addressed the room.

"I'm a mechanic. I fixed Mr. Sweeney's cars for years. He was very fond of German motors, Audis and BMWs."

The mechanic had several teeth missing and such a strong country accent that some people in the room had trouble understanding him.

"A while back I was hit by a big legal claim. It was enough to put me out of business."

He flashed a gap-toothed smile.

"I needed thirty thousand pounds but couldn't get access to that sort of money anywhere. When I told Brendan about it, he said he would be happy to lend me the cash. Without hesitating, he wrote me a check for the entire amount."

When the mechanic had finished, a woman stood up.

"I'm a neighbor of Brendan's," she said. "Without him, we would never have got planning permission. My husband wanted to build a house beside his mother who was sick. She had a large farm to run. Even though we owned the land, we weren't allowed to build there.

"After we told Brendan about our predicament, we got a phone call from the planning department telling us to put in for a good site on the brow of a hill."

She sat down and everyone was quiet again. Several mourners got up and talked. They all told stories about Sweeney's kindness and generosity. It was as though the old man had bowled through his seventy-one years, flinging out loans and favors like a one-man charity, smoothing out bureaucratic wrangles and ensuring the survival of nearly every Catholic-owned business in the area.

Daly took advantage of a pause in the stories to slip upstairs to the toilet. The IRA man was still blocking the corridor to the front door, forcing people to sneak past him. From downstairs, Daly heard a door being slammed and the sound of stifled laughter. He was surprised there was no queue at the bathroom. Perhaps the mourners were frightened of missing something. But what? he wondered.

When he returned, a group of people had moved their chairs away from where he was sitting, leaving him alone with the woman with the stained teeth. She looked up as he sat down, but this time she did not smile.

She leaned over and nudged Daly. "You're Frank Daly's son. Tell us what you remember about Brendan Sweeney."

"Me?" said Daly. "I don't know what to say."

"Don't let us stop you," said the man opposite, "we're all mourners here. Everyone here is free to say what he or she thinks."

His voice was gentle and encouraging, but it also carried a warning note of authority.

The seriousness of his expression suggested to Daly that this was not an opportune moment to play the stranger. Not for the first time that evening, he wondered how many of the mourners knew he was a policeman. Slowly, he stood up.

"There is one thing I cannot ignore about Brendan Sweeney," he began. "It happened when I was a young boy. I was playing at the bottom of the lane when he strolled up one evening. He was wearing an old coat and a pair of green wellies. Even though Sweeney was the wealthiest farmer in the parish, he was never happier than in a pair of old boots talking about the price of cattle.

"He said he liked to tell things as they were and wanted to chat with my dad. He gave me a pound note and walked into the house. Dad was having a shave before going to Mass. I think it was the end of Lent. The bathroom window was open and I could hear snatches of their conversation. Dad kept on shaving. He told Sweeney that he was in a hurry to get to Mass. This must have angered Sweeney.

"He began accusing Dad of something. I couldn't hear the words, but it must have been serious. The tap in the sink kept gushing water.

"'I won't give a damn penny to murderers claiming to be Irishmen,' was all I heard my father say.

"Later when Sweeney had left, I came in and saw Dad phone his solicitor. He was holding a handkerchief to where he had cut himself on his neck. They never spoke to each other from that day on. A few weeks later, an IRA gang hijacked my father's car. They wore balaclavas and told my father Sweeney had sent them to collect their dues.

"That's all that I remember."

When Daly sat down everyone went quiet. The woman beside him nibbled at a leftover sandwich and the man opposite answered his glance with a cold stare.

From an unexpected visitor welcomed to the wake, Daly felt himself become an undesirable element in their midst. The man opposite kept staring at Daly, his cheeks flushed red. It was as though they could not bear to have Sweeney's reputation questioned in any way. In their eyes, he could do no wrong. Inwardly, Daly groaned.

From the back of the crowd, an anonymous voice spoke up.

"Sweeney was an extortionist and a blackmailer all right. And he bankrupted anyone who had the courage to cross him. He might have been a great Catholic, but he would have shot you as soon as look at you."

An old man pushed his chair forward in response. Butter dripped down his chin, but he appeared oblivious to it. His rasping voice trembled in his throat.

"What Brendan Sweeney did to my family was a crime," he declared.

"Tommy was our only son, and he was nineteen. He was never any trouble. He was somebody we could rely on and trust, and he lived for cars. That was his whole life. I never thought he would die pleading for mercy. Brendan Sweeney ordered his execution. Tommy was blamed for causing a car crash that left the daughter of an IRA man badly injured.

"The men who killed Tommy all wore boiler suits and surgical gloves. It was a planned operation, and they broke every bone in his body. Afterwards Sweeney said no one was allowed to speak to the police about what had happened. He said he would take full responsibility for the murder.

"That man was nothing but a coldhearted butcher. Most people if they had to put down a cat or a dog would walk away with some feeling. I wanted to know if he ever felt remorse. Now I'm at his wake. I used to dream about this day, but all I feel is sadness."

The old man's voice rolled about in his throat, and tears streamed down his face.

"In this part of the world life is cheap; you won't find it cheaper anywhere else. Sweeney was a monster. It would take years to list all the terror that bastard waged upon his own people."

In the tense silence that followed, a young woman stood up, placed a coat over the old man's shoulders and wiped his chin. "Let's go home, Granddad," she whispered. "Don't cry on his account. It's too late for that."

Egged on by the old man's grief something broke loose among the mourners, a pull of emotion that passed from person to person like an electrical current, bringing a woman to her feet, her chin stuck out defiantly.

"My nephew was kneecapped by Sweeney's gang for getting into a fight at a pub with a bunch of IRA men. That mistake ruined his life. His mother had just bought him a new pair of football boots. They lifted him from the football ground and took the laces from the boots and tied him up. He's never kicked a football since."

She sat down quickly and immediately a man took her place with another story. It was clear Sweeney had a split personality, wronging as many people as he had helped.

The mourners began quarrelling. One side claimed Sweeney had been a generous patron of the parish and a good Republican, the other that he had terrorized his neighbors and turned the parish into his personal fiefdom. Daly got up. He quietly slipped from the room into the kitchen, and out through the back door.

The rain that had been falling all day had lightened, but the drizzle still enshrouded the view from the back door. The mountain behind Sweeney's house was obscured but a nearby gully and its rumbling water could clearly be heard. Sweeney must have woken to its perpetual roar every day of his life. Perhaps that was where the old man got his edge, Daly thought, that intimidating sense of violence, as he rolled from house to house along the gentler slopes of the valley below.

The latch of the back door clicked shut as someone else left the house. The IRA man slowly moved into view, inspecting the space around him, discreet but without making an effort to be quiet. His steel-tipped boots echoed on the cobbled yard. Too late, Daly realized he had walked into a trap.

"Why are you here?" he asked, squaring up to Daly.

"Brendan was a neighbor of my father's."

"No, I mean what are you doing here?"

He prodded Daly in the shoulder.

"I'm a police detective and I wish you'd stop doing that," said Daly.

"You're not a detective here. You can be a mourner come to pay his respects but not a policeman. You can't come here and poke your nose into a dead man's life."

"I understand," said Daly, trying to hold the terseness in his voice. He did not want to signal surrender, only a growing awareness of how complicated the situation was. He glanced tentatively toward the kitchen door, but it was shut. Dusk was advancing, and even though the IRA man had removed his beret and sunglasses, his face was difficult to see in the fading light. He poked Daly again in the shoulder and began circling him, jabbing him here and there as though inspecting what sort of stuffing he was made from.

Before the detective could brace himself against an attack, a cigarette flared in the darkness. Someone stepped out of the shadows and beckoned the paramilitary to return to the house. The new arrival had a peaked cap, and the collars of his coat were drawn up. Dressed to draw the minimum of attention to himself. He pushed his face forward for inspection and Daly recognized the tufty beard and shining eyes of Owen Sweeney.

"Sorry about that," said the politician, glancing at the retreating back of the paramilitary. "They're like gun dogs quivering with excitement at the scent of prey. You're lucky, you know. The next time you saw your face could have been in a mirror on a hospital ward."

A grimace creased Sweeney's face and he gestured toward the house. "Typical Irish wake, eh? My father's not even buried and they're tearing his reputation to shreds. It's disgusting."

He rocked back on his heels, drew heavily on his cigarette, and allowed himself a rueful grin. "All the same, Dad could be a sick old bastard when he wanted to be."

There was an air of potent self-assurance about Sweeney in the shadowy light. Daly had seen that smug confidence before in senior Republicans, former paramilitaries who had done time in prison and were now celebrated politicians in the Northern Ireland Assembly. Men who believed they held the balance of power, sure that the dealt cards favored them.

Together the two men watched the signal light of a helicopter flash in the murky sky.

"How could the British ever defeat us?" said Sweeney, softly, almost wistfully. "We were stubborn and showed them we meant business."

He turned and concentrated his gaze on Daly.

"Glad you could make it, by the way, Inspector. Dad would have been pleased to have a policeman praying over his body."

He tossed away the cigarette. "Also, I've something I want to show you."

Sweeney's self-satisfaction slowed his voice into an intoxicated drawl.

"But that can wait. You know, at the time of the cease-fire we weren't losing the battle. British soldiers had to walk backwards on the streets of every town in Armagh and Tyrone. And you don't do that if you're winning the war."

He licked his lips as though the words had left a sweetness behind he desperately wanted to savor. From his pocket, he took another cigarette and lit it.

More smoking and silence.

When Sweeney spoke again his voice was still low but less intimate.

"Let's get down to business. Tell me what you make of Devine's murder. I hear it was quite a crime scene."

"Officially it's too early to say. Unofficially, I'm working hard on the angle that Republicans were involved," said Daly.

"I wouldn't get too excited about that avenue of investigation."

"Why not? There's enough about Devine's past and the way in which he was killed to justify such an inquiry."

"Republicans had nothing to do with his murder. An incident like that would have far-reaching political consequences. The whole peace process might unravel. Anyway, we had no intelligence that Devine was an informer. He wasn't even on the radar. If you're interested in finding his killers, you'll have to spread your net a little wider. Devine had in his possession sensitive information which could have done damage to a lot of people."

"You sound well informed, better than Special Branch themselves."

"Who? Donaldson and his cronies?" said Sweeney derisively. "They couldn't investigate the whereabouts of their boots."

He crushed the cigarette, and his face grew animated.

"Since the cease-fire we Republicans and the intelligence organizations have been working by a set of unwritten rules. One of them is that we keep an eye on each other. Trust is in very short supply. We strike a balance, look after our own security, and everyone gets on with promoting peace."

Sweeney turned his big-boned face at Daly, all trace of enjoyment gone from his features.

"Unhappily, you were assigned Devine's murder, and ever since you've been trespassing on everyone's territory. It's time to stop taking an interest in Republicans, Daly. There's a lot of uncertainty in the ranks and your investigation is stirring up all sorts of conspiracy theories."

"I'll suspect anyone I want," replied Daly.

Sweeney looked at him fiercely and then a twinkle of mirth flashed again in his eyes. From the inside of his jacket, he produced a sheaf of papers.

"You know Devine was kneecapped in his youth. He'd been pestering some girl and the order was put out to give him a little tickle on the knee. I fired the bullet. Looks like I should have aimed it higher."

He rolled the papers into a baton and smacked them into the fat of his palm.

"These are the legal files you retrieved from Devine's house. They make interesting background reading. Nobody wants a bloodbath unless it's really necessary. Devine wasn't murdered out of blind fury or revenge. He was killed because it was necessary. And the orders must have come from very high up."

"Who are you talking about? The intelligence services?"

"Who knows? But don't expect any help from them. Their brief is to ensure the investigation goes 'round in circles until people like you get tired of pursuing it. Devine has no family, so the expectation is there'll be no campaigning relatives to keep his case in the spotlight."

He handed Daly the papers.

"Want to know something you'll never see written down in any report or file? One of your lot tried to recruit me once. A Special Branch officer nicknamed the Searcher."

"What's he got to do with it?"

"His name was David Hughes, the man who's leading you a merry dance at the minute. I remember him as a self-righteous prat with a strong sense of duty and no mercy. But I hear dementia has made him much more pleasant to get on with."

It was turning out to be an evening of the strangest questions and confessions, thought Daly.

He glanced at the papers. "What about the pager?"

"The pager?" asked Sweeney. "I had to return it to its rightful owners."

"Who are they?"

"Your friends in Special Branch," he answered with a laugh. "Property of the British Security Services. They're very precious about things like that. I didn't want to get a bill and an angry letter from them."

22

Reconstructing the past was proving a tougher task than the visitor had imagined. At times David Hughes couldn't remember the identity of his companion, let alone what had brought them together. Moreover, as each day went by the net of their investigation seemed to expand, taking in a wider circle of informers. Now he was back to talking about ducks again. The old man's illness made it feel as though they were trying to walk over deep black water. Time was running out.

"I've had enough. Stop talking about those bloody duck decoys." The visitor lost his temper.

Hughes looked at him from the corner of his eye, as though he wanted to say something but was restraining himself.

"What is it?"

Hughes sighed. "If only I could escape."

"From here?"

"No. From my conscience. Now that the truth is close, I wish I could escape."

"And you think that hiding from the truth will bring you freedom?"

"You wouldn't understand. My conscience has got very big, too big for the old wreck of my mind. It keeps challenging me to a fight." He began to shake his head as though a fly were annoying him.

"Do you believe in God?" asked the visitor.

Hughes was silent. He scratched his head vigorously.

"If I believed in God, I'd also have to believe in the devil, and hell, too, and that would cause a whole lot more complications than my muddled mind can deal with." He looked at the visitor. "What age are you?"

When the visitor told him, the old man laughed.

"And you believe in God and angels and that we all have souls and good intentions?"

The visitor felt ridiculed.

"You've led too pure a life to realize that man is a brute," said Hughes. "Give him a gun and any kind of uniform, and he'll trample all over you."

"If you don't believe in God, then why listen to your conscience?"

"My conscience is my major flaw. It'll kill me quicker than any illness."

The visitor got up and stood at the window. The darkness outside was thick and foreboding. He felt a sudden squeeze of panic in his guts thinking of what Hughes had said. We are like two blind mice scurrying on the pantry floor, he thought to himself.

He was unable to rest so he put on Hughes's old overcoat and sat up, waiting for the moon to rise. The pockets were full of duck feathers. He seized a thought that had been floating around the edge of his consciousness. Devine's last message had made an unusual reference to flight. He didn't know why the description had stayed with him, but then he saw the connection.

He went over to the bed and roused the old man. They were about to make a late-night trip, and for the first time they were going to be accomplices to a crime.

23

Now that he had worked out the meaning of Devine's last message, the visitor's mind was as clear and simple as that of a poker player with a winning hand. What a moment of inspiration it had been, coming out of the blue when his search for the truth had seemed so dark and complicated. Now, as he drove the borrowed jeep along the overgrown lane, he felt freed from any shadow or notion of fear.

Hughes sat beside him with his vacant hunter's face, impermeable to weather or words. He kept looking straight ahead as if searching for an indication of rain or inclement weather. During that first meeting in the room of comfortable armchairs, the old man had let slip his nickname, the Searcher. It was apt. Even though illness had dulled his personality, his gaze still burned with a stubborn intensity.

The visitor did not say anything. He just followed Hughes's directions. A person had to know when it was right to stay silent. It was no longer possible to have a full conversation with the old man anyway. His illness interfered too much with the organization of his mind. He had to be patient, and ensure they made the most of their new lead.

They drove on as a cold rain snuffed out the dusk. They wanted to avoid the police patrols that might be watching their intended destination, so they followed forgotten lanes that were no longer marked on maps. The jeep sloshed through the downpour. They slipped unnoticed through a small forest. A screen of thorn trees swung back, revealing the cottage and the light from the back porch throwing into jagged relief a circle of unkempt garden.

"Where are we?" asked Hughes. They had been silent so long the old man had forgotten their mission. He looked about him as though he might be on one of those artificial outings designed to break the boredom of the long winter evenings.

The driver sighed. "The truth is always near, within your reach."

After a minute of silence, he tried another tack.

"To catch two birds with the one stone. What does that mean?"

"I know that. It's simple. This is usually what people try to do. Because they want to catch too many birds, they find it difficult to stay focused. They end up not catching any birds at all."

The driver waited, counting his breaths, keeping his impatience in check. During his bouts of confusion, the two of them clung to a few wisps of shared conversation. Swapping proverbs and playing word games had become a vital form of sustenance to their friendship.

"The man with two birds," said the driver. "This is his house."

"Of course, I remember now." Hughes looked around him as though he was just coming to consciousness from a long nap. "Switch off the headlights. Keep the engine running. This will take just a minute."

The old man walked furtively toward the back door. The visitor leaned back and thought of Joseph Devine, a man he had never met but who had fundamentally changed the course of his life. Devine had held more than one bird in his hand. He had been the center of a secret organization of spies and informers. But in the end he had made a mistake. And that had cost him his life. He knew that any mistakes made by him or Hughes would be punished in a similar way, such was the dangerousness of their operation.

Eventually the old man reappeared, creeping out of the house. The driver flashed his headlights. Hughes stood in the dim gleam of the porch light and took his bearings. A look of confusion darkened his face. Over his shoulder was a bulky bag. The driver held his breath. The old man put down the bag and walked toward the front of the house, his posture changing abruptly from skulking to leisurely. The driver felt the blood drain from his body. He flicked the headlights twice, and then again. He was convinced the detective in charge of the case would have posted a patrol car at the front of the house.

The rain spattered the windscreen, obstructing his view. He rolled down the window and, straining his ears, heard only the washing sounds of the lough. He felt a moment of terror in the darkness. A tremor of the mind as disabling as Hughes's fits of confusion. The heavy trees and the brooding cottage all converged upon him, shutting out any means of escape.

Something moved at the other side of the house, a prowling silhouette. Hughes had returned. He held out his hand as though he had just discovered it was raining. The headlights lit up his grizzled face. He was dripping wet. Ducking back toward the porch, he threw the bag over his shoulder and hurried back to the jeep. In one swoop, he opened up the back door and heaved the load inside.

It landed on the floor with a heavy thump.

As the jeep slowly reversed, he glanced at the driver with a twinkle in his eye.

"Bet you never saw an old fool burgle a house before."

"Not like that, anyway."

"You're an accomplice to robbery now."

"If the police ever question me, I only gave you a lift."

"That's right. I could be carrying anything in that bag. A load of sticks or a bale of hay. Anything at all."

The driver peeked into the sack and saw Devine's collection of duck decoys glinting back at him. He grinned at Hughes.

24

When Daly got back to his cottage there was a message for him on his answering machine. Constable O'Neill had asked him to phone her at the station.

"What's happened?" asked Daly, expecting grim news.

"Nothing too serious," she replied. "I thought you might like to know. Eliza Hughes rang earlier looking to speak to Inspector Irwin. No one else would do. When Irwin got the message, he left in a hurry. That's all."

"Did she say where she was calling from?"

"No."

"Thanks. Keep in touch if you hear anything else."

Eliza's secret meeting with Irwin was suspicious enough to merit further investigation. Wishing he had eaten something at the wake, Daly got back into his car and drove to Washing Bay. He met her on the way, driving fast, an expression of alarm on her face. She did not appear to have noticed his car. He reversed in a lane and took off after her in a flurry of mud. As he drove in the twilight, the dark blues of the lough reasserted themselves, the pine forests lagging behind. She was following the lough shore, Daly realized, keeping off the main roads.

The idea that she might have something to hide was psychologically disturbing for Daly. She was Hughes's long-suffering carer, an elderly woman who had devoted herself to her brother's needs, not someone who organized furtive meetings with Special Branch.

As her brake lights gleamed ahead, something pressed upon a nerve in his subconscious. Her responses had struck him as odd on the night of Hughes's disappearance. A stillness and silence when he asked about any enemies David might have had. Daly's hunger was replaced by a gnawing unease.

Her car turned left, and after ten minutes of driving turned left again into a forest. There was only one possible destination, and that was Joseph Devine's rundown cottage. Daly pulled his car into a passing place and waited for her lights to disappear through the trees. It was a calm moonlit night. In a field, he saw two hares running together. After a few minutes, he took off again, slowly following the road through the forest.

He parked in the shadow of a high plantation of fir trees a short distance from Devine's cottage. The first thing that struck him as strange was the absence of a patrol car guarding the house. He rang through to the station on his mobile and discovered that Irwin had reassigned the officers to a burglary in Portadown.

The lights were on in Devine's cottage, and the front door lay slightly open. The night was dark and cold, and the cottage still offered a residual sense of welcome that even the owner's grim murder had not quite dispelled.

It had rained earlier and the thorn trees dripped heavily as Daly brushed beneath them. He wasn't looking forward to several hours of cold, wet, stooping surveillance.

Eliza Hughes was briefly silhouetted in the doorway, her hair tied up in a bun, before she scuttled within. He saw her again framed in the front-room window, talking to someone. A few days ago, she had been Hughes's stricken sister, a detached but recognizable figure. Now she was a woman of intrigue with a hidden life. The upturned collar of her coat and the formal arrangement of her hair made her look efficient, like a woman dressed to carry out a difficult assignment.

Daly watched her head turn to survey the room and then back to continue her conversation. He was amazed he had not noticed this side to her personality before. He felt an overpowering sense of curiosity and was about to walk up to the cottage when the figure of Irwin appeared in the window. Daly heard the detective shout suddenly. Eliza crouched with her arms raised protectively to her head as a horrible clacking sound echoed from inside the house. Irwin stood behind her, waving his arms wildly in the air.

It was no time for chivalry, but Daly did not want to see the woman hurt. He tensed his body and was about to run toward the house, when the motive behind their violent pantomime became apparent. There was a trapped bird in the room, its dark shape swinging between the walls like the shadow cast by an erratic candle flame. Its wings thrashed frantically against the windowpane as Irwin tried to help it escape. But the bird was too frightened. It fluttered its wings through his hair and swung its beak at his face. In the background, Eliza appeared with a broomstick and managed to shove the distressed creature out the opened window. Daly crept back into the hedge, half smiling to himself.

For the next twenty minutes, the two conducted what appeared to be a thorough search of the house, even stripping at the grim wallpaper. Daly watched, waiting for someone else to appear. Nothing made sense to him. He couldn't imagine Irwin at the helm of a conspiracy with Eliza as an accomplice.

Eventually another figure appeared in the room. A tall, sleek, well-groomed man with a razor-blade smile. Daly wondered where he had been during the search. His presence in the room was like a sudden shift in gravity. It appeared to galvanize the efforts of Irwin and Eliza Hughes. They proceeded with more haste throughout the house, emptying shelves, pulling out boxes, upending furniture.

Watching the growing desperation of their search, Daly had a hunch that whatever they were looking for was already gone. The secret life of Joseph Devine was entangling more and more people. His mind flashed back to the black BMW that had followed him from Mitchell's house, and the note pinned to his door. It was more than an attempt at intimidation. We can follow you and we don't care if you see us, the note seemed to suggest. But behind it, he also sensed a growing agitation as his investigation dug deeper into Devine's past and the connections with David Hughes became evident. Perhaps they were trying to distract him from something.

He walked back to his car. He had gained an advantage over Irwin, and he wanted to make sure he made the most of it.

It rained heavily throughout the night. The next morning, Daly's car sped along the lough-shore roads on white wings of spray. His eyes took in the flooded scenery of the countryside, the huddled gables of outhouses, wet ribbons of water forming in the fields, and cattle sinking up to their knees, but his mind was elsewhere.

So familiar was the route to Hughes's cottage he could have driven there in his sleep. A furniture-removal van crammed the lane. Two men waited in the cab and watched as Daly parked and got out. He felt as though he had stepped into an unfamiliar water-bound landscape. The sound of hidden water filled the air, gurgling in gullies and clefts along the lane and behind the hedges. He made his way up to the house, scrambling between dry land and the flood's rising tide.

When Daly called at the door, Eliza Hughes's face registered a kind of cold dismay. In the morning light, she looked to have aged. She was haggard, the smudges beneath her eyes were coal-dark, and her forehead was heavily lined. She seemed to have lost weight. Her neck did not quite fit the collar of her polo-necked blouse.

She nodded quickly at Daly and stepped aside for him, as though she had been expecting his visit. The kitchen table was stacked with half-filled boxes. Cupboard doors and drawers lay open, their contents gone.

"I don't have much time to talk," she told him. "Busy packing."

Daly surveyed the rifled kitchen. "Every step I take forward in this investigation seems to produce more and more complications," he remarked.

The cottage was quiet but full of shadows. It occurred to Daly there might be someone lurking in the next room. The ever-present sense of danger was what distinguished the lives of these people, he realized. He looked at Eliza and she produced a distant smile for him.

"Do you mind?" he asked, getting up to close the door.

She said nothing and stared at him, her eyes widening.

"Is anything wrong, Miss Hughes?"

"Nothing," she said, turning away. "I've been unable to sleep. The loneliness has got to me. I'm moving back to Belfast, until they find David."

"Who's 'they'?"

"I mean the police. Yourselves." She looked around the room as if giving it a mental farewell.

"I visited your house last night, but you were gone. What were you doing at Devine's cottage?"

She was less distracted now, listening carefully to Daly's every word.

"From the first night I came here, something has not quite added up. You've been hiding the truth from me. In fact, I believe you've delayed and hampered the progress of this investigation all along." He waited for his words to sink in. "But, I suspect you were put in an impossible position."

Eliza switched on the radio and turned up the volume. On her way back, she staggered slightly. Daly wondered if she was on tranquillizers. Her face was ashen with weariness, and her voice sounded groggy. Through the window, the flooded fields looked like the gray ice floes of a frozen landscape.

"I should have told you the truth that first night you arrived. David wasn't just a farmer. He worked undercover for Special Branch. The East Tyrone Support Unit was his brainchild. He set it up with eight other officers. They operated in plainclothes and in unmarked cars, and mixed with the local community. He was a recruiter of informers, one of their best. Devine was one of the men he enlisted." Although her voice shook at first, a practical tone reasserted itself. She was like a survivor reconstructing the scene of a ghastly accident.

"I used to work as an administrator in the security forces, and had special clearance. When David became ill, I was assigned to look after him. After all, I was his sister and I knew how much he wanted to live here by the lough. I kept in contact with headquarters, and they routinely assessed him. Though he was confused at times, he wasn't deemed a security risk. I thought I could keep a handle on his dementia, but David had his own plans.

"My brother believed that Devine had made a note of all the operations he was involved in. The typical legal type. Everything recorded down to the last detail. That's what we were doing at his cottage, looking to see whether he had hidden the information somewhere."

As she spoke, Daly noticed the lines of tension dissolve from her

162

face, and he guessed she was telling the truth, or at least that part of the truth she knew.

"I need to know if anything unusual happened to David in the weeks before he disappeared," said Daly. "Did he have any strange visitors? Did he talk to someone he shouldn't have? This wasn't a prison. You couldn't shut him away completely from the world."

She looked away and reached for a bottle of window spray on the table. Daly got there first. He grabbed the bottle and placed it out of her reach. She stared at him in surprise.

It was a small but important victory against the woman's obsession with cleaning. The way in which she used it to tidy away unruly feelings and unwanted thoughts.

"Remember, this is David's last chance," said Daly. "To the people who murdered Devine, life is cheap. Especially an old man's life."

She stared at him, her face motionless. She appeared to be waiting for more. He tried a different tack.

"Noel Bingham's life was cheap too. I suspect his death was no accident. It was linked to his meeting David the morning after he ran away."

Eliza shook her head. "Don't you see what's going on? Bingham knew everything. He was David's driver when he worked undercover. Bingham was in contact with Special Branch, and was meant to bring him in. Somehow, David guessed and managed to get away while Bingham was phoning for help."

She reached her hand into a cardigan pocket and fumblingly withdrew a cigarette.

"The last few months have been hell. I took on far more than I could handle. David became obsessed with the past and the informers he had recruited. He didn't seem to notice me at all. It was as though I had become a shadow in the cottage, walking through his darkest memories.

"The weeks dragged on and became months. His illness didn't get any better, nor did it seem to deteriorate. I began to feel I was the one under surveillance. Living in a prison. David was writing notes to himself and leaving them littered across the hedgerows. I couldn't sleep at night with the worry.

"Last November, I went to my GP to get some sleeping tablets, but I broke down in his surgery. It was the one moment in the last six months that I lost my self-restraint. Before I knew it, the GP had organized a fortnight's respite for David at a nearby nursing home. An ambulance was waiting for him when I arrived home. I had two weeks of blissful sleep at night and desperate elation during the day. Even then, I had a dread that my rest was going to be paid for at a very high price. I didn't tell Special Branch, of course.

"When David returned, he appeared less confused. He was full of humorous remarks about how quick I was to abandon him. I was relieved and glad to get back to the business of caring for him. I convinced myself I had done no wrong. Special Branch believed their security measures were watertight, up until the night he disappeared. I committed my second error that night by ringing the police in a panic. My instructions had been to contact a special number if David went missing, but it was the middle of the night and I couldn't think straight."

Her eyes filled with tears. "You've been so helpful and I've been such a hindrance."

Daly shook his head. What he saw was a guilt-ridden woman swept into a land of shadows.

She stared at Daly. "I'm worried about David. You'll find him, won't you?"

"You did the right thing that night, calling the police," said Daly. "And I'm glad I was the detective on call. But I have to be careful. Special Branch is watching me, as well. I want you to give me twenty-four hours before you tell them about David's respite stay. Now, I need the name of that nursing home."

25

The silence observed by the residents in the nursing home was like that between competitors at an interminable game of chess. It hung in the air, forming an invisible barrier between them as Daly made his way through the day room to the nurse manager's office. Some of the faces of the patients looked vexed, others had relaxed into the half-grin of senility. Nurses carried out their duties with an air of organized tranquility. Underfoot, the thick carpet decorated with the shapes of flowers gave off a synthetic smell of roses.

The nurse manager stood waiting for him, as his urgent call had requested. Her mild, maternal eyes scanned his face with an expression of puzzled amusement.

"What sort of emergency heralds a lone policeman in an unmarked car?" she enquired.

"I'm sorry for taking you away from your work," said Daly. "This shouldn't take too long. I understand David Hughes spent a fortnight's respite here back in November. I'm just following up any leads that might help us locate him."

"David Hughes," she said with an understanding nod. "We were all concerned when we saw his photo in the papers. The staff warmed to him while he was here."

"I need the details of anyone who came in contact with him. Staff, visitors, other residents' relatives…."

She went to a filing cabinet and produced several files. "All our employees are vetted by the police these days. Their information is in these files. I can let you read through it, if you want."

An old man walking up to one of the windows in the nearby day room caught Daly's eye. It was dusk outside, and the old man's focus was short. He appeared to be examining his own reflection rather than the darkening view of the landscaped gardens. Saliva drooled from his mouth.

"Mr. Hughes enjoyed his stay with us," said the manager. "It was a surprise he did not come back. I think he needed more space and time to work things through."

"Work what through?" asked Daly, raising an eyebrow.

"He still hadn't come to terms with his illness. Sometimes the residents gain a new perspective, a different angle, when they come here. Sometimes it forces them to see what they've been ignoring all along."

"Like what?"

She shrugged. "We've all got unfinished business, Inspector, things we try to push to one side and ignore."

Daly felt his shoulders tighten. He found himself staring down at his shirt.

"Take that gentleman over there," she said, pointing to the man at the window. "He's in the early stages of Alzheimer's. Like Mr. Hughes. To anyone who'll listen he'll tell a terrible story about his brother-in-law, and the morning they found his mutilated body in a roll of carpet floating in the river Bann. I've no way of knowing if his story is true, but the details never change."

"Did David ever talk about his past?"

"No. He was very reticent in that regard," she said. "He was more of a wanderer than a talker."

The manager left him alone to search through the files. He took down names and contact details. It was like searching for a needle in a haystack. He was going to have to interview every staff member and find out what they knew about Hughes. Then he would have to start on the residents and their relatives. Even then he could not be sure he had talked to everyone who had met Hughes during those two weeks. How could he? Perhaps he was just fooling himself. Eliza's revelation about Hughes's stay in the nursing home had seemed promising at first. However, he feared it might lead him down a dead end.

When he got up to leave the office, the old man was still standing at the window, peering into the unfathomable depths of his reflection. He glanced over at Daly. The corners of his mouth were dragged down by what might have been sadness.

"Do you shave with a razor?" he asked.

"No. Should I?" Daly rubbed his jaw line.

"I need a razor myself. I haven't had a proper shave in weeks."

Daly noticed the man's jaw was smooth and stubble-free. A bit of dried shaving cream was stuck in one of his nostrils.

The old man raised his hand. He was holding a crumpled piece of paper.

"Do you know what this is?"

"No."

"It's my secret. You didn't know I had secrets."

"Everybody has secrets."

"But mine are special."

"What are they?"

"I can't tell you. Only the visitor is allowed to see."

"The visitor?" Daly's voice changed, grew careful.

"Yes. The young man that comes and writes down our secrets. Are you waiting for him too?" he asked, analyzing Daly's face.

"No. I'm not."

"Does he frighten you?"

"No." Daly made an effort to relax

"Good. He doesn't frighten me, either."

"What's his name?"

"Who?"

"The visitor."

"That's his name. The visitor."

"Are you going to show him your secret?"

"Maybe I won't. It might be too horrible."

"Will it frighten him?"

"Let's wait and see."

Daly turned away.

"Do your best to find him," the man said. "I've been waiting for too long."

Daly assured him he would.

The manager was signing sets of sheets by the medication trolley in one of the lounges. A humming noise filled the room. At first Daly thought it was a trapped insect, but the noise was too loud. It continued, hanging elusively in the air. It jarred him when he realized it was a high-pitched wail coming from an old woman with closed eyes. Another old woman looked up at him, blessed herself, and began reciting the rosary. The patient next to her leaned forward and with vehemence began chanting: *"Fuck the pope and the IRA."*

"Oh dear," said the manager. "That's the only phrase he remembers."

A care assistant helped her remove the disturbed patient from the room. She returned with a harried look on her face.

"You didn't tell me about the visitor," said Daly. "The young man who writes down secrets."

"The visitor?"

"The patient in the dayroom is waiting for him with a piece of paper."

"He must be talking about one of the pupils doing voluntary work."

"What pupils?"

"They come here at weekends. They add a new dimension to the residents' lives. Sometimes they write up people's life stories, or play games. There's a big difference in the residents' moods afterwards."

She glanced impatiently at her watch. Daly moved in with the important question.

"Tell me about the boy who writes down secrets. Did he spend time with David?"

"Yes, there was a boy who wrote down his memories. His company produced a big change in Mr. Hughes. He was more settled afterwards."

"What's his name?"

"His grandmother is a resident here: Rita Jordan. He's a quiet boy. Dermot's his name. Dermot Jordan."

Daly left the nursing home in uncertainty and confusion. Dermot Jordan, he thought to himself. Could he be behind Hughes's disappearance? The question opened up a depth of anxiety within him that immediately demanded a remedy.

In spite of his suspicions, he could not help but feel a protective concern for the boy. If it was true, the boy was out of his league, playing a dangerous game of hide-and-seek with the security forces and a host of other nefarious groups. They might not be as powerful and belligerent as they were during the high noon of the Troubles, but they were tenacious in their desire to tie up loose ends, and their powers were secretive and arbitrary. He didn't imagine Dermot could withstand an interrogation. He worried about the state of the boy's mind and, more pressingly, that Tessa Jordan was somehow entangled in the subterfuge too.

26

Minnie and Bill were a pair of larger-than-life duck decoys, the most ancient set Joseph Devine had in his collection. Minnie had at least twelve coats of paint plastered over her, and Bill had a fissure that ran down the center of his back, but in spite of their decrepit condition, David Hughes handled them with care and delight.

"They're a motley pair, and at least fifty years old, but there's plenty of game left in them," he declared. "You can't beat the old ones."

Dermot drew closer. "'For further arrangements, contact Bill.' That's what Devine's obituary said."

Hughes wasn't listening. He had already found the map. It was slotted inside the hole in Bill's back like a half-posted letter.

The old man grinned. "'If that old bird could talk, the tales he would tell.' How right Devine was."

He and Dermot Jordan pored over the map. The boy sensed that a decisive watershed had occurred in his life.

"Devine must have asked a lot of questions to come up with this," remarked the old man.

The map showed a square mile of bog land above the village of

Cappagh, in the foothills of the Sperrins. The dead informer had managed to narrow the search for Oliver Jordan's burial place.

Dermot felt the truth was very close. Now all he needed to do was take Hughes out to the bog land and hope the journey would jog his memory. He breathed deeply. No point in getting excited now. There had been so many false starts in the past few months, so many leads that took them nowhere.

"You must be able to recall some landmark. A tree, a stone, a river, something?" said Dermot.

Hughes said nothing.

"Can't you remember anything at all?" the boy shouted in exasperation.

They were close but yet so far.

Hughes turned his back to Dermot and lay down to sleep. His last conscious thoughts brought him deep into the fog of his memory as he struggled to recall the details the boy had requested.

In one of his dreams, he found himself stepping out through the back door of his cottage into pitch-darkness. The door gave onto the black wind. Voices whirled and echoed in the howling air. He realized his eyes were closed against the darkness. Opening them, he gradually made out a sky of dim stars. But the brightest thing in the night was a flowering thorn tree sitting in the middle of a dark hedge. Its naked black branches were laden with white blossoms, shining like clusters of stars. A line of ghosts shuffled along the hedge toward the tree, as though it offered some form of protection. He saw Oliver Jordan climb up into the tree, then others, like stowaways boarding a boat, reaching up on their tiptoes, hugging the twisted branches while the blossoms stirred in the dark wind like a set of sails.

A sense of relief and happiness overwhelmed him. Nothing was lost. No one had died. For forty years he had worked as a police officer; so many colleagues had been killed, as well as informers, not to mention the countless civilian victims. He saw the thorn tree gather them all up safely into its branches, ready to bear them off to a safer haven. But there was something anchoring the tree, something buried amid its roots, preventing it from carrying its cargo of lost souls heavenward. He gripped the gnarled base of the tree and tried to shake it loose, begging it to uproot itself, but it would not budge. The branches grated together as if in pain. He began digging with a tiny silver trowel, scratching at the stony soil.

He was still digging in his mind when he awoke. It was not soil he was sifting through but memories. He dug deep, until he found what he was looking for in his mind's eye, the site of Oliver Jordan's grave. He could see it clearly now, on a strip of mountain bog, a whitethorn tree marking the spot, its scant blossoms fluttering in the breeze. It had been early spring when the IRA men buried his body, and the white flowers of the tree had provided the only colorful things for their eyes to rest upon. It was the one living landmark in the expanse of lifeless bog. The siege of his memory was ending.

27

A frost was already forming when Daly pulled up at the farmhouse. In the distance, he saw a pair of rear lights melting into the still-red sky. He lurched up the lane wishing he had worn a thicker jacket. In fact, he wished he had given more thought to his clothes in general. He had been wearing the same shirt, tie, and trousers for the last few days, and they were beginning to look crumpled.

In spite of the cold, he felt a thin layer of perspiration on his forehead. He rubbed his moist hands and paused for a moment to get his breath. What in God's name was going on in his body? He had made an important breakthrough, yet here he was, sidling about anxiously in the dark like a lovelorn youth. He was Inspector Celcius Daly, chief investigating officer in a murder case. He glanced tentatively at the caravan door. It was just as well dusk had advanced. The shadows might conceal the red glow in his cheeks.

He froze just before knocking on the caravan door. A thought struck him. Had he exaggerated the importance of Dermot's relationship with David Hughes? For a moment, he feared this new development was just a sham orchestrated by his heart to prompt another visit to Tessa Jordan's caravan. The impetuous thumping of his heart felt undignified for a man approaching his fortieth birthday. The rush of blood was another clue that his feelings were taking over the investigation.

He stood in the dark feeling a helpless sense of indecision. And then the caravan door opened in front of him, and Tessa Jordan leaned out her dark head.

"Go away! Get out of there!" she shouted in his direction.

Daly stood his ground.

"Clear off, I said!"

"Not until I've spoken to you about your son, Mrs. Jordan."

She half-screamed, half-giggled in surprise. Her hand ran up to her throat, and then shakily covered her mouth.

"It's you," she said.

"Thanks for the welcome." Daly's voice had an injured tone.

"I wasn't talking to you," she exclaimed. "I was shouting at that old goat. She keeps breaking out and digging up my plants."

She drew back into the caravan but left the door half open.

Daly was reassured to see that the goat was indeed sharing the darkness with him. In the dim light its strange eyes stared balefully back at him.

The caravan was cramped and untidy. There was no sign of Dermot or any of the things that a seventeen-year-old boy might be interested in. She waved him to the one seat that was not covered in clothes.

"Does the caravan get cold at night?" he asked, to break the silence.

"No. It's very snug. Reminds me of holidays in Donegal. Especially when the wind and rain batter it at night." She had a dreamy, vacant look in her eyes.

A gust of wind shook the caravan, and he felt the closeness of her body. It was snug, all right. In the confined space, he felt surrounded by her smells and textures, the sound of her breath, the fragrance of her hair. It was a more intimate interior than her living room on Woodlawn Crescent. Only the picture of Oliver Jordan leaning against the window kept his passion at bay. His thoughts scuttled away into crannies.

"Is Dermot around?" he asked.

The question fell a long way in the short distance between them.

"You just missed him."

"I need to discuss something very important with him." He felt the sweat return to his brow. "In fact, it might even be a criminal matter."

The radiance in Tessa Jordan's face drained away. In the moments before she could compose her face, he saw fear, loss, and a wild look of recognition take shape as though she had been preparing herself for this revelation.

"Is this about the arson attacks?"

"Perhaps," he replied, intrigued by what she was referring to.

The words came rushing out, as though they had been building up a pressure in her throat.

"Dermot always loved playing with fire," she explained. "As a child he messed around with matches and cigarette lighters. He could hold a match until it burnt down to his fingers. I thought it was something boys did just to test themselves; challenge the steadiness of their nerve."

Daly nodded. He had played around with fire as a teenager too. Until he discovered the incendiary potential of girls.

"Then he started lighting fires in the house and in the garden. Anything he could get his hands on. Newspapers, clothes, even pieces of furniture were burnt. I took him to see a psychologist. He said it was attention-seeking behavior."

She paused, giving Daly time to work out where this was going. The revelation hit him like a series of encroaching bombardments. Not too heavily at first, but then closer as the truth began to dawn on him.

"He was a teenager without a father," continued Tessa. "What could I do? Make him some herbal tea when he was angry? Then last year, the fires became more serious. I wanted to protect him. He was old enough to face criminal charges. Spending time in jail would have spelled the end for him. So I had to cover up for him. What else can you do when you have an arsonist in the family?"

The word "arsonist" rolled through his mind as he replayed the events of the past few weeks. The fires at Woodlawn Crescent, the men dressed in black, the smoke alarm with the battery removed. Each memory was like a fresh wave of breaking thunder. He needed to go somewhere private to absorb this unexpected development and its ramifications.

"So the men dressed in black never existed? Except in Dermot's imagination?"

She bit her lip.

"Has Dermot talked to you about what he's been up to recently?"

"I'm the last person he would talk to. He looks up to you, though. I thought you might have…" Her voice trailed away.

Daly sighed. "You should have told me about the fires. A judge might have decided a custodial sentence was not in Dermot's best interests. I could have arranged for him to get some help. Instead, you wasted police time. I have enough real work to do without policing dysfunctional families and their problems."

"Well, you can save yourself any more trouble and leave now," she said abruptly.

Daly wished he could rewind their conversation and start again. He had been wrong-footed by Tessa's revelation. He wondered what else Dermot had been concealing.

"Before I go, I need to know if Dermot is linked in any way to the disappearance of David Hughes. Dermot met him when he was in a nursing home last November. They built up a friendship."

"Dermot has nothing to do with that, or with you for that matter. What he does is none of your business."

He shook his head sadly and closed his notebook.

"If that's the case, I doubt if there's anything I can do to help him. If he does know where Hughes is, the two of them may be in great danger. Hughes was a Special Branch agent. He knows enough secrets to have signed his own death warrant."

He sat square and immobile in his seat. A vague glimmer of doubt began to glow in the green irises of Tessa Jordan's eyes, but it was extinguished as quickly as it had appeared.

She scowled at Daly. "I don't need you to do anything for Dermot. Save that for the informers and your colleagues who recruited them. They're the ones who need help."

He stood up, dismayed. "Why do you think I came here in the first place? Don't you realize I'm on your side? I want to find out the truth too, not get involved in another cover-up."

"What do you mean by 'another cover-up'?" she countered. She stood up in front of him, her body strong, lithe. Her face was inflamed with anger, the clear skin with its spatter of burning freckles, the green eyes like a storm-churned sea. Tiny beads of perspiration formed in the groove of her upper lip.

Daly paused. His tongue felt thick, inert in his dry throat. "Cover-up" was the wrong word to have used. She had thought he was referring to her concealment of Dermot's arson attempts. The suggestion that a mother's love might mirror a dirty war against terrorists had riled her.

When his voice returned it was quieter, appeasing.

"I'm here because I'm concerned about Dermot. It's up to you to help me. Anything you can tell me about what Dermot's been doing in the last few weeks would be helpful. Here's my home number. You can contact me anytime. When you see him next, talk to him, find out as much as you can about his state of mind."

"If what you say is true, you won't be able to help Dermot."

"Why not?"

"This is Special Branch territory. An agent on the run, and an informer murdered. It's their area of competence. They won't want you involved."

Daly thought of Irwin. Their area of *incompetence*, he wanted to say.

Before leaving, he tried one last shot at enlisting her help. "I'm here as a friend, Tessa. A friend of your son's. I'm not interested in the arson attacks. I just want to know that he's safe. Special Branch isn't far behind me, and God knows who else. They might not share my concerns."

"If you're no longer interested in the fires, then there's no reason for you to be here." Her gaze was level, cold. She had clammed up. There was nothing else he could do.

He sat in the car afterward, rubbing his stubbly cheeks in the palms of his hands. He toyed with the idea of returning to the caravan and imploring Tessa to help him find Dermot, and launch a search party immediately. Then he thought better of it. Home, he decided. As quickly and discreetly as possible.

Later, as he lay in his bed, the night filled with the sound of crows, hundreds of them, moving out of the trees around his father's farm, to wherever they spent the spring months. Just as he was about to fall into sleep, he was jerked back into consciousness. The crows had left, and the house was still. He listened for the sound that had awoken him, then realized that the disturbance had come from within.

177

28

When Daly left the police station at lunchtime, he found two men loitering by his car. Irwin was leaning against his driver's-side door chatting to a man in a dark suit as if they were old friends. Their relaxed demeanor put Daly off his guard. He walked straight up to them.

"You want to jump in and go for a ride?" he suggested.

"No," said Irwin, regarding him with a sardonic smile. "We just want to get inside your head and fix the loose screw in there."

Daly surveyed the two of them, trying his best to look unimpressed. Irwin with his long, relaxed face and slick grin, and the other man, fair-haired, all business, his face lean and expressionless. Daly recognized him as the man with the razor-blade smile who had orchestrated the search at Devine's cottage.

He held out his hand to Daly, leaning forward grimly, automatically.

"Inspector Daly. Inspector Fealty, Special Branch."

Fealty was a different animal altogether from Irwin. He looked like a man who spent time making sure not a hair on his head was out of place. His blue eyes burned into Daly's.

"What can you tell us about Dermot Jordan?" he asked.

"Nothing," replied Daly. "Until you tell me why you want to know."

"Just interested in his movements," replied Fealty casually. "We've placed him on our list of suspects. I would suggest you do as well."

"Thanks for the tip. Anything else?"

"Just wanted to help, that's all." Fealty paused and examined Daly's face. "After all, you've no suspects, no witnesses, no motives, and Devine's been dead for a fortnight. You're hardly a credit to the police force."

Irwin flashed him a look of disgust. "I hear you're doing a number with Tessa Jordan."

Daly didn't answer. Fealty watched him closely. His lips looked too fastidious to join in Irwin's line of questioning.

"What were you doing at Tessa Jordan's last night?" asked Irwin.

Daly faltered. Nothing in his life was private anymore.

"For how long has following me been a priority for Special Branch?"

Irwin smirked. "It's always a pleasure to watch a fellow officer enjoy his work."

"Is that your brief? To distract me from my purpose and get me to shift my investigation away from Oliver Jordan's murder?"

Fealty switched the line of questioning. "What was the rationale behind bringing Dermot Jordan along to Mitchell's house?"

"He was on work experience from school. His mother wanted me to help him as a favor." Daly's face grew hot as he realized how lame his explanation sounded.

"We're well aware of Tessa Jordan's influence on you and this investigation," said Irwin.

Fealty snapped in. "Here's the situation, Daly. Dermot Jordan's fingerprints were found on a postcard sent by David Hughes. We have his details on record. It appears he's a very troubled boy. Quite the little fire starter, in fact. When he was thirteen, he set fire to a neighbor's shed and then his car. The charges were dropped on condition he receive psychiatric counseling."

The boy really was troubled, thought Daly.

"You don't look surprised."

"Of course I am."

Daly felt the odds had been dramatically increased against him concluding the investigation successfully. They clearly had the advantage on him. He could see it in Irwin's gloating smile.

"Looks like Tessa Jordan's dropped you in a right little mess," he said.

"The thing is, Daly," said Fealty. "I wish the boy had stuck to lighting fires rather than getting mixed up with Hughes. This is a very dangerous game. And judging by the psychiatrist's report on Dermot Jordan, he's not good in a crisis."

Fealty watched Daly's reactions. He sighed. "Listen. We need to find Hughes as soon as possible. Otherwise, all hell is going to break loose. Is there anyone else you can think of who knows Hughes and might have an insight into where he might be hiding?"

"Yes," replied Daly. "But unfortunately he's dead."

"Pity. Anyone we knew?"

"You should," said Daly caustically. "Noel Bingham. He used to work for you."

The lines around Fealty's eyes tightened. His voice grew taut. "Of course."

"Try to see it from Special Branch's point of view," interjected Irwin. "If everything Hughes knows gets into the wrong hands, we could have a stack of corpses on our turf."

"Who, exactly, are we talking about?"

"Don't play the naïve policeman with us, Daly. You ask too many questions."

"Well, if it's answers you want, you've come to the wrong place. Questions are what I specialize in."

"Just get on with being a detective, and stop pretending to be Dermot Jordan's social worker," said Fealty. "You're working for the police force, just the same as us. Don't forget that."

29

They had trekked all morning without coming across a whitethorn tree or any other recognizable landmark. And then the sound of a car approaching made them look up suddenly. In all that time there had not been a human sound in the expanse of mountain bog land apart from their labored breathing.

David Hughes was the slower of the two, walking with head bowed and feet dragging as though he were pulling along the ropes and chains of an invisible harness.

At times his companion felt like they were two sleepwalkers drifting toward the edge of the world. At other times, that they were far out in the silence of a great sea. There had been a gentle wind, and the heather and bog cotton waved serenely under a low sky. However, there was nothing serene about the strip of bog they were searching for. The turmoil of the human world had seen to that.

Dermot gazed anxiously at the road cutting across the bog field. The car was still far off. It was the wind that made it sound close. He relaxed a little and watched the old man struggle to get his breath. The slowness of his progress had helped focus his mind, which had been ruthlessly driven by the desire for revenge. He had adjusted to the slow pulse of the old man's thinking and was now content to walk side by side with him, matching his earth-heavy footsteps. Strangely, he found the emotions, which had cut so deeply for years, were growing less painful in his company.

"Let's go back to the road and walk to the other side of the mountain," suggested Hughes. "The tree might be there."

"It's a long hike," said Dermot. "All the way up there and down again."

"Well, it's a long story."

"Never mind that. You've got to tell me more about what happened that day. What other landmarks do you remember?"

"I remember following them for hours as they carried the body. Even back then, it was a grueling journey. They buried him under a thicket of whitethorn trees. It was early spring and the bare branches were brimming with white blossoms. Like stars against the blackness. That's all I remember."

A fissure in the bog opened before them, with a pool of black water far below. They tracked west, and the fissure grew into a wide trench filled with sphagnum moss and weeds. A soft drizzle fell on Dermot's head and shoulders. He could hear water gurgling under the peat beds. He listened to the sound of countless droplets cascading down crevices that in his mind became deep trenches of darkness that threatened to open up before him. As they had opened up for the bodies of the disappeared, the murdered men and women whom the IRA had tried to wipe off the face of the earth.

"There's only me left," said Hughes. "The last time I counted there were six of us, but little by little, we've been falling away."

Inwardly, Dermot groaned. The old man was unraveling quicker than he feared. Soon he would lose all sense of orientation. Dermot wished he could force the old man to remember, as one forces a hopeless piece of machinery to keep functioning.

Hughes turned in every direction, taking in the windswept arena.

"Maybe God doesn't want us to find the tree," he said. "That's why he made this damned bog land so big."

The sound of the approaching car caught their attention again. It had disappeared from view where the road knifed between two embankments of bog. Then it rose toward them on an open stretch, the wheels spitting gravel and clouds of dust.

The driver was going much too fast, thought Dermot. Perhaps the lonely mountain road and featureless horizon made him less conscious of his speed and the need for caution. Instinctively, he hid in a culvert by the road.

When the car drew level to where Hughes was standing it braked suddenly, as if the driver had recognized the old man.

Rolling down the window the driver leaned out and shouted: "Can I give you a lift?"

Dermot ran unnoticed along the culvert. Then, inching his way, he crept along the side of the car and crouched behind the driver's window. He stopped just out of view of the wing mirror and waited. He was on tenterhooks.

"I'm only going as far as Cappagh," shouted the driver.

The old man hurried as fast as he could toward the car, his wet trouser bottoms flapping. He bent at the passenger window and blinked, a look of confusion clouding his eyes.

"I'm only going to Cappagh," said the driver again, a note of impatience creeping into his voice. "Sorry."

"How far?"

"About three miles."

"It's OK. I'm not ready to go yet."

Hughes's fingers still gripped the edge of the opened window.

"It looks as if it's going to rain soon," said the driver. "You'll get wet."

Hughes hunched forward, pushing his face further into the car.

By now, Dermot was fairly sure the car was not part of a trap. Yet he was unable to relax, listening to the two men trade apology and politeness. He could see Hughes's face, his features fumbling as he tried to grasp what the driver was saying.

"You'll get wet with no shelter," said the driver with concern raising his voice.

"I don't mind the rain. As long as it doesn't snow."

Hughes paused again and stared at the driver. The lines of his face deepened as he sifted through memories.

"I remember one year the snow was so high it covered the hedges all over Tyrone."

The driver began to feel awkward with the old man's contorted face leaning into the car. However, curiosity kept him asking questions.

"What are you doing up here?"

"I guess you could say I'm in hiding."

Dermot's heart shriveled. His worst fear was that the old man would start divulging their secrets.

"In some kind of trouble?" asked the driver with a puzzled smile.

"You could say that. I had to leave my house in the middle of the night. Ever since I haven't settled anywhere. But it's been that way my whole life. Not just a few times. My whole life."

"Everyone should be allowed to enjoy their old age in peace."

"That's what I thought." Hughes sounded pleased to receive a measure of sympathy from the driver. "But they won't leave me alone." He cracked a smile. "Where did you say you were going?"

"Just up the road."

"Cappagh, was it?"

"That's right."

"You know this bog well?"

"I pass here every day."

"Nothing much to see is there?"

"Not when you know it like the back of your hand. I keep an eye out for strangers, though. We get a load of people up here trying to dump rubbish. That's all they think this place is. A tip to discard what they would rather forget. I thought you were one of them."

"No. I'm trying to find something I lost. I came here one day and found a whitethorn tree. I think it was a fairy tree. Its branches were all shrunken and pointed in the one direction. A dog came out of nowhere and tried to take a lump out of me. Christ. I had to thump it before it would leave me alone."

"There's a fairy thorn like that up at O'Neill's bog. And that sounds like a dog he once had. If you went anywhere near his strip of turf you had to carry a hell of a stout stick with you."

Hughes almost jumped into the passenger seat with delight. His reaction bewildered the driver.

"Can you tell me how to get there, to O'Neill's bog?"

The driver supplied a few directions. Hughes thanked him, but he had already released the clutch and was moving off.

Dermot came up to Hughes, his face grave, after the car had disappeared out of sight.

"You shouldn't have spoken to that driver. Now he's suspicious."

"Nonsense," said Hughes dismissively. "I can still judge a trustworthy character. That's always been my way. Anyway, I like talking to strangers. Especially when I'm worried about something. Remember, that's how we met. That driver was a gentleman."

The old man was angry, his face crammed with darkness.

"You know, I shot O'Neill's dog that night, right between his eyes. I saw his bared teeth just in time. I always had the luck to see everything in time. No man or animal has ever caught me unawares."

Hughes's profile was like a blind slab of rock. He set off, following the directions to O'Neill's bog.

The sun's edge disappeared behind the clouds, and they came across a drift of flowering bog cotton, woolly blobs of new whiteness against the darkening peat. The old man moved in a purposeful mood while Dermot hung back a little, picking his way carefully over the shards of old turf that lay hidden in the grass. Every now and again they paused for breath. Then Hughes would look up and set off at such a fast zigzagging pace that Dermot suspected he was trying to get away, or at least discourage anyone from following him.

The bog on the north side of the mountain turned primeval. They could hear the roar of perpetual streams coursing through rocky gashes. After a further half hour of trekking, the old man came to a sudden halt and raised his arm to signal to Dermot.

"We're almost there." His breathing was hard.

They had found the stunted thicket of whitethorn, its twisted branches raising a wild bouquet of blossoms no one wished to accept. Farther along, in a bleak valley where little sunlight fell, they discovered the pit of dead bodies. It was as though even the mountain had turned its back on the horrors it contained. Dermot almost swooned at the stench of death and petrol fumes.

30

The priest was straining his eyes to read his prayer book when there was a knock at the door. The abbot of the monastery appeared, framed in the doorway, looking tired and anxious.

"Father Fee, there is a man waiting in the hall to see you about an urgent matter."

Fee looked up in surprise. "In the hall?"

"Yes. It would be helpful if you would take him back to your room and talk to him here." The abbot's voice was drained of its usual benevolence. "We don't want to disturb the peace for our other guests."

The priest followed the abbot down a corridor toward the stairs that led to the entrance hall. The walls were flaking and peeling. From a large prayer room to the right wafted the reassuring smell of beeswax polish and incense.

Inspector Daly's first sight of Father Fee was of a gray-faced, elderly man in a black gown worn to a shiny veneer.

"Father, I'm glad to meet you at last," said Daly, stretching out his hand. "I'm here to talk about Joseph Devine."

The features of the priest's face bulged with anxiety, like a shellfish too big for its cavity. He clung to the banister.

"You're too late. He's dead."

"I know. My name is Inspector Celcius Daly. I'm investigating his murder."

Again, the priest's pale face appeared to undergo a slight expansion and contraction. "You had better come with me," he said quickly.

Daly was led to a small, sparsely furnished room. He sniffed a complex holy odor compounded of incense, wine, soap, and old books, which brought him back instantly to his schooldays. A desk was covered with papers, and an opened sketchpad showed an unfinished drawing of the monastery's landscaped gardens. In a corner sat an unused easel and a set of watercolors. An image of the Sacred Heart on the wall drew a gloomy mantle of suffering around itself.

"It had always been a plan of mine to take up painting when I had the time," said the priest, following Daly's eye.

"I thought it would be a good excuse to sit for hours doing very little other than observing nature. Unfortunately, I've found it very unsettling for the mind."

By now the priest seemed to have collected himself. A faint color pulsed in his cheeks.

Daly thrust forward with the purpose of his visit. "You were called to the scene of Mr. Devine's murder to give the last rites. I need as much information from you as possible about the telephone caller."

The priest folded his plump white hands on the rounded perch of his belly. "The caller only said a few words. Enough to identify the location, nothing more." He furrowed his brow. "From what I remember, he spoke in a monotone, as though he was mouthing a prayer. I couldn't place the accent."

"We've been anxious to speak to you for the past fortnight," said Daly. "Why did you come here so quickly after finding the body?"

"I just needed to recharge my batteries. Call it sick leave. I had booked myself in several weeks before."

The priest appeared to have stopped breathing for a second. As though bracing himself against an upsetting revelation.

"Mr. Devine was a parishioner of yours. Did you know him well?"

"Well enough." Father Fee glanced away. "Or, at least I thought I did."

"Did Devine ever speak to you about his past?" Daly's eyes steadied on the priest's face, which had slipped into shadow. In his black clothes, and with his face in the dark, the priest looked to have crossed the line between day and night.

"You should know that priests keep their confidences close to their chests." The priest's voice was thin. "The confessional booth permits glimpses of the soul's privacy, which I am utterly forbidden to disclose."

Daly studied his notepad.

"I'm not looking for details, Father. Just your impressions. Did he seem afraid of anything or worried about his safety?"

The priest switched on a lamp.

"Joseph was a hard-boiled character, but lately his conscience had been troubling him. In this part of the world, the worst thing a person can be is an informer, of any type. Whether it's to do with smuggling, or someone doing the double, anything at all. What Joseph did, however, was beyond the pale. He knew he was living on borrowed time."

"Did his death come as a shock?"

The priest slumped in his chair. "There's nothing as absolute and awesome as death."

"But what was your reaction when you realized the dead body was Mr. Devine? Was it surprise? Anger?"

"Surprise, no. Regret, perhaps."

Daly looked up sharply. "What do you mean, regret?"

"I didn't have much of an idea about what Joseph was involved in, or who his victims were, but I fear I had a hand in his murder."

"How?"

"I'm not sure. The last time I spoke to him was in the confessional. I'm afraid I can't divulge what either of us said." His face was grim. "But I'm convinced I sent him to his death."

"I need more details. You can't make a statement like that to a detective in a murder investigation and expect it to be left unquestioned."

"I wish I could tell more."

"I'll get to the bottom of this, sooner or later, even if it takes a court of law." Daly tried to keep the threat out of his voice.

The priest stood up. "I've been trying to make sense of Joseph's death for the past fortnight. Trying to make it hang together according to some divine law."

Daly said nothing, letting the silence reel out wider and wider.

Father Fee was standing at the window. "Every morning, the monks here tidy the rooms. They clean the toilets, plump up the pillows, replace the towels. Their satisfaction lies in caring for the troubled souls who come here on retreat. It reminds me of the pleasure I used to get from the confessional. Listening to parishioners' tales of woe and betrayal. Providing a soothing word here, a formulaic penance there. I was able to construct a jigsaw image of the outside world from their stories. Better listening to it than inhabiting it, I told myself." He sighed. "But after the Troubles ended, a new type of penitent started coming to my booth. Former paramilitaries, mostly. Men and women trying to pick up the threads of ordinary life again."

Daly nodded. It wasn't for nothing that Northern Ireland still had some of the highest Mass attendances in Europe.

"Hour after hour I listened as these men and women hid behind the metal grille and squawked and gibbered their terrible crimes. They came in droves seeking forgiveness. As if salvation could be guaranteed that easily. It was a terrible burden that made me tremble and weep. I felt uncertain about what I was doing, and I suppose that left me malleable to human weakness.

"Joseph Devine's confession was the first time I ever withheld an absolution. Six months ago, I would have handled his revelation differently. His story was not that strange or evil, and his soul was already beginning its tortuous journey back to salvation. But it was the depth of winter, and I felt old and tired. The booth reeked of alcohol and his sweat. Instead of the usual penance, I asked him to contact a relative of one of the men he had sent to his death. Make some form of reparation and ask for forgiveness. Undo the evil of his actions, so to speak. After he had done that I told him he could return to the confessional and I would finish the sacrament."

"I need to know who he contacted."

"I left the choice to him. We only talked in the abstract about his crimes. I knew he was a marked man. Not that that will ease my guilt or give me any peace. It won't make me feel better thinking he would have died anyway or that he might have been killed a month or two or a year later. I've confessed my sin to the abbot, and I've prayed harder than at any other time in my life. Forgiveness is not that easy, though. This is my penance. To think that he suffered because I decided not to grant him God's absolution."

Daly nodded.

"I want to know where this ends." The priest's voice echoed in the bare room.

"What?"

"Your investigation."

"Cases like these sometimes never end."

The priest swallowed.

Eventually he asked, "Do you believe in divine intervention?"

"I only piece events together," replied Daly. "I don't believe in any pattern or explanation beyond that of criminal motive."

"What do you believe in, then?" asked the priest, his face inquisitive.

Daly felt suddenly wrong-footed. He gazed out the window. "I believe in death. And life, of course."

The priest coughed. "As a priest I have to believe in a greater pattern, the possibility of a more mysterious explanation. I saw it perfectly on the morning I gave the last rites to Joseph. Unfortunately, it vanished quickly afterwards, the feeling that God had planned his death, and that I was an intimate part of His intervention."

The priest appeared embarrassed by his disclosure and joined Daly in looking out the window. The two men stared at the wide lawn dotted with yew trees and lined with laurel hedges. Small groups of men and women walked up and down the paths, deep in thought.

Fallen angels who'd suddenly found mortal shoes, thought Daly. He could almost identify with the priest's agonizing sense of plummeting, his fall from grace into confusion and self-doubt.

"Are all these people from the religious life?" Daly asked.

"No. They're from different walks. Mostly they've experienced some sort of short-circuit in their relationships or career. They find consolation in the monk's routine of prayer and meditation."

The priest glanced at Daly. "You should try it sometime."

A bell rang somewhere. A door opened and slammed. The figures walking in the garden slowly returned indoors. The air in the room felt oppressive. It smelled of dust and the musty days of winter.

The solution as to why Devine was killed appeared simple enough. Prompted by a troubled conscience and a misguided priest he had revealed his past to someone and they had sought revenge, or employed someone else. The irony of it produced a grim smile on Daly's face, which he hoped the priest did not notice. The informer had finally informed on himself.

Daly's eyes were drawn back to the view from the window. It was like a picture with a message for him, holding back some sort of a secret, like the postcard from David Hughes. A line from it rang in his mind: *My kind hosts are looking after me. If only they would stop talking about God and salvation.* Daly surveyed the lawn closely, but the people in the garden had disappeared.

"I need to see the abbot, now," said Daly, trying to keep the urgency out of his voice.

31

Dermot Jordan and David Hughes made their way along the ridge of whitethorn trees until, suddenly, out of the mist, a grotto of death appeared. The heavy stench of rotting flesh and the buzzing of flies hit them as they approached the edge of a disused quarry. For one nightmarish moment, Dermot wondered whether the smell of decomposing flesh could be from his father's corpse. Then he saw the gaping carcasses of chickens, and the bodies of bloated sheep melting back into the earth amid split bin bags and piles of rubble.

Hughes explained to Dermot how the IRA men had brought his father's body to this godforsaken place and buried him in the bottom of the pit.

Dermot shook his head. He wished he had never discovered the location. Never had a landscape produced such a sharp mood change in him. The anticipation and sense of adventure he had felt all morning was transformed in an instant into a dark, suffocating depression.

Over the years, the quarried hole had been turned into a grim bunker of illegally dumped rubbish, and judging from the smell, the waste products from laundered diesel. It was a dump, a place for criminals to discard what they would rather forget. Like a ghastly tapestry of death, the bodies of chickens hung from the blackened thorn trees growing along the sides.

Before them lay a sea of black bin bags, more animal carcasses, and, incongruously, several prosthetic limbs like the ones in Mitchell's back room, sticking out at odd angles from the rubbish. It would take months to excavate the quarry to find his father's body, and even then, the bones would be lost amid the skeletons of dead farm animals. It would be a revolting and painstaking search for the truth.

A series of dry retches gripped his stomach, but he remained where he was, trapped by curiosity and a wish to burn upon his memory the details of his father's burial place.

Hughes edged away on his own, counting under his breath, scanning the pit for terms of reference, a familiar rock or shrub, something for the mind to hold on to and trigger a memory. He circled the edge of the hole, then disappeared from view.

Dermot's clothes felt cold and clammy. Right then he realized that all these years what he had been searching for was a window, a window offering light and warmth, and a view of his father, the man whom he had wanted to love dearly but who had been taken away from him. He had never seen his father, but still he had an impression, an inverted memory of him, an illusion based on the stories he had heard and the photographs he had studied. But in the dark pit before him all he saw were the shadows of evil men. How easy it would be to give the old man a push and send him flailing into that pit along with all the other horrible secrets of the past. A sense of foreboding rose in his chest. Had he come all the way up this mountain just to follow in the footsteps of his father's killers?

"Let's go back." Hughes had reappeared. He stood close by, a fine rain drifting between them.

"We should have turned back a long time ago," mumbled Dermot.

32

By the time Daly entered the abbot's office, he was accompanied by Inspector Irwin, and two squad cars of police waited at the monastery gates.

The abbot nodded politely at their request and began explaining how the monastery ran its retreats.

"Catholic monasteries used to be regarded as strange or the stuff of medieval myth," he said. "The irony is that at a time of dwindling congregations around the world, our monasteries are being besieged by people seeking some form of retreat. In fact, we're oversubscribed for the summer. Our guests stay in former monk cells, and payment is made on a free-will basis." He smiled at the two detectives and steepled his fingers together. "No accommodation can promise silence and serenity like a monastery. Our only problem is keeping the growing hordes down to the genuine spiritual seekers, not just vacationers at 'Club God.'"

"We haven't come here for the tour guide," snapped Irwin.

The abbot's face froze. He blinked. In a cold voice, he said, "I'm glad you don't plan to stay with us, Inspector. The Benedictine motto is to treat all guests as you would treat Christ himself."

Daly spoke. "We're looking for a man called David Hughes. We have reason to believe he may be a guest here."

He handed the abbot a photograph of Hughes.

"His life may be in danger. As might the lives of those he confides in."

The abbot studied the photo for a moment.

"It's an old one," added Daly. "Mr. Hughes may have changed in the meantime, shaved his beard, or lost weight."

"No, no, he hasn't changed at all," said the abbot. He raised his hands in a gesture of bewilderment. "How can such a harmless old man cause such drama?"

"An informer called Joseph Devine was murdered a fortnight ago. Mr. Hughes was his handler, his point of contact with the security forces."

The abbot got up and began fussing over a heavy folder.

"I think you'll find," he said, addressing Daly, "that the gentleman you're looking for is in Room 204."

There was a heavy creak of leather as the abbot sat down wearily.

"He's still registered as a guest here, but I haven't seen him for a few days. His grandson used to come and take him out for trips."

Dermot, thought Daly. It had to be him.

The cast-iron radiators hummed with heat, and Daly felt the sweat gather on his brow as he and Irwin hurried down the long corridor.

An old monk came hobbling toward them, walking with two sticks to help carry his weight. Though he looked to be in pain, his smile as they passed him was pronounced, unwavering.

The abbot had supplied them with a key, but the door was already ajar. Irwin gingerly pushed the door wide with his foot. He took a step into the room with the air of someone assuming control.

The bed had been made, and a chair sat neatly at a bare desk. The carpet was spotless. A pile of clothes lay folded in an opened suitcase. A fly buzzed against the windowpane, a black dot of anger in an otherwise empty room.

"For someone with Alzheimer's, Hughes has a tidy streak."

"More likely it belongs to the person helping him," murmured Daly.

He walked over to the bedside cabinet and picked up a leather-bound notebook. It appeared to be a journal written by Hughes over the previous six months.

One of the first truths of detective work was that the unexplainable almost never happens. Even a vulnerable old man disappearing into thin air turns out to have a perfectly logical explanation. Daly could see that now. The monastery had been a perfect hiding place with its fixed routine and unwritten code of privacy. Guests were looked after without too many questions asked. The behavior of a confused old man might not appear so strikingly out of the ordinary. Most of the guests were probably fleeing some sort of pain or disturbance in their spirit. If one of them rambled a little, it might only be because he was trying to shake off some burden of guilt. And if a guest seemed unsure of himself, wasn't it because, in a fundamental sense, everyone on a retreat feels lost or undermined or no longer certain of anything? And then there was Dermot, posing as Hughes's grandson, able to wander in and out like a shadow as the guest ate, prayed, and sang hymns.

The boy was resourceful, Daly had to hand him that. He had established a refuge where he could patrol and keep an eye on Hughes, unbeknownst to anyone else.

"Now that the boy knows we're on to him, he'll turn himself in," remarked Irwin.

"I don't think our presence here is going to stop their mission."

"They're not on a mission," snorted Irwin. "This whole thing is an elaborate schoolboy's prank. He's using the old man to get attention. Just like his arson attacks."

"That doesn't sound like the Dermot I know. He's trying to extract information from Hughes. Dangerous information."

"You're thinking like a sane person."

"I'm thinking full stop. That's what we're paid to do."

"You can't think sane with a disturbed teenager and a senile old man. Trust me on this."

33

Daly decided to hand over responsibility for the surveillance operation at the monastery to Irwin and Special Branch. It was not because he thought they could do a better job. It was because of something more personal—the thought that his involvement with the Jordan family had reflected badly on him as a detective. He worried that he had lost the necessary intensity of effort and concentration that should have alerted him earlier to the boy's secret life. How could he penetrate the darkness surrounding a possible suspect when he felt he was walking in pitch-darkness himself?

He went back to the station. He planned to spend the next few hours going through the investigation, searching for any more mistakes, or leads he might have overlooked. Then he would start reading through the journal he had recovered from Hughes's room.

It had been a long day, with many surprises, and it was barely afternoon. He postponed lunch and sat down at his office to read the journal. He quickly found himself absorbed by the old man's words. Few things are as captivating as other people's nightmares.

October 22

It has been a week since I last was able to pen my thoughts.
I misplaced my diary and was worried sick Eliza had found
it. Fortunately, I found it at the bottom of my suitcase. Things
aren't getting much better for me since the last time I wrote.
The ghosts keep appearing on the appointed nights. They ask
me questions about old cases, and often I cannot remember.
Sometimes they're gone by the time I get outside. Then they
leave newspaper clippings of old cases hanging on thorns to
haunt me. Last night I locked myself out of the house and
Eliza got mad at having to let me in. She said I shouldn't be
out wandering in the dark, and took the front door key off me.

November 2

I awoke last night to the sound of heavy rain drumming the win-
dow. My calendar tells me the ghosts will appear again tonight,
but Eliza has made me a prisoner in my own home. Earlier, she
locked the bedroom door, and threatened me.

"I've got to sleep, David," she told me. Her hands shook as
she fitted the bars on my bed. "I'll look in now and again, and if
I see that you've tried to get out I'll have to ring the police. You
understand that, don't you?"

When I awoke later I used up a whole hour just listening to
make sure she was in her room. I heard her settle into bed, and
waited for any further creaks. Then I moved to the bottom of the
bed and squeezed past the sidebars. I pressed my ear against the
key hole of the door. Not a sound. I took out a key I had hidden,
and unlocked the door. The only noise I could hear was the blood
rushing in my head.

The dark wind from the lough was blowing again, bringing
with it the voices of ghosts. I could see through the whitethorn
hedge a man wearing an old RUC uniform. The badge on his
cap glinted in the moonlight. He was carrying a rope. He se-
lected a branch and tied the rope to it. Before he placed his
head in the noose, he turned towards me, keeping the features
of his face hidden in the shadow of his cap. When I returned

*from the thorn hedge, my clothes were so wet I had to wring
the water out of them.*

Daly read on. In a series of rambling entries, Hughes described
his conversations with the ghost of Oliver Jordan. He had recognized
Jordan from the blue electrician's boiler suit he was wearing, and the
details he supplied about the unexploded bomb that had signed his
death warrant. Then on November 5, Hughes noted in capital letters
that he had been *INSTITUTIONALISED*. Daly assumed this referred
to his arrival at the nursing home. There were no notes for the following week, except the comment that the other "inmates" seemed
to be drugged or asleep.

Then on November 12, he started to write at length again.

*They wheeled an old woman in beside me today in the sitting
room. Her eyes were directed past me towards the window, and
they had a dull look. Her hair was a spool of downy grey and
the features of her face were lined with a throng of wrinkles. A
young man came in and asked her could she hear him. He was
persistent but well mannered, but the old woman seemed asleep.*

When the old woman eventually spoke, her voice was faint.

*"I know why you've come here," she whispered. "You're dredg-
ing the past for ghosts. Go home and forget about where they
buried him."*

*For a moment, I thought the old woman was doting but
something in the boy's expression made me wonder: "Buried
who?"*

*I looked at him closely, and then the sweat began to form on
my forehead, and I felt my neck begin to itch. His face looked
oddly familiar. A coughing fit overcame me, and when I looked
up again, the boy had disappeared, and the old woman was
asleep again.*

November 13
*In the afternoon, I awoke in the sitting room. The sun hadn't
come out all day. I had lost my watch, and felt disorientated. This*

illness hangs over me like a curse. There was light from the tall windows moving the shadows about, and from their position, I tried to work out the time. The old woman was sitting beside me in an armchair with dirt-encrusted wheels. I had heard the nurses call her Mrs Jordan. By now, I had guessed she was Oliver Jordan's mother. The coincidence was too horrible to bear.

"You're caught," she said suddenly, turning her head slightly towards me. "You've come to a dead end. First you made the mistake of getting ill, and then coming here where you're boxed in by other dying people towards your own coffin. Get out while you still can."

The words of her final command trembled in her mouth. She was breathing heavily. Her eyes were barely open, and I was unsure if she was addressing me.

I must have fallen asleep because my next memory is of seeing a cold cup of tea and a buttered scone sitting on the armrest of my chair. There were crumbs on the old woman's chest and her eyes were open and fixed on the opposite wall. It was an empty wall, and during the long afternoons, it acted like a blank screen, shimmering with the images of the past. A tangle of memories floated to the surface. I saw the headlights of a car swimming through a foggy night, a body bundled out of the boot, torches winking across a wild bog, and a man's bare feet dragged through the mud.

The old woman shifted in her seat.

"I didn't get a chance to say goodbye to Oliver," she said. "The last time I saw him he was sleeping." She pointed at the wall opposite. "Sleeping in that bed there. The same bed he used to sleep in when he was a boy."

I thought of offering some form of sympathy, but could see no consolation in that, not after all these years.

"I didn't sleep for days," she added. Her face screwed tight against the memory.

My mind started filling with more images from that dreadful night. It was almost impossible to speak. I worried about how I was going to frame what I wanted to say.

At last I spoke. "I may be the only one left who saw your son's body being buried that night."

A nurse pushed a medicine trolley past the door, and a bed alarm echoed down a distant corridor.

"I'm the only one left," I repeated.

The old woman's eyes were shut. Her mouth had folded upon itself as if the words had chewed her up. If she was breathing, there was no sign of it. She was gathering her strength for what was coming next. She stooped forward and gripped her hands on the armrests of the chair as though she might fall to the floor. A cup of cold tea fell across the carpet. She released a long breath, and then she turned her dim eyes towards me.

"Who are you?" she asked. "Why have you come here?"

Her arm reached out towards me, as though an electrical current had taken hold of it. I recoiled. Afraid that some shock of grief or sorrow might suddenly leap from her wrinkled skin.

"I worked for Special Branch," I began to explain. "We were monitoring the movements of Republicans. I watched them that night dig a pit and bury your son's body. I wasn't able to intervene because it would have endangered the operation. It was too late for your son, anyway. He was dead."

The old woman sank back into her seat, and shut her eyes. For a long time, there was not a sound in the room. We were like two people isolated on an island of grief. I watched the sky darkening to twilight. Night was approaching. Her grandson would be making his way through the gloom, on his way to the nursing home, seeking his answers.

"I always believed that one day news would reach me," said the old woman. "That I would find out where Oliver was buried." She paused, caught her breath, and turned towards me.

I told her that my memory was failing, and that I could no longer recall the exact location of the grave.

"But you must remember," she said. "You must. Let him be given a Christian burial. So I can finally rest." Emotion gulped in her throat.

"I will do my best," I replied. There was no one left who

could help her. I sank back into my chair, surrendering myself to the task. I was going to have to return to the gap in the thorn hedge, and step back into the black wind where only ghosts wandered.

"Let me talk to your grandson," I told her. "Let me see what I can do."

The next entry was a few days later. In the meantime, Daly surmised, Hughes had introduced himself to Dermot Jordan and passed on the few details he could remember. After that, the entries described Hughes's regular conversations with the boy. Then on November 19:

My last day in the nursing home. I sat waiting for the ambulance to take me home when Dermot appeared. It was our final meeting.

"Are you going already?" he asked, a note of disappointment in his voice.

I felt the same. Our friendship was ending. Or rather, our usefulness to each other was waning. It was ridiculous to believe we could build on the conversations we had shared during my short stay in the nursing home. I could see the boy was reaching the same conclusion. After all, I was an old man with a rapidly fading memory, who hadn't been able to answer his most pressing questions.

He accompanied me on a short walk through the nursing home grounds. It was a cold winter evening. Not a trace of wind in the air. Soon a frost would form on the neatly mown lawn and the conifer trees.

"I must find out where they buried Dad's body," he said.

"I've forgotten. That's the simple truth. My memory is going. Anyway, I was never the type to look back and revisit old scenes. I must have blotted out the details of the entire incident."

The ambulance pulled up.

"You have to tell me if you remember anything more," he urged.

"Of course. You have my address."

I got into the back of the ambulance. It drove me slowly through the darkness of the lough shore, with no siren lights or wailing noise, through a wind swathed with snowflakes, dissolving into the blackness like the trapped faces of ghosts.

The notes after Hughes's departure from the nursing home became more disjointed and confused. There appeared to be a marked deterioration in his condition. His handwriting became hard to make out, and he switched to writing in pencil. In one entry, he noted that the ghosts had left him feeling apprehensive but determined. The next few pages were roughly torn out. Thereafter there was only a sentence or two in each entry. Daly could feel a chill seeping from the barely legible words. At one point, Hughes wrote that he was afraid of dying, and that only the thought of seeing the duck flocks fly over in spring kept him going. There was little further mention of his investigation or of the location of Oliver Jordan's grave. Each day seemed to have become a grim survival against an unknown fear.

34

Irwin stood smoking by an unmarked car in a lane opposite the entrance gates to the monastery. From there he had the best view of both approach roads and was invisible until the last moment to passing motorists. Officers had positioned themselves on the grounds of the monastery and in the rooms next to 204.

Irwin could have swamped the surrounding roads with checkpoints, but he wanted to bring the boy into custody himself. He was looking forward to quizzing him about his relationship with Daly. As for Hughes, who cared about a senile old man? Alzheimer's was a death sentence anyway.

The lane led to a few sagging outhouses with rusted tin roofs and stone walls that had lost their mortar. A black dog bounded out and began sniffing at his feet.

"Get lost!" he shouted, kicking out at the animal.

"Don't mind him." A young man appeared from one of the outhouses, carrying a feeding bucket. "He'll not bite."

The boy started calling to the herd of cows in the adjoining field. Irwin stood still, wondering how he was going to explain his presence. No point in lying, he decided. The boy might have seen something that might be of use. Better to tell him the truth and enlist his cooperation.

"Is that your car?" asked the boy with a simple grin. "It looks fast." There was a lopsided look of simplicity to his face.

Clearly the result of inbreeding among farming folk, thought Irwin.

"Yeah," he said with a smile. "You should see it accelerate when I hit the motorway."

The boy regarded him with such a look of innocence that Irwin began to wonder whether he was seriously retarded.

"I haven't seen you here before," said the boy. His brow knitted in puzzlement as though trying to count something in his head. "You're not from the school, are you? If you are, I'm not going back." His face was strained with anxiety, and he shied away from the detective.

"No. I'm not from school," explained Irwin. "I am trying to catch someone though."

A flash of cunning appeared in the boy's face. "Is that why you've a fast car?"

"Yes," said Irwin. "You're a quick learner."

Again that happy, ill-made expression of stupidity appeared on the boy's features, his face like a wrongly shaped bowl rejected by a potter.

"I'm looking for a boy about your age and an old man. They've been staying at the monastery for the past few weeks." Irwin showed him a photograph of Hughes.

A mouthful of delighted laughter shot out from the boy. "I think I've seen them. I live in the house back there with my da. He lets me feed the cows in the evening. I've seen them leave the monastery in a jeep."

"I'll let you go for a ride in the car if you can tell me more," offered Irwin.

"Da talked to the old fellow a few times," said the boy, thinking hard.

A voice yelled from farther up the lane. A high-pitched, demanding voice, contorted by illness or old age.

"Let me feed the cows first," said the boy, a flicker of worry appearing in his face. "Then we'll go up and talk to Da."

Irwin nodded.

The boy swung his leg with practiced ease over a gate and marched up the field, calling all the time to the cattle. Very soon, he had disappeared over the brow of the hill, the herd of cows lumbering behind him.

Irwin waited. He smoked a cigarette, and another. Then he returned to his car and sat in silence.

One by one, the cows returned over the hill and jostled against the gate as if they were still hungry. They stared at Irwin with their stupid faces. There was no sign of the boy. The detective sat forward with a new attentiveness. The cows pushed harder against the gate, hooves stamping, eyeballs swiveling. Hungry animals getting hungrier. Irwin went over the boy's actions in his mind. It occurred to him that the bucket had probably been empty. The boy had duped the animals into following him over the hill. They weren't the only ones who had been fooled, he was beginning to suspect.

He got out of the car and walked up to the outhouses. There was no sign of a house beyond, or the boy's father, only a muddy lay-by with a fresh set of tire tracks. Irwin followed them, his stomach churning with unease. They led back down onto the main road. He stood and stared across the fields, hoping to see the figure of the boy return. After a few more minutes, he returned to his car and phoned the station. An officer sent an image of Dermot Jordan to his phone. When it came through, Irwin turned to the baffled herd of cows and performed a passable imitation of a man shooting himself in the head. One of the animals responded with a despairing "Moo."

When Daly arrived, Irwin was still wrestling with embarrassment at letting Dermot Jordan slip through his fingers. Daly's request for the precise details of their conversation had the younger detective writhing on a mental skewer. He watched with interest as the hostility in Irwin's face drained away completely, replaced by a squirming look of failure, which broke through his hardened features like a hooked fish pulled from the depths.

"How could you let it happen?" asked Daly.

Irwin recounted the incident methodically to Daly, like a new recruit doing what he was taught to do. "I swear he looked simple. I thought he was just a farmer's son sent out to feed the cattle."

"Simple? That's the last word I'd use to describe Dermot Jordan. What kind of vehicle did they drive off in?"

"I didn't see a car. I already told you."

Daly shook his head. "Jumping to assumptions is an extremely unreliable trait in a policeman. Just because the boy was carrying a bucket, it didn't automatically make him a farmer's son. It didn't mean you could abandon all your suspicions." He realized he was shouting. He turned his back on Irwin and groaned to himself.

A female officer was standing guard by the outhouses. She looked at Daly as if he might be in pain.

Daly tried not to let his antagonism show.

"I think I saw a pair of eyes in there," she told him, pointing into the darkness of the outhouse.

"Perhaps it was an animal," he suggested.

"What if it was a rat?"

Daly took out a torch and directed its light into the byre.

A half-spilled sack lay in a corner. Motionless eyes glinted in the light of the torch. He walked in and discovered a heap of duck decoys. Some of them were damaged, split into pieces. He shouted for Irwin to join him.

"This is where the paths cross," said Daly. "These decoys are the point of connection between Hughes, Devine, and Dermot Jordan. We don't yet know their significance, but I suspect Hughes and Jordan stole them from Devine's cottage."

Irwin ruffled his hair.

"I want you to find out why they were stolen," added Daly.

35

Pulling into the station, Daly saw Fealty get out of his car and hurry into the building ahead of him. Daly sensed he was going to have another confrontation with the Special Branch inspector. Since their conversation about Dermot's past, they'd had no further contact, but in his mind, Daly felt he was engaged in an ongoing war with Fealty.

However, he was surprised when the inspector met him in the corridor and invited him for a coffee. Daly thanked him but declined. Staring at Fealty's pinched, jaded face, Daly wondered if it had been proper to thank him. To be grateful placed him in the position of a subordinate.

Fealty did not seem to have heard Daly's refusal. Instead, his bleak eyes stared through Daly, as if to some point of doom behind. He drew close to the detective and began talking about how important it was to find Hughes and Dermot Jordan. He asked Daly some routine questions about the search, but the detective got the impression he knew the answers already. Fealty's earlier arrogance had disappeared completely. He seemed deflated, unsure of his next move. His haircut looked too short for his narrow face.

When Daly had finished, Fealty looked at him and waited for something more, his eyes two hungry black dots.

"What fresh leads have you?" he asked sharply.

"If I had any, you would have heard already."

Fealty looked offended. He seemed to be expecting a measure of sympathy and cooperation from Daly.

"You know, Inspector, this country has undergone a fundamental change in the last few years," said Fealty. "There's a whole generation of people like David Hughes, who have lost their way. You don't need to have dementia to feel unsure of what's going on in this country. Or question what was the point of risking your life as a policeman. The Troubles went on too long, but there's a prevailing feeling they ended too easily. You were lucky you got away to Scotland. Your perspective is not so distorted by history. That's why I think you bring something useful to this investigation."

Daly raised an eyebrow. "My father sent me to live with an aunt in Glasgow after my mother was killed. She was shot in crossfire during a police ambush on a band of IRA men. It left me grief-stricken. As angry as an only son can be. My father was afraid the loss would politicize me and propel me into Republicanism. But I never escaped. Even in Scotland. It was more like my history was stolen."

Fealty nodded stiffly. "That kind of tragedy is hard to comprehend. It can put tremendous pressures on the mind."

"What about David Hughes's mind, and Joseph Devine's? What kind of pressure was put on them?"

"That's Special Branch business. As you know, David was a spymaster, the main point of contact for informers like Devine. He retired after the cease-fire. Like many people, he thought that was it. War over. Safe to hunt ducks and tend to his farm to the end of his days."

"Let me guess, Special Branch thought differently."

"We had to take precautions. There were too many loose ends left hanging. We recruited his sister to keep an eye on him, report on his state of mind, that sort of thing. It was our insurance policy. We thought we had nothing to worry about, until six months ago, when the Alzheimer's came to light."

"You were worried he might divulge some dangerous secrets."

"I won't lie to you. He held damaging information about how Special Branch ran its operations. We asked his sister to monitor his conversations, check his movements, keep a lid on him generally."

Daly thought, When people tell me they're not going to lie, what follows seldom sounds very convincing.

"How about this for a theory? Special Branch were worried that Hughes might compromise a higher-placed informer in the IRA. A senior politician, for instance? Who else did you send to monitor him? You must have taken more precautions."

"We had an arrangement with some former operatives. Some of them wanted to mount their own surveillance. Hughes was their worst nightmare come back to haunt them."

"I take it one of them was Joseph Devine."

Fealty nodded. "The irony was not lost on us. Devine was the perfect candidate for that kind of surveillance. He had similar interests as Hughes. For the last six months he had been spying on the man who once recruited him."

"But there were others. More than Devine. I get the feeling you are supplying me with just enough information to satisfy my curiosity."

"If there were, they are of no interest to your investigation."

"Not if they were witnesses to a crime or know of Hughes's whereabouts."

"You keep trying to fit Devine's murder with Hughes's disappearance. As though the two are part of one jigsaw. You're wrong. You'll never make them fit together. They belong to two different puzzles."

"According to his priest, Devine was cracking up. He believes Devine confessed his crimes to the relatives of one of his victims, and this led to his death." Daly watched Fealty carefully for a flicker of interest, but the Special Branch man looked nonplussed.

"That didn't give you the fright I thought it would."

"Our main worry is finding David Hughes. Devine is dead. And dead men don't talk. Until we find Hughes we're prepared to turn a blind eye towards Devine's killers, whoever they were."

"What about the rule of law? Are you blind to that as well?"

Fealty had recovered his former vigor and stared resolutely at Daly. A slight frown was the only clue to his earlier anxiety.

"There's only so much law and justice a society like this can take.

People have to get used to those lofty concepts first."

"Is that why Special Branch administers them in such miserly doses?"

"We're all striving towards a more just state."

"But what are we doing right now if it's not just? Either we uphold the law to the letter, or we're no better than the criminals and terrorists we're meant to police."

Somewhere a door opened. A bunch of trainee officers filed out of a room. The sound of their walking and talking filled the corridor. Daly waited for Fealty to reply, but he remained silent.

"That's all for now," he said after the young officers had trooped past.

"And there was me thinking we were making progress," remarked Daly.

Fealty, walking away, turned back briefly. "That's right. We were. But you're not going to disentangle Hughes's past in a single conversation. The same goes for Devine. Finding out the truth is a long and complex process. There are no shortcuts for policemen anymore."

"What about Noel Bingham? Was he another loose end?"

"What about him? He was a drunk. Killed in a hit-and-run."

"The driver made sure he got his man."

"Inspector, you should know that people die in road accidents all the time. You've been spending too much time dabbling in the world of spies. Now you're beginning to think like one. Forget your conspiracy theories. The hit-and-run was just the final twist in his tragic life. An inescapable twist."

36

As Daly approached Joseph Devine's cottage, a stray black dog lurched up to him as if it had a secret to divulge. It was almost twilight and a vibrating veil of midges hung in the air. Daly ruffled the dog's itching neck. He opened the front door and paused for a second, staring into the gloom. If anyone had been there since his last visit, they had left no sign or trace. He stepped inside. The wind followed behind, sending a few dead leaves and scraps of paper scuttling across the dirty floor. He was instantly aware of the cold inside, and the smell of dust, and something sharper. Old ashes, old sweat, the smell of an elderly man and the inevitable damp that crept indoors during a lough-shore winter.

He picked up one of the scraps of paper. A torn piece of old newspaper. Nothing more. He looked through the cupboards and a wardrobe in the bedroom. Devine had been a man of rough comforts. In the drawers, he found a folded pile of linen, washed well beyond softness.

Daly sat down on a dirty leather chair as the dog prowled about outside. He felt the sides of the chair, looking for he knew not what. He found nothing at all, and paused, sinking back into the chair. Devine must have made contact with someone in the days before his death, an old enemy, a still-grieving relative, a former colleague....

The dog was whining and scratching at the door. The house had been searched several times but no one had found a safe or strongbox. This perplexed Daly. He thought that a suspicious man like Devine must have had a secure place to hide his most important belongings.

In a cardboard box, he came across several theology books. Perhaps there had been a religious dimension to Devine he had not noticed before. Daly thumbed through them, noting the passages Devine had underlined. The dead informer appeared to have read only the first few chapters of each book. There was plenty of evidence that he had been undergoing a spiritual crisis and frantically searching for answers, but it was a skittering, heedless search with only enough momentum to carry him through the first twenty pages or so of each book. He weighed the books in his hands. They represented the high-tide mark of a very private terror. The idea that Devine had undergone a spiritual crisis sparked Daly's interest. He made a note of some of the quotations Devine had underlined. Later he would find Father Fee and ask him to explain them. Or perhaps he should simply forget about them. After all, they had more relevance to his own curiosity than to the murder investigation.

He still had religion on his mind when he walked out to where the dog was prowling. The wind had picked up, and he could hear the washing of waves at the dilapidated jetty where Devine had moored his boat. The dog set off in the direction of the lough, and Daly followed behind.

There is nothing worse than a long, drawn-out wait for something to happen, thought Daly. Whether it's waiting for the results of some tests from a doctor or the executioner's ax to fall. Daly supposed that retirement had become a private hell for Devine, a state of suspense that finally sweated him into informing on himself. It was thoughtful of Special Branch to assign him the task of monitoring Hughes. Like getting a prisoner to eavesdrop on the agony of a tortured inmate in the cell next door. Watching Hughes struggle with his guilty conscience, as Alzheimer's systematically dismantled his personality, must have had a profoundly unsettling effect on Devine's own state of mind.

The water surged against the jetty, creating a wash that left the tethered rowing boat heaving like a frightened animal. Past the slipway sat a small boathouse half-hidden in a thicket of alder and willow. The setting looked familiar. He recalled the photograph of the duck-hunting club and realized he was standing close to where the photo had been taken.

The door to the boathouse refused to budge. Daly kicked it with his boot, and it flew open. A bird flapped noisily in the bushes nearby. Daly hunched inside and looked around carefully. The interior of the shed looked smaller than he had expected. Disappointingly, it was empty. He was about to leave when something caught his attention. A small nut and bolt was attached to the back wall of the shed. He walked around to the outside of the shed, roughly measuring its dimensions. After checking and double-checking, he reckoned the length of the shed on the outside was about two feet longer than the inside.

He retrieved a wrench from the boot of his car and used it to remove the nut and bolt. A plywood section freed itself and slid up against the roof, revealing a hidden compartment. In a suitcase he found a pile of neatly folded clothes, an old RUC uniform, a set of blue overalls, a battery, an alarm clock, and bundles of old newspaper clippings like the ones he had found in the hedge at Hughes's farm. The overall effect of the cache was extremely unsettling, as if his entire investigation had been based on an elaborate hoax.

He took out a pen and picked through the clues, trying to extract from them an inevitable order, a final arrangement. He wondered whether the objects were genuine items of evidence linked to the crimes outlined in the newspaper clippings.

From the pile of clothes, it looked as though Devine had dressed himself up as the ghosts that haunted Hughes at his farm. Had the informer spent the last few weeks of his life tormenting a confused old man? Daly shook his head. It seemed more sinister than a practical joke. However, Devine did not appear to have been the type of person given to practicing cruel japes. Later that night, reading over Hughes's journals again Daly became convinced that Devine had dressed up in the uniforms for one purpose only—to extract information from Hughes.

Had Devine approached the old man in person, Special Branch would have been alerted immediately. But by dressing up as a ghost he had counted on the fact that no one would bother to investigate their meetings. Special Branch had already taken Hughes's stories of ghostly intruders as proof he was beginning to lose his mind. It was the perfect setup for Devine to pry into the old man's mind without fear of capture.

37

The black hedges around his father's farm were heavy with the foaming branches of whitethorn blossom. Daly stared at them with a profoundly unsatisfactory sense of time hurrying by. It was March already. His eyes were distracted by the surges of brilliant white flowers lit up in the morning sun. The narrow fields around his father's farm seemed to swell and shimmer, reconfigured into softer, more mystical dimensions.

Patience, he thought. It's been a long winter. He drew a deep breath and looked down at the sink. His mind was heavy with thoughts of Dermot and Devine's subterfuge. He looked back at the whitethorn-bounded fields, and a line from a Patrick Kavanagh poem floated into his mind. Something about not growing old unless he walked outside his whitethorn hedges. He hoped that within the vigorously flowering hedgerows there might be space for a tired mind to grow again.

He felt a tension in his shoulders as he drove up the lane to Tessa Jordan's caravan. The worried clucking of a flock of hens greeted him as he stepped out of the car. The sweet stench of rotting manure hung heavily in the air.

Pots of herbs and flowers were arranged by the caravan door. A sign that her temporary living arrangement was gaining a more permanent footing. The farm looked deserted. He paused only long enough to check the caravan was empty too.

A car pulled up alongside his, and Tessa Jordan climbed out.

"I don't know what gives you the right to walk around my sister's property when there's no one here!" she shouted. Her voice was indignant. "Aren't you supposed to have a search warrant?"

"I was just about to leave," explained Daly, feeling his temper flare.

"You haven't answered my question. What are you doing here if you haven't a search warrant?"

"I just want to find out where Dermot is."

However, Tessa Jordan did not seem to hear him.

"How long have you been here? Are you spying on me?"

"I haven't been spying on you. I just have some questions to ask, and then I'll be on my way."

"You'd better come in, then," she said grudgingly.

Daly stood in the cramped caravan. "I was with Dermot when we found out why your husband was killed. I took him to Mitchell's house. I feel a responsibility towards the boy, and I need your help. This is too serious."

She sat down. Something inside her had collapsed.

"He seemed so contented recently," she said. "I had almost stopped worrying about him. I never thought he would run away like this. It's like his father's disappearance all over again. This morning I stood at the sink and said the Rosary over and over again. It was all I could do to keep myself sane."

Unwilling to test himself against her eyes, Daly studied her lips. There was a disturbingly tremulous jut to the lower one. He felt his defenses break.

"Nobody has kidnapped Dermot. He can still be rescued from danger."

"I've heard policemen make those promises before. They're worn out. I can't lose Dermot as well."

Daly heaved a patient sigh. He had not been trained as a family therapist. They had never told him he would be dragged so often into the internecine war of emotions families waged upon themselves. He longed for the simple life of catching bad guys and saving the good ones. Sometimes the questions he had to ask of relatives felt like minor acts of war.

"Is Dermot seeking some kind of revenge?"

Her eyes blazed at him. "For what the security forces and Republicans did to his father? If he was like that, you would have been the first to find out."

"I need to know if he is capable of violence."

"There's violence in all of us."

"Let me reframe the question. Would he break the law and harm another human being?"

"I don't think he's concerned with the law in this country. For that matter, neither am I."

"But the law is concerned with your son."

"Why? Dermot hasn't committed a crime. The only crime I can see is the one committed against his father by people like you."

He was losing her again. He felt her recede into the simplistic perspective of the past, the black-and-white world of the Troubles, with victims pitted against perpetrators and the security forces, and grieving widows embattled on all sides.

Daly tried to control the edge in his voice. "We need to find Dermot because he has some form of control over David Hughes. We suspect he was the man who handled the agents responsible for your husband's death." He paused before continuing. "We also need to assure ourselves that nothing bad has happened to Dermot."

Tessa was quiet. The momentum of her anger had dissipated. A vagueness clouded her features. Her every move reflected an intense desire to not betray her son. Daly watched as her eyes fixed upon him.

"What do you want to know?" Her attempt at helpful compliance was unexpected.

"What vehicle is Dermot driving?"

"His uncle's jeep. The registration is KBZ 1648."

"Does he have any other relatives he might call on?"

"No."

Daly stared hard at her. He had the impression that he was looking into a mirror that had once been transparent glass. There was no sign of the Tessa Jordan he had known, only an ugly sense of his plodding pursuit of the truth.

"When was the last time you saw Dermot?"

"Two mornings ago. He left very early. Before dawn."

"Did he say where he was going?"

"No. I didn't know he was leaving." She sounded evasive. "My sister heard him leave."

"He must have planned this through carefully. Let's think about it. What is he hoping to achieve?"

"Perhaps he's scared and in hiding."

"Possibly. What did you think when he didn't return?"

"No news is good news with Dermot."

She was talking calmly, matter-of-factly, which he found the opposite of reassuring. The lack of concern in her voice, its lightness, after the earlier drama, posed too sharp a question for him to ignore. He looked about the caravan. It was clutter free, the shelves and cupboards tidy and ordered. Someone with a composed mind had been working hard.

"It would take months to tell you all the escapades Dermot has hatched over the years," said Tessa. "Frankly they're not months I would care to spend, even in your company."

He nodded as she continued speaking, wary at her demeanor, sensing that somehow she knew her son was safe. A coolness flowed from her that suggested a mind at ease with itself.

"What I need to know is whether or not he's planning to harm anyone," he said abruptly.

There was silence. Nothing happened to her eyes. Nothing happened to her face.

"When he was a child he used to burn insects," she said eventually. "Then he moved on to setting cats' tails alight. He seemed to smell of smoke all the time. The psychologist said it was an avoidance mechanism. What he really wanted to hurt were the people responsible for his father's disappearance."

Daly surveyed the caravan again. "This place could go up like a matchbox." There was an unpleasant frost to his voice. "Aren't you frightened he might set you alight, because of his 'avoidance mechanism'?"

Something in her fed on his coldness and rose up in defense of her only son.

"That's a ridiculous and cruel thing to say. I can still tell you to leave. You haven't a search warrant, and I'm not under arrest."

"If you were really worried about where your son is, you wouldn't even consider asking me to leave."

"What are you trying to suggest?"

"That you know where Dermot is, or at least he's been in contact with you recently."

"I've told you all I know." She rose imperiously. "Are you finished now?"

"No," he replied. "You have to do one thing for me."

She considered it for a moment. "What is it?"

"Dermot's going to call you and ask if I've been here."

"He won't."

"I think he will."

"Well, don't worry. I'll not tell him anything."

"No. I want you to tell him I was here."

She looked at him in surprise.

"And tell him that I know what Devine was doing in the weeks before he died. I'll be at home all weekend."

38

Dermot drove along flooded fields that resembled shards of sky strewn over a landscape of small farms and disappearing lanes. The tracts of water soaked up the gloom of the darkening clouds that massed overhead, threatening another burst of rain. His companion beside him was something of a specialist on floods in this part of the country, a hoarder of memories of disgorged rivers, the steep sheen of the lough after a storm and the elaborate patterns of newly created lakes stalked by duck hunters in the dawn.

However, neither Dermot nor David Hughes had ever seen a flood like this, with many of the lough-shore roads cut off by arteries of pulsing water. Only the twisted tops of hawthorn trees, their branches like fallen stags, marked the direction of the submerged roads. They were unable to follow their preferred route to the house and had to work their way along the fringes of Lough Neagh, its wide advancing loneliness making them feel they were adrift in a flooded land without bridges or stepping-stones.

They almost missed the house in the murk of the gathering storm. A jugular of muddied water coursed down the side of the road, forcing them to abandon their vehicle on a ridge overlooking the house.

"This is the worst flood I can remember," said Hughes.

His eyes were swimming in the cold, but his voice was clear.

"What I see bears no relation to memory. I need landmarks and fixed points on the horizon, but all these are missing. I might as well be lost at sea." He closed his eyes.

In the distance, uprooted bushed and young trees revolved in patches of disturbed water. The untidy shoreline had a look of exhauted turmoil.

"If that's the case, then so am I," replied Dermot.

They were like two sailors spinning in a whirlpool, he thought.

The noise of the floodwater got louder and closer as they watched it pour in big, gurgling streams over the banks of the Blackwater River. The old man stared at the moving abyss of water with a stillness that suggested he could have stood there for hours without getting tired of the sight.

Dermot thought the old man's stature had shrunk over the past few weeks, his body grown thinner. He was like a frail raft disintegrating because the currents were too strong. They were almost out of his medication and would have to see a GP soon. But first Dermot would find an answer to the questions Hughes had been unable to answer. He would get the solution to the cruel mystery that had overshadowed his childhood.

Above the roar of the water, he could make out the sound of cars approaching and leaving the house. Curious, he watched as people slowly entered and briskly left through the building as though a burden had been removed from their shoulders. The house itself was plunged in darkness, with not a light on in any of the windows.

"Come," said Hughes, interrupting his thoughts. "Let's go and see what this man has to tell us. See how all his surroundings have given way to the lough, as though the land is trying to pull away from him. Keeping the secret of your father's grave has been too heavy a responsibility for him. He's had bad luck."

No one troubled them as they joined the file of people moving through the front door into a candlelit hall where a man in a black suit was shaking hands forcefully with those at the front of the queue. Although the queue was long, he greeted everyone with unchanging gravity, thanking them all as they offered their condolences.

Dermot waited nervously behind Hughes, realizing they had

arrived in the aftermath of a funeral. He was unable to detect if the man recognized Hughes; his rolling voice showed the same rehearsed formality to each of the visitors.

Hughes shook the man's hand. "Bad weather for a funeral," he remarked.

Owen Sweeney produced a stock smile in reply, one that politicians practice to show they are still human.

"The dead are past caring about the weather," he said, holding on to Hughes's hand.

"Mr. Sweeney, I'd like you to meet a young man who's anxious to speak to you. You knew his father."

Sweeney rubbed his beard and smiled like an overbearing relative, a look of curiosity starting to enliven his features. Dermot gave him a quick, nervous grin in return. Just then, a group of women in a nearby room struck up a rosary chant. Sweeney mumbled along and reached out to shake Dermot's hand, at the same time surveying the faces farther down the queue.

"Everything's going from bad to worse here," he said apologetically.

"We were just getting over Dad's death when the floods came. Then this morning the storm put our electricity out. Hence all the candles," he said, sweeping his hand into the house's gloomy interior.

"My name is Dermot Jordan, my father was called Oliver," said Dermot.

Sweeney didn't seem to hear. He leaned closer to the boy.

"You know, the sound of the river bursting its banks woke me right out of my sleep. I thought the walls of the house were going to cave in."

"We've found where the IRA buried Oliver Jordan, and now we want to hunt down his killers."

At the mention of Jordan's name again, Sweeney straightened up like a puppet on unsteady legs, his eyeballs turning and twisting upon themselves as he took in the old man and the boy.

"At least you have the luxury of visiting your father's grave. Knowing where to lay a wreath of flowers," said Dermot.

Sweeney turned to Hughes in recognition, his mouth crooked, his eyes belligerent.

"Surprised?" asked Hughes.

"That my father's funeral has been disturbed by an enemy of the IRA? No, that happens all the time."

"Would you have talked to us if I had arranged a meeting?"

"Probably not."

Even under the thick beard, it was possible to see Sweeney's upper lip stretch into a sneer.

"You should be in a nursing home or under armed fucking guard, not here in my house, drooling like an old bloodhound," he said.

"Don't worry about me. I can take care of myself," replied Hughes.

"What else have you been taking care of?" Sweeney's voice was a hoarse whisper. "A man with your secrets should go to the grave quietly, without trying to drag as many as possible along with you."

"Secrets? There are so many." Hughes touched his fingers to his forehead. "But don't worry. My memory is poor, and many of the details are not as clear as I would wish. That's why we've come to you."

Sweeney noted the sleepwalker's tremble in Hughes's eyelids, the dirt-lined fingers stroking his creased brow, and the food stains discoloring his beard. Some of the fear and tension lifted from his face. He had worked out that the old man and the boy did not present an immediate threat to his physical safety and that they had come unaccompanied. Nevertheless, the two of them were a nuisance, a source of irritation, and they would hamper the way in which he conducted himself in front of the crowd of mourners. He needed to get rid of them as quickly and skillfully as possible. He took Hughes's arm in his hand. It was thin, little more than skin and bone, and Sweeney's confidence that he would handle their unexpected arrival was reinforced. The old man made no attempt to pull away as Sweeney led them into a side-room.

"It's not a good time to talk about these matters," he chided them.

"My questions can't wait," said Dermot.

Sweeney seemed to think for a moment, and then smiled.

"Now I understand," he said.

"What do you understand?" asked Hughes.

"Why that jeep has been parked outside my house several times this past week."

Dermot nodded. "We've been trying to meet you. As I said, my questions are urgent."

Sweeney sat down and lit a cigarette, his movements careful and meticulous. After he had taken a few drags, he fixed his gaze on Dermot.

"Really, you should come back after I've had time to grieve."

He watched the boy's reactions.

"However, I'm a patient man. And the two of you seem to be running out of time. I will tell you what I know, without adding anything or leaving anything out."

As he spoke, his gaze bore into Dermot, weighing up his responses, trying to read his state of mind.

"Firstly, I have no idea where your father's body was buried. The IRA doesn't have an archive section where you can dig out a document on every single operation."

He showed his empty hands and chuckled to himself.

"All you can rely on are my memories and those of other activists. And all this is off the record, OK?"

"I'd like to hear you say that in an interrogation room," interrupted Hughes with sudden venom.

"I haven't heard an invitation like that for years," replied Sweeney coolly. He got up, removed a bottle of whiskey from a drawer, and poured himself a glass.

"As I said, none of this is cast-iron. That's the thing about memory. Some days it can be less reliable than others. But there's nothing unusual in that for men of our age, is there David?" he said, his grin expanding. He knocked back a cheekful of the amber alcohol.

"I know my own mind," said Hughes. "Sometimes I don't recognize the man using it."

"I'm feeling sorry for you now," said Sweeney with a rebuking shake of his head. His silver curls settled against the stiff collar of his shirt. "But then that's probably your intention. Soften me up a little. You always were a cunning bastard."

He returned to examining Dermot. The boy looked sad, depressed almost. But then, so did most teenagers. Adolescent angst was a shield, as inaccessible as a mask.

"About your father, Dermot. I've overheard some things to which others have added more details. At the time I was unaware of how much I actually knew, but over the years I've been able to build up a picture of his last days."

"The facts, not bullshit," warned Hughes.

"Though they will never publicly admit it, the IRA is genuinely sorry for what happened to people like your father," Sweeney continued, composed now, on practiced ground. "And I am too, but that won't save you from your anger, or grief, or prevent Republicans from feeling guilty or give us any peace. For your father, his troubles are over and his soul is at peace.

"Believe me, Dermot, if I had known he was an innocent man I would have freed him. But what did I know? I'm not a mind reader. In those days, I didn't have the influence I have now. I was just a foot soldier, ignorant and trusting.

"The IRA never wanted to admit to your father's murder because he wasn't properly handled by the thugs who kidnapped him. Aidan Corr was the main man, but he was drunk. All he did was ask a few stupid questions and then he got his comrade, Danny O'Shea, to dress up as a priest and extract a confession. After that, Corr pulled the trigger. If they had really believed your father was an informer, he should have been tied up, guarded, and handed over to more senior personnel. The IRA would have had a field day if their suspicions had been correct.

"But Corr claimed to have got your father to confess to everything, so they shot him. The murder calmed Republican nerves, convinced them that the leak had been dealt with.

"Corr was later imprisoned for withholding information. A year after he was released his car collided with a cement mixer on the same road from which he abducted your father. His accomplice, O'Shea, was killed in 1986 by the IRA for using weapons for unauthorized criminal activities. His maggot-infested body was found in a ditch in South Armagh, a fertilizer bag wrapped around his head. The secret of what happened to your father's body died with them. You could say that the IRA brought his killers to justice, the most summary form of justice there is.

"Does that make a difference, Dermot? Knowing that the men who killed your father led violent, miserable lives? Nobody cried at their funerals. Have you gained anything from knowing that?"

"I appreciate your frankness," said Dermot with a surly tone that suggested he did not appreciate it much at all. "But the account's not settled."

"Something tells me you know more about Oliver Jordan's death than you're letting on," said Hughes. "You were the third man in the IRA gang that included Corr and O'Shea. Where were you when the kidnap was taking place?"

"That's your problem, Hughes," said Sweeney, his mouth teetering once again on a bitter sneer. "You always suspect the worst in others, if only because your own career was based on such deception and dishonesty."

"I have a sneaking admiration for people like you who build a successful career on their own lies," growled Hughes. "I've watched you closely over the years. Followed your development as a politician. Seen how the media practically jumped into your lap and combed your hair for you. Television becomes you, like any actor. But you're not going to wriggle out of telling the truth now."

Sweeney ran a hand pretentiously through his silver hair and sighed.

"That sounds like the David Hughes I remember. So let me level with you."

"Is that not what you're doing already?"

Sweeney paused and stared at the ground briefly. A look of darkness passed across his features. Then he raised the glass of whiskey into the air. The gap in his thinking had been small but noticeable, and the movement with the glass had helped him cross it.

"Naturally, I wasn't there when they took Oliver Jordan away," he continued. "That's all there's to it. The only piece of evidence I have to prove that is the testimony of my estranged wife. You can check with her. She had just given birth to our first son. The baby shut my mind against the rest of the world. I didn't want to be bothered with anything else. All this is true."

"Somehow I think there's more to come," said Dermot, leaning forward as though he wanted to slap the whiskey out of Sweeney's hands.

"No," said Sweeney curtly. "That's it. We're through. As the politician said to the journalist, I've nothing more to add at this moment."

"What about the files you have stashed away in the shed outside? Confidential information about the investigation into my father's murder."

Sweeney balked. "Legal files? In my shed?"

"Yes."

He took a step back. "Who's been snooping?"

"I told you we came looking for you last week. The door to the shed was unlocked and I went in. I found the file and read it."

"I returned that file to Inspector Celcius Daly a few nights ago. He was snooping 'round as well," said Sweeney, still floundering.

"Daly reopened the investigation into Dad's death. I can see why he wanted the file. But why did you have it in the first place?"

"The police aren't the only ones interested in revisiting that investigation," said Sweeney, recovering from the shock of Dermot's discovery. He was like a swimmer returning to the surface with expert strokes. "We Republicans have been conducting our own enquiry into your father's death, and why the investigation went nowhere. In some respects we consider it one of the most important cases in the history of the East Tyrone brigade."

"Don't tell me you're having your own truth commission," interrupted Hughes.

Sweeney laughed, part belch, part smoker's cough.

"If you must know, we're just as lost in the labyrinth as you are. For years, we've been trying to uncover the identity of the top-level informer your father was killed to protect. We think Devine's murder is somehow linked to him. Devine had a special connection to the case. Perhaps his killer had as well."

"What have you discovered, then?"

"I was holding on to the files before passing them back to the police. But I can put you in touch with someone who has a more thorough knowledge of the case."

"Who?"

"A very gifted professional. A man of enormous patience and inquisitive powers. I think he will be able to help you."

"He must be a bloody clairvoyant," said Hughes.

"I can arrange for you to meet him," said Sweeney, ignoring the sarcasm. "I happen to know he's free this evening. You can meet him here if you like."

"We're not leaving until we get answers," said Dermot.

39

Daly noticed an orange dome of light shining on the night skyline as he went out to feed the hens. The birds tilted their heads and made no sound as he ushered them into their coop. It was as if they sensed the danger carried on the evening air. There was not a single cluck or scratch from them as they made their way across the half-frozen ground.

His mobile rang.

"Daly?" The caller's voice was frantic.

"Yes."

"I'm not far from you." It was Irwin. "At Owen Sweeney's house. You'd better get over here quick. There's trouble." Then he hung up.

When Daly approached Sweeney's house, all he could see on the horizon was a blaze of light floating between two pools of darkness, the lough on one side, and the boggy hinterland of Maghery on the other. A fire was raging through the two-story building. As he jumped out of the car, a section of the roof collapsed before his eyes, sending a torrent of flames leaping into the sky. An explosion of embers spat out the stars, and he instinctively ducked.

He heard the sound of running feet and saw Irwin's tall figure, bent in two and scurrying, lit up momentarily by the flames. Another blast

of heat hit Daly in the face and he backed away. He heard Irwin pant-
ing beside him. The Special Branch officer's face was white as a sheet.

"Can't get in. Fire's taking hold. I think Sweeney's still in there. God
knows who else."

"Who raised the alarm?"

Irwin, still breathing hard, explained. "We got a call from Sweeney.
Said he was with Hughes and the boy. At his house. When we got here
we saw this. Place stank of diesel. The back door was open but there's
no sign anyone escaped."

"Did Sweeney say he was in any danger?"

Irwin studied the flames sucking at the darkness. "No. He just said
to hurry. He didn't know how long he could keep his visitors. They
were anxious to get on their way."

"'Anxious to get on their way.'" Daly repeated the words. They hung
in the air for a long time.

The two men stood, peripheral, numb, as the fire intensified.

"The smoke will have done them in first," remarked Daly.

Two fire engines arrived at the scene. The darkness grew dense with
moving bodies and shouts. Jets of water and billows of smoke illumi-
nated by searchlights screened off what remained of the house. Soon the
sound of gushing water began to replace the roar and crackle of the fire.

After about an hour, the firemen managed to smother the flames.
Daly scanned the ruins, the drenched wreckage steaming in the artificial light.

It was dawn before the firefighters, searching under the collapsed
walls, found a body. The morning sun drained away the darkness, but
the burnt corpse remained as black as the night. It was the body of a
middle-aged man. He was neither small nor big nor deformed in any
way, but the fire had made a monstrosity of his corpse. It lay slumped
in the charred remains of a chair, its mouth agape like an astonished
spectator at the fire's pyrotechnics. They said that Owen Sweeney had
been untouchable as a politician because he knew more dead colleagues than living. Unfortunately, he had crossed to the wrong side
of that line himself.

40

It was the nature of Terence Grimes's job that he remain hidden on the sidelines. After all, that was where he did his best work. A light rain fell on his head as he ambled along the fence and examined the building. He had circled the grounds several times in the past few days and had learned all he needed to know about the nursing home's routines— what time the nurses changed shifts, when they did their handovers, how long visiting time lasted. He was carrying a basket of fruit and a box of chocolates to help him carry out his mission. The gun in his shoulder harness represented plan B.

There was a sun room by the front door where three people sat, strapped into wheelchairs—all old men in pajamas. He raised a hand to signal a greeting and in response got three vacant stares. There was no one to stop him at the front door. That was the thing about nursing homes, he thought, designed to keep people in rather than out.

He smiled to himself. The concept of the nursing home was a useful one. A business based upon caging the old. And very necessary, too. Contrary to first impressions, the elderly were a dangerous and trouble-some lot. Take David Hughes, for example. All that time on his hands with only his memories to keep him company. They should have tied the old bastard in a wheelchair and shoved him in a corner, thought Grimes, rather than let him wander the country, stirring up all kinds of anxieties. If only he'd had a stroke and lost the power of speech.

At the far end of the corridor, an Indian nurse sat at a desk, her head bent as she read. Grimes presented the basket and chocolates to her. "I'm here to see Mrs. Jordan. These are from the family. We want to thank you for her care."

The nurse smiled at the gifts, glancing only briefly at Grimes.

He hovered for a second. In the mirror behind, he examined the cold features of his face, his mouth and eyes, the helmet of blond hair combed back immaculately. It was a face grafted onto the nightmares of countless paramilitaries with secrets to hide.

"Is she in the sitting room?" he asked, smiling at the nurse.

"No. She's in her room. Number 6," said the nurse in halting English.

Rita Jordan was sitting in an armchair as though expecting his visit. She appeared calm, serene. Had the boy been talking to her recently? he wondered.

"Nurse?" she asked, staring in his direction.

"I had to tell her to leave," he whispered. A staff member passed the door, and he squeezed the old woman's hand fleetingly.

"I came to see you, Rita Jordan," he said, unable to resist a mock formality. "All the way from Her Majesty the Queen, just to see you."

"Who are you?" she asked.

He ignored her question.

"I've come to find your grandson. I've looked for him at home. I've searched for him at school. I've visited all his little haunts, chatted to his friends, the few that he has. They tell me he has run away. And so, finally, I've come here to see you."

"What do you want?"

"I've come a long way to see you." He sighed and sat back wearily in a chair.

"Well, you've seen me now. I've had better days, but I'm fine. You don't need to worry about me." She adopted the tone of someone addressing an insincere relative.

Grimes looked around the room. A smile played on his lips.

"You're not hiding him under the bed, are you?"

"I'm not hiding anyone. What do you want Dermot for? He's not done anything wrong, has he?"

Grimes allowed her question to hang in the air. He wanted her to remain in a state of uncertainty for as long as possible. Allow her imagination to apply its own pressure.

"He's safe, isn't he? Nothing has gone wrong. Has it?" Her cracked voice trembled.

"I hear that he has got himself mixed up in bad business. He's keeping the local police force, not to mention Special Branch, very busy."

"He's in bad trouble."

"What about Hughes, the old man, have you seen him?"

"No," she lied.

"Did he sing for you? I hear he has a lovely singing voice. Especially for strangers."

The old woman didn't answer. She closed her eyes and pretended to be asleep. Grimes sighed. She was well into her eighties. Almost a decade older than Hughes. People of that age became stubborn and unyielding, even if their judgment day was close at hand. He stood up. Nothing of their conversation would be of any use to him. He glanced at his watch. Visiting time was over.

The old woman opened her eyes and watched Grimes draw closer. Her voice quavered, high-pitched and defiant.

"Dermot will never give up until he has found the truth. His father's grave matters to him, and to me. It matters because we're of the same blood. We'll never give up looking for him, as long as we're still alive."

"I came all the way to see you because I wanted to leave Dermot a message," said Grimes. He had a pillow in his hands.

"What sort of message?"

Grimes squeezed the pillow over her face.

"This is his message: It's going to be dark very soon."

In the quietness that followed, he could feel a throbbing beneath the pillow, her muffled cries and the submerged struggle of her breath as it faltered and slipped away. After a few moments, he lowered the pillow to check her eyes. They grew dark. Whatever light was left in them was being wiped away and stamped into the darkness of death.

Something caught his eye. He removed a loose strand of hair from the pillow's cover sheet. Then he smoothed its creases. It was the minor points like this that repelled him, the untidiness and inattention to detail, which tended to distract him from an important task at hand. A nurse walked by the door and glanced in.

"The old dear's fallen asleep again," he said, smiling. Hurriedly he placed the pillow behind the old woman's limp neck and walked out of the room.

41

When Dermot got the message from his mother that his grandmother had suddenly slipped into unconsciousness at the nursing home, he and Hughes sped off in the jeep. He approached the sharp bend at Maghery and thought he had come to a dead end. It all happened quickly. He lost control of the vehicle and the hedge loomed toward him so abruptly he did not have time to brace his body. He steered to the right but the jeep did not answer his touch. Instead, it slewed to the left, and he struck a tree, side-on. A shifting weave of vegetation, shattered glass, and torn wood enveloped him. There was something sharp and singular about the tree as it ripped through the vehicle. In his mind's eye it was as hard to look at as the sun. He felt the air zipping around his face, surprisingly fresh and clean, and heard, all around him, a horrendous smashing noise. He could not remember his flight through the windscreen or recall encountering any stiff resistance but somehow he blacked out and came to consciousness lying at the side of a wet ditch.

There was a humming noise like a giant bee above his head. It took him a while to realize it was the still-spinning tires of the jeep. There were other sounds, the tinkling of broken glass and water dripping, and the willing combustion of diesel and plastic. The radio was playing loudly, the jagged nighttime voice of Bob Dylan floating through the shredded windscreen. Something about the soothing tone of Dylan's voice made him feel that everything was fine, and that he would be safe soon. Sinking back into blackness, he heard someone sigh, and opening his eyes briefly saw the gaunt face of Hughes hovering above him, a tenacious presence, his dark eyes like a pair of sea creatures sucking at the final threads of his consciousness. The last thing he remembered was a snarl forming on the old man's lips.

When he returned to consciousness again, it took him a while to work out what had happened. He tried to focus on the event in which he had been a central protagonist. A scene of higgledy-piggledy violence lay before him—upended thorn trees, twisted metal, lumps of glass etched with a spidery delicacy. His impression was vaguely of a flogging, of a lumbering metal beast having succumbed to the scratching intensity of thorn trees. His mouth felt dry, and when he rubbed his lips there was spittle hanging at the corners. He stood up. A fit of dizziness made him stagger.

The swish of unseen cars passing on the road above alerted him to his whereabouts. The jeep had ended up on the far side of the hedge, below the level of the road. He moved back to the jeep, which was heavily crumpled along the driver's side, and removed the ignition key. He brushed the glass from the leather folder containing the map of the bog.

There was something else that should have been there. An important piece of evidence. He checked for his mobile phone and found it in his pocket. He stared at it for a moment or two, hoping that it would help him organize his mind. Something vital had exited the accident scene, somehow floating away through the mesh of thorns and cracked glass.

He tried to coordinate his memory, running through the series of events, the jeep skidding, the flight through the branches, and then he remembered. The old man. He recalled Hughes's face hovering above him and wondered if it had been some sort of vision. Had he survived the crash and simply wandered off? He took in the accident scene with greater intensity now, saw the scars in the earth where the tires had slithered, the snapped branches and skinned bark, the jeep destroyed beyond repair. He had been lucky to survive the crash, but what about Hughes?

His panic widened in concentric circles from the crashed jeep, spreading outward as he searched for a sign of the old man's body, in the ditch, along the roadside, in the field, until he was scanning the near horizon in all directions.

42

When his mobile rang, Daly was trying to find some peace and quiet by digging up the potato patch in his father's front garden. His spade hauled up stones and the previous year's rotten tubers. After stooping for an hour or so he straightened his back and thought of having a lie-down. Not for him, his father's epic daylong efforts with a spade. He fumbled to find his phone. He checked the screen but it was smeared with clay.

"Hello."

"You said you would help me," said the voice. "Does the offer still stand?"

"I never go back on my word," said Daly, recognizing Dermot's voice.

"I can't talk for long. My battery is going to run out. Do you have a pen and paper?"

Daly hurried back into the house. "I'm writing this down as we speak."

"I crashed the jeep at Maghery corner. I can't remember what happened but when I came to, David was gone. He must have wandered off."

"What do you want me to do?" asked Daly, playing for time to think.

"Organize a search party or something. He can't have got far. There's a man called Grimes. He's tried to kill us already. I had to rescue David from Sweeney's house. Before it went up in flames."

"Hold on a minute," said Daly, trying to conceal the concern in his voice. "There's a lot of things need sorting out. First, you might be injured from the crash. It's my duty to bring you to hospital and inform your mother."

"I have to find Grimes first."

"This man sounds dangerous. You need help."

"And where would that come from? Special Branch? The PSNI?"

"You can't do this by yourself."

"I've already found my father's grave. Something you people have been trying to do for the last fifteen years. At least Grimes is above-ground. I have to hang up now. I want to save the battery."

"Wait," said Daly. "You haven't given me a proper description of Grimes. I want to launch a manhunt for him. Plus it's getting dark. Where will you sleep tonight?"

There was pause at the other end of the phone. Daly pressed on. "I'll be at Maghery as soon as I can. Twenty minutes."

"OK. Thanks."

"You don't need to thank me. I'm just doing my job. Anyway, you and I need to talk. I want to know if you're hiding any other secrets from me."

When Dermot climbed into Daly's car there was a remote fugitive's smile on his face. He turned to face the windscreen, revealing a jagged cut above his ear, fragments of glass and congealed blood matting his hair. The blood ran down the side of his ear and stained his T-shirt.

"That needs looking at," said Daly. "And your mother's going to ask questions when she sees that T-shirt in the laundry. But that's the least of your worries right now."

Dermot touched his wound gingerly. "You could call it Sweeney's revenge."

"Sweeney is dead."

"I know. He was dead when we escaped the fire."

Dermot looked away as shadows swung over the recesses of his face, his features too gaunt for an eighteen-year-old. Daly felt the acid rise in his stomach and wondered to himself if his passenger had brought more dangerous excitement than he could handle on his own on a Saturday evening.

"What the hell's been going on? I never thought it possible that a schoolboy could cause so much aggravation. Special Branch is trying to finger you for Sweeney's murder."

"Is this an interrogation?"

Daly held his impatience. "I'm not trying to incriminate you. But it's clear a lot has been going on that I know nothing about."

A spasm contorted the boy's face. "Why should I trust you?"

Daly glowered at him and sighed in exasperation. "Don't you see? We're both too deep in this to hold back any secrets. For Christ's sake, I'm breaking the law right now to save your skin. That jeep is a stolen vehicle. Right now, I'm aiding your escape from the scene of an unreported accident. Not only that, but you're also wanted in connection with arson and possible kidnap charges. I would think it's clear I'm the only friend you have right now, apart from a seventy-six-year-old man with Alzheimer's, and he's just run off on you."

Dermot shot him a look of sullen fright. "I've done nothing wrong."

"No doubt. But I need you to answer my questions truthfully."

"What do you want to know?"

"You could start by telling me what happened at Sweeney's house."

Dermot threw a cigarette lighter onto the dashboard. "I set it alight. There's your evidence. Now arrest me."

Daly shook his head in annoyance. Driving a suspected arsonist to a place of safety was hardly normal procedure for a police detective.

"Let me assure you that if this was a proper investigation you'd be in handcuffs right now and on your way to a prison cell," he said.

A tight-lipped smile formed on Dermot's lips. He lifted the lighter and put it back in his pocket.

"I risked my life going back in to rescue Hughes," he told Daly. "We were at Sweeney's house, digging for information. Sweeney said he would introduce us to someone who could help. Then this man called Grimes arrived. He spoke with an English accent, and he was angry. He accused Sweeney of not following his instructions. I knew he wasn't to be trusted."

"An English accent?" remarked Daly. "Then he definitely wasn't to be trusted."

Dermot paused, wondering if Daly was being prejudiced or ironic.

"I managed to escape but realized I had to save David. They were holding him captive. The only thing I'm good at is lighting fires. I needed a diversion and there was fuel in Sweeney's garage. There was nothing else I could do. I'm not the SAS."

"So you set the place alight and managed to get Hughes out?"

"Yes. When I went back in, the fire had taken hold. David was tied to a gas cylinder. Sweeney was sitting in a chair, shot in the forehead. Hughes told me that Grimes hadn't wanted them to burn to death. He'd just wanted their guts blown sky high."

Dermot paused. "Fortunately I got in with my act of arson before Grimes could blow the place up."

"Why was Sweeney shot?"

"Grimes is trying to tie up all the loose ends from Dad's murder. That's why Hughes is still in danger."

They drove on in silence for a while.

"Grimes is one of your guys, isn't he?" said Dermot. "He's working for Special Branch."

"Let's not try to jump to any conclusions just yet," replied Daly.

"It's the only explanation that fits."

"Somehow I don't buy it. Not yet, anyway. I need more proof that Special Branch is prepared to kill Hughes. Or wanted Sweeney dead."

"Sounds like you don't know Special Branch very well."

"I can't see Special Branch killing its own people." Daly was resolute in rejecting the theory.

"The only person I know who has a motive for killing Sweeney is you, Dermot." Daly looked at him.

The boy was silent.

"Here's my theory for you," continued Daly. "This Englishman called Grimes doesn't exist. Just like the men who were supposed to have burnt your house down on Woodlawn Crescent don't exist. Neither your nor Hughes's lives were ever in danger. You set fire to Sweeney's house to kill the two remaining people who had a hand in your father's murder."

"Exactly," said Dermot. "That's what they want you to think."

"What proof could you give a court of law that you're telling me the truth?"

"Hughes will back me up. That's why we need to find him. Why else would I have contacted you?"

When they got back to the cottage, Daly asked Dermot for the cigarette lighter.

"I don't want you losing vital evidence," he joked, placing the lighter safely in his pocket. In truth, he was worried about what might happen if he fell asleep with Dermot as a houseguest. His father's cottage was insured against fire, but not one started by a boy with a track record of arson. From the hallway, he phoned headquarters to organize a search for Hughes. A helicopter was mobilized to sweep the fields and roads around the scene of the accident while officers were dispatched to carry out house-to-house inquiries. The police officers would have their work cut out for them. The moon had yet to rise and the darkness was dense. Anxious to dispel his sense of hopelessness, he brought the boy into the living room and made coffee.

Over a turf fire, Dermot opened up about his feelings.

"All I ever wanted to know was where my father was buried," he told Daly. "I didn't care about his killers or what happened to them. As long as I never had to meet them. It was a case of out of sight, out of mind. Then I learned from Hughes that Sweeney was involved in Dad's abduction. The great politician and peace broker. It sickened me to see he was still alive, feeding his rotten soul with the illusion he was a man of peace. I couldn't forgive him. Now that I knew who he was and where he lived, I wanted to finish him off. It enraged me to think he had profited so much from the Troubles. He should have spent the last thirty years of his life hiding like a leper."

The turf burned quickly, inflaming their eyes with its sweet smoke. Outside a branch cracked and an owl hooted in the darkness. Dermot crouched by the fire, wanting to give himself up entirely to the comfort of heat.

"But he's dead now," he continued. "I thank God it wasn't me that did it. He wasn't worth it. I would have slipped to his level, fallen into a hole with him, never to get out again."

A lump of bog root burst into flames, sending out a shower of sparks. Daly's head felt light and fuzzy. The blue smoke of the turf was redolent with so many memories.

"My mother was killed in crossfire between an undercover police unit and the IRA," he said. "The police said she was in the wrong place at the wrong time. But she wasn't. I was only ten and even I knew that. She was in the right place at the right time. She was coming home from work." He stopped suddenly, regretting the words he had let slip, as if he had betrayed a secret and now wanted to recover it. Dermot's anger had ignited a childhood anger within him.

He had let that anger go, as he had let everything else go. Never putting up a fight for anything. All he had wanted to do was look after himself, no one else. In the same way, he had let his wife go. Work had just been an excuse, a means of avoiding getting too close to anyone. He had walked alone all his life, like an escaped convict, shackled to his fear. Cramped up by the dread of losing another loved one.

The fire burned down to its embers. Daly went out for a fresh load of turf. The darkness was filled with the sound of the wind howling through trees. He felt the wild air of the lough blow through him. He was surrounded by memories, the wind puncturing holes in the darkness through which ghosts could stream.

"Tell me about David Hughes," he asked on his return.

A grim expression appeared on Dermot's face. "What is there you don't already know? He's a confused old man carrying a load of terrible memories. Like a boat that can't find a safe harbor. He's plagued by ghosts and visions from his past."

"Some of his ghosts are substantial enough, whatever you might think. I ran into a few of them myself."

Daly described his suspicions that Devine had dressed up as the ghosts that appeared around Hughes's cottage.

"Why would he do a thing like that? That's sick."

"He wanted Hughes to talk about the past. A bit like what you were doing in the nursing home. Call it reminiscence therapy with a supernatural twist."

"Why didn't he just ask him straight-out?"

"And have Special Branch alerted? Devine knew that however Hughes might try to explain their secret meetings along the hedge, the whole thing would always sound unreal, ghostly, even to Hughes himself. Remember, Hughes had just been diagnosed with Alzheimer's. He didn't believe his own eyes, so how could he persuade anyone else?" Daly threw some more turf onto the fire. "Hughes had once been the spymaster, but now Devine was pulling the strings. This time it was the informer who was extracting the information from the spymaster."

"Was there a pattern to his visits?" asked Dermot.

"What do you mean?"

"Did they occur at a particular time of the day or week?"

"I don't think so. According to Hughes's journal, the ghosts came anytime they pleased."

"He told me he could always sense when they were due."

Daly took out the journal and they examined the entries. There were no obvious clues of the ghostly visits following a timetable or plan. Dermot took the book and began leafing through the pages. He only paid attention to the dates and began writing them down.

"Have you a calendar?" he asked.

Daly retrieved one from the kitchen wall. He gave a low whistle of surprise as Dermot marked down the dates. They corresponded with the nights of the full moon. They sat quietly for a moment, taking in the pattern.

"The last full moon was February fourth," said Daly.

His finger followed the days until he came to the start of March.

"We need to get going. There's a full moon tonight. Hughes might be waiting for a rendezvous with his supernatural friends as we speak."

The wind that blew from the lough was cold, the moonlit sky clear of clouds, the water gleaming silver in the distance. The cottage lay abandoned, and the fields empty of human life. Lurking in the corners of the field were the whitethorn trees, their blossoms pale in the moonlight.

As Daly and the boy skirted the hedgerows around Hughes's cottage, he had the impression he was approaching the advance posts of a hidden enemy. He hoped to find the old man quickly so they could all return to his house, eat, sleep, and build up their strength before dawn. A new day would give him the chance to clear his head and put everything right. Perhaps he would take the cowardly approach and lay the entire case at Inspector Fealty's feet. Absolve himself of any responsibility for what happened after Dermot and the old man had been found.

In the moonlight, he could see the figure of a man sitting on a stone. He had his chin propped on a stick and was gazing out at the lough.

Daly called to him, but the person did not hear. He went up close and saw that it was Hughes. He looked up at Daly and shook his head.

"Joseph Devine and then Owen Sweeney, both dead. What's bad is that I pushed Devine when he didn't want to carry on. He begged me to let him go. He wanted a green card, and a new life in the US. But I kept jerking him into the air. Like a puppet. I kept him walking and talking the way I wanted. I told him he could never leave. His only way out was to tie a stone around his neck and throw himself into the lough."

"Don't talk like that," said Dermot, appearing at Daly's side.

"I can't ignore what's in my heart. Your friend here and the ghosts need to hear this. I went to your father's memorial service all those years ago, and I watched your mother cry. Now I feel her weeping inside me. It's as if she's wringing out my soul."

He caught Dermot by the arm. "Tell the ghost I didn't mean to do all those things. They were just orders I was obeying."

"Tell who?"

"The ghost that's come to sniff out its killers."

"There are no ghosts," said Daly. "It was Devine impersonating dead people all along."

Hughes's eyes grew terrified. "Devine? Has he come back too?"

The old man looked at Daly. "Do you know what's going on? What secrets are you hiding?"

There was a soft cough in the darkness behind them, like a cork popping out of a bottle.

Then the flare of a match as someone lit a cigarette.

"Excuse me, but I couldn't stay quiet for much longer," said Grimes, striding toward them, the cigarette blazing and the steel muzzle of a gun gleaming in his outstretched hand. "Though I have been very discreet up until now."

He studied Dermot's frightened face. "I respect your resourcefulness, but it's the end of the road for you now, young man. You've run out of options."

Daly tried to appraise the situation as quickly as possible.

"Whoever it is you're trying to protect, they're safe," he said. "No one's interested in unraveling Hughes's network of spies. The boy just wanted to find out where his dad's body was buried. There's no reason to do away with any of us. Nothing to be gained, a lot to lose."

Grimes appeared to listen. He blinked at Daly. He looked down at the old man for a while, weighing up his silence and confusion, the loneliness that was plain to see in his gaunt features.

"I'm taking on board what you're saying," he replied. "But you see, I've been made an offer. An opportunity to make some really big money. Plus I've a gilt-edged reputation as a reliable hit man. Letting you lot go would do it serious harm. Now, tell me why should I risk that?"

Daly searched for an answer and found it. The answer was he shouldn't. Of course not. All three of them were expendable. All three of them were tarnished in some respect, and discredited. The teenage arsonist, the senile spy handler who talked to ghosts, and the police detective with the flawed judgment and misplaced loyalties. Had he only known it, Dermot had done Grimes and whoever was paying him a favor by entangling Daly in the trap. There'd be no one left to question the circumstances of their deaths. No one else in the police force pointed in the right direction. It was an overwhelmingly persuasive argument from Grimes's viewpoint.

"How well do you know the people you're working for?" asked Daly. "Can you trust them?"

"What do you mean?"

"Do you really think you're going to be able to grab your money, take off, and disappear? Have you not thought of what arrangements they might have made behind your back?"

"You're trying to distract me from my mission. Maybe even buy yourself some more time. It's to be expected. I'd do the same in your circumstances."

Daly persisted, hoping to press home his advantage. "You're doing all their dirty work for them. What's to stop them from eliminating you, too? Look at it from their perspective. It's the only way to ensure the truth will never come out."

"I'm getting tired of this silly conversation," said Grimes, a forced smile playing on his lips. "You don't need to worry about me. I've made my own contingency plans. I treat all my employers with the utmost suspicion."

"I hope you're relying on something more than their goodwill. Just think about it. Three unexplained murders are going to raise a lot of questions. People will want a scapegoat, someone to blame."

"I can give you some reassurance that won't happen. Unfortunately, it might not be to your liking." He paused to take another drag of the cigarette and fill his lungs with pleasure. "This gun I'm holding is a Glock 19. There's nothing special about it. It's as good a killing device as any other gun. Except that it's registered in the name of David Hughes. For his personal protection."

Daly went cold.

"I'm keeping to my agreement. I've told you that already. Do you still have any reason to doubt that?" He smiled at Daly, coaxing him to join in his good humor. It looked like checkmate.

Daly realized he had just one remaining chance to save the three of them. And he needed to take it while he still had strength.

Grimes lined the three of them up and made them walk down toward the lough. They gave little resistance as he started tying them up, first Hughes and then Dermot. Grimes had no reason to be impatient. He took his time, making sure the knots were strong. It was a misconception that fear made people unpredictable, he thought. On the contrary, it was like a numbing drug. Fear made its victims very boring.

Finally, it was Daly's turn. Grimes pushed him to his knees and leaned over him with the rope. Daly raised his hands upward and then at the last moment let them drop.

"Lift them up!" barked Grimes.

Daly leaned back into a squatting position and raised his hands slightly, luring Grimes closer.

"Sit up."

Grimes paused but Daly refused to budge. Cursing, he swung his boot at the detective's ribs. Daly dodged the blow and waited until the arc of Grimes's kick flew into thin air, then rammed his body into the hit man's standing knee. Grimes saw it coming and tried to cling on to Daly's propelled body, but his leg buckled from underneath. The hand carrying the rope fumbled in the darkness for a grip before he fell back with a heavy thud.

Daly wondered if he should take another swing at Grimes, for good measure, but he feared his physical strength might not be enough. Instead, he flew forward. Keeping his head low, he scurried for cover. Soon he was running into the darkness of a hedge, a hail of thorns pricking his face and hands.

He scrambled along the roots of the hedge, feeling as though he had spent the entire month in the shadow of thorn trees. Running up and down, doing little more than beating the hard winter ground harder. Grimes's flashlight tracked back and forth behind him.

"If you don't come back, I'll shoot the boy," warned Grimes.

Daly lost time pausing to get his whereabouts, searching for the gap in the hedge that had been sawn down months ago. The hole through which the ghosts and Hughes's dark wind had blown all winter. A crashing sound alerted him to Grimes's approaching presence. He flung himself deeper into the hedge, fearing each moment was going to be his last. He crawled along the muddy track of a ditch. Even if he managed to escape, Grimes would undoubtedly go back and shoot the old man and the boy. Running away was pointless. Instead, he had to find another way out, one that would include the rescue of his companions. The moon came out and an owl hooted nearby. He was close to the gap in the hedge and its uninterrupted view of the cottage's back door. Somewhere in the wizened branches above him lurked the hidden eye that had tracked Hughes's movements through the winter.

He fumbled through the earth and wet leaves until he found it—a heavy metal object buried like a log in the hedge bank. He pulled at it and a cable sprang out of the earth. He had located the battery pack and lead for the surveillance camera that he'd guessed had been concealed somewhere in the branches above. The device had probably been operating for months, Daly reasoned. It had been monitored by Special Branch, who alerted Devine via the pager whenever Hughes had wandered from the house.

It was easy to disconnect the lead from the battery pack. He watched as a warning light flashed silently on the pack. Eyes on target no longer.

The wind picked up, sending the branches slashing sideways. The scent of the ditch's leafy dregs rose from the disturbed earth, filling Daly's nostrils. A pang of doubt and anxiety overcame him. Perhaps all he had done was ensure that his final moments at the hands of a bloody assassin would never be recorded. He turned and walked back toward the torchlight with his hands raised in the air.

When Grimes had tied Daly securely, he dragged him back to where the old man and the boy were kneeling. Only Hughes struggled now, twisting and turning his body in an attempt to loosen the ropes, knocking shoulders with Dermot, grumbling in desperation. His confusion no longer seemed irrational or berserk, but necessary in a blind, stubborn way. Perhaps it was this refusal to give in that had helped him stagger through the unwinding events of the past few weeks. The boy was kneeling beside Hughes, his head bent, like the prow of a boat cleaving through the wake of madness stirred up by the old man. It seemed to take all his effort not to fall forward.

Daly felt as though he did not quite belong to this final scene. The old man and the boy might be father and son, their huddled silhouettes merging together in the moonlight. Daly knelt on his own, waiting for the darkness to be punctured by the rip of gunfire.

"It was you that murdered Devine," said Daly, still playing for time.

"Please," said Grimes. "Murder is not a kind enough word. I eliminated an individual who betrayed countless victims and thought he had evaded all his enemies."

"He left a message behind. In a newspaper obituary."

"And what good did that do him?"

The patience of Grimes's wait, the mildness of his movements as he took the final drags of his cigarette seemed unbearable to Daly. The way in which Grimes was dragging out their execution was the mark of a man who took pleasure in never hurrying.

Hughes's breath rose and fell like the bellow of a bull about to die: sharp, and hoarse, and then sharp again. The old man had given up his struggle. He was exhausted.

But when the shots went off, they sounded farther away and higher up than Daly expected. From behind them, there was the sound of a rotten branch being kicked. He turned around and saw Grimes's body fall to the ground, his spine crumpled by a series of high-caliber bullets. Daly crouched against the ground and closed his eyes.

When he looked up again, he saw two soldiers with night-vision goggles breathing heavily and staring at him, semiautomatic guns nestled in their arms. Another two soldiers were helping Hughes and Dermot to their feet.

One of them introduced himself to Daly as Captain Shane Kerr, the head of an SAS unit that had been dug in at an abandoned cottage nearby. Their mission had been to pick up Hughes if he ever returned to the house. They had been monitoring the camera and its view of the cottage when the alarm went off, alerting them to the fact that someone had tampered with the equipment.

"What took you so long?" asked Daly angrily. Even though it was cold, his clothes, covered in mud and leaves, were soaked in sweat.

"We didn't want a general slaughter on our hands. You should be grateful we got close enough to hit our target. Before he hit his."

Twenty minutes later Inspector Fealty arrived, along with an ambulance.

"I was beginning to think we would never find our assassin," he said, inspecting Grimes's body.

The Special Branch man's face was gravely pale and weary. He lifted his eyes toward the thorn trees, where the surveillance camera was hidden.

"If you've damaged the camera, Daly, we'll be sending you a hefty bill."

"Don't worry. I just switched off the power. I assume it was recording all the time. Even on the night Hughes disappeared."

Fealty nodded solemnly. "That's correct. Think of it as our baby monitor. Special Branch always likes to know exactly what's going on."

"So you knew the old man had escaped, even before the police arrived."

"Even better. We helped him get away. Ripped the back door open and frightened him out of his wits."

Daly gave him a look of surprise.

"It was a calculated risk we took. The old man could have wandered off at any point. At Special Branch, we don't like losing control of a situation. The decision was made that Hughes needed inpatient care. He was a liability in that cottage. So we planned his escape. It was the only way we could convince Eliza her brother was no longer safe in her care. We figured that separating them for a night or two would have shocked her into agreement."

"But Hughes managed to shake you off. Noel Bingham was hardly up to the task of keeping track of him."

Fealty looked pained. "In spite of his drink problem Bingham was loyal. A man to be trusted. But he let Hughes slip through his fingers. Also, we hadn't counted on the old man befriending Dermot Jordan."

"You've made my police team look like fools," said Daly bitterly. "You should have disclosed the truth to us at the start."

"You've nothing to regret. Hughes has turned up, along with Devine's killer. The case is successfully closed."

"We've still Noel Bingham's murder to investigate."

"Like I told you earlier. Bingham's death was a nasty accident. Nothing more, nothing less. That's your problem, Daly, you think too much."

"Unlike you desk men at Special Branch."

"That's right," said Fealty with a sudden smile. Success and adrenaline had made him overconfident. "Thinking too much can be bloody dangerous."

"So who hired Grimes to kill Devine?"

Fealty shrugged his shoulders. "Dissident Republicans? Who knows. The success of our operation was measured according to whether or not we found the man who killed Devine. The media needs the identity of a killer, and so does the public. The rest is speculation. That's the official line, anyway."

"What are you afraid of? Upsetting the people who ordered Devine's death?" Daly suspected that someone in a powerful position was being protected.

"Don't try and complicate things, Inspector," warned Fealty.

"A lot still needs sorting out. We need to know if Oliver Jordan was killed to protect a high-ranking mole in the IRA."

"If you've still got questions, you can come to the morgue and ask Sweeney himself," said Fealty. He behaved as though Daly's obstinate search for the truth was a disturbance that had to run its natural course.

"Can't you see, Daly? That's the problem with investigating the past. There's always one more damned conspiracy theory lying hidden inside every shocking revelation. If we keep on, we're going to end up chasing an infinitely improbable and powerful villain, who we'll never be able to capture because he's also part of us. Perhaps it's time you learned to live with a little uncertainty."

The Special Branch inspector walked off. The tug of tension pulling at one side of his face might have been a grimace or a lopsided grin.

The paramedics were busy helping Dermot Jordan and David Hughes to their feet. The old man was resisting help, refusing to be lifted into the ambulance. Still fighting for his independence.

"I don't want to go anywhere," he said. "I need to think."

Daly had the sense they were still prisoners surrounded by a net of darkness, all of them struggling to find space to think. It was a very crowded net. In a sense, it included every civilian in the land, everyone who trusted in democracy and hoped for peace. He tried to work out how it would all end. Back to the bombs and shootings, to sectarian murder and revenge or into a bright new future of prosperity and forgiveness. He didn't know. He was left with a hollow sense of hope as he watched Hughes and Dermot support each other and step into the ambulance, the blue siren light dancing across their tired faces.

Daly got to his feet. His own legs drew strength from the distinction he made between good and evil, even though it meant his mind might never rest.

ACKNOWLEDGMENTS

I thank my agent, Paul Feldstein, for his kind support and for so diligently protecting me from the physical and emotional realities of publishing a book; Eileen and Kevin for setting their own compass and pointing me in the right direction; my old friend Phelim Cavlan for his mine of encouragement and the deep shifts he clocked up in my company over pints of Guinness; Paul and Kerri, Rhoda and Garry, Nuala and Gerald, Jim and Rosemary, and Charlotte and Martin for their invaluable support; my children—Lucy, Aine, Olivia, and Brendan—for their sustaining laughter, and for showing me that sleep deprivation does have an upside (those long night hours in your company helped think this book into shape); and Frank O'Connor, who listened to my stories and gave as many back. And finally I thank Clare—the secret heart of this book belongs to you.

BORDER
ANGELS

ANTHONY J. QUINN

1

She knew about border country. There were wolves, bears, and buried land mines in the one she had left behind, those snow-covered oak and pine forests that divided her homeland from the outside world.

During her enforced stay in the decomposing cottage, she dreamed of her homeland until the shadows of its trees stretched as far as this new border country. She could almost picture, in a dark corner of her mind, the forgotten light of her grandmother's farmhouse at the edge of the alpine forest. But when she opened her eyes, all she saw was a cracked windowpane glittering in the moonlight, and the figure of yet another man hitching up his trousers, tucking in his shirt, and stumbling out the door.

As a teenager, she had been hungry for journeys, to be on the road to interesting, colorful places. She wanted to escape the forests that bounded her village, to travel where war had not, where politics bored people and music played all night long. She passed her time waiting for true love, or an adventure, one that would transform her life and help carry her to new destinations. Little did she realize that one man's cruelty would do the job much more efficiently.

After two months in the farmhouse brothel, she was no longer interested in what happened to her for its own sake. A part inside her could not be touched or changed. She just watched. It was November. The sloe berries in the thorn hedges dripped with heavy drops of rain. From her window, late at night, she could hear the roar of a deep river devouring the darkness along the Irish border.

2

A sinuous flow of headlights made its way to and from the border brothel on weekend nights. Jeeps and expensive German cars snaked along the overgrown lanes, shifting down the gears, the barely controllable nature of the motorists' urges resulting in haphazard parking; tires sinking into mud and gurgling ditches; handbrakes pulled abruptly; bonnets lurching one final time under the sodden thorn trees.

Jack Fowler was in no mood to be discreet. He drove up to the farmhouse in his flashy Mercedes, knocking the wing-mirrors of a Land Rover and a BMW along the way. He looked the part of a shrewd businessman in expensive clothing come to spend some of his hard-earned money.

Horseflies spun round him as he trudged into the farmhouse. In spite of his unsteady gait and the drops of sweat forming on his forehead, he had the air of a man who was in perfect control of the world, and his own life. In truth, however, his mouth was filled with the bitter taste of defeat. Deep down, his soul grieved over his avarice and the string of mistakes he had made in the property market. It was too late now to retrace his steps and correct the pivotal error of his greed. The value of his investments plummeted as each day rolled in with more news of job losses and business failures, one black wave after another, sweeping him closer to ruin.

He had knocked back several whiskies before seeking out this border hideaway, and already he could feel the approaching drum of pain behind his forehead. The cottage swam toward him, the door flapping open as if pushed by a gust of wind. A guilty feeling of transgression drafted through him. He closed the door behind and waited for his eyes to grow accustomed to the dim light.

At first, he was just anxious to talk to someone. The women whispering behind the red velvet curtain turned out to be Eastern European. Not many of them knew English well enough to carry on a conversation. He introduced himself to a girl called Lena, noticing that her eyes were clear, free of hate or disgust, or the signs of drugs.

She responded to his attempts at conversation not to please him but out of loneliness. Sometimes she went through the entire day without speaking to another soul. When they ran out of small talk, he paid the money and left. It had been the most expensive conversation he'd had about the weather in his forty-two years.

When he came back the next week, he asked specifically for her. This time they had sex, and afterward he fell asleep on the bed.

When his time was up, she poked him awake.

He roused himself quickly and searched for his clothes, but something made him stop. He leaned toward her, startled.

"Did I hurt you?" He sounded horrified with himself.

She hesitated for a moment. "No."

"Those marks on your body." He reached out to touch a line of bruises, dark blue smears against the pale marble of her rib cage. She had tried to hide them but there were too many.

She dragged the blanket over her shoulders.

"The man who guards this house came up last night. His name is Sergei. My presence makes him feel like a coward. So every now and again he takes his anger out on me." She reached for a cigarette.

"How can you stay in this place?"

She did not reply.

"I came here seeking pleasure but . . ." He opened his mouth, closed it, and tried again. Nothing came out. His eyes were bright with confusion. He was like a man underwater trying to avoid suffocation.

She finished the sentence for him. "But all you've found is pain." She lit her cigarette. "Pain of the ugliest type. The pain inflicted by men who hate women." Her voice sounded different, savoring the words like the cigarette smoke she was inhaling.

"Is there another type? Can pain be anything but ugly?"

He reached out to touch her but she flinched.

Yes, of course there was. The pain caused by nature was never ugly, like when you ran barefoot in the snow, but she did not tell him that.

"You're right. There is nothing but pain here."

She closed her ears to his soul-searching.

"How do you keep going?"

She took a deep drag of the cigarette without taking her eyes off the opposite wall. "You know how the cliché goes. The one about separating the personal from the professional."

"I've never understood that one."

"The truth is I'm no longer afraid of anything."

He stood up, made to leave, stopped at the door.

"How long have you been here?"

She flicked the cigarette ash. "I wish I could say. I don't know. A couple of months. It feels like a year."

His silence was more uncomfortable than the silence that usually came over her clients. She tried to dismiss him with her eyes.

"If you want to be left alone, just say so."

"Yes. I mean no. I don't want to be alone. Why have you stayed? What else do you want?"

He dropped into a chair in the opposite corner of the room.

"I want to help you."

"Then save me from this hell."

The minutes passed and neither spoke. The word *save* seemed to echo in the air between them. She was his prisoner, trading this intimacy for the promise of freedom.

"There's nothing I can do right now," he said eventually. In the half-light he appeared as solemn as a priest. He sat down on the bed next to her. Her face looked empty. He pulled her toward him, his fingers fumbling, light and then rough. He tried to wrap his arms around her. He almost overpowered her. Several times, she felt she might lose herself in his embrace, but then she crept away to the bottom of the bed. She felt relieved to know she had not yet crossed that territory where a man might care for her. She began to think there might be a way back to her old life after all.

A fierce gust made the cracked windowpane shift in its frame.

"This is a dangerous place," she said. "The people who run this house are violent and evil."

He stared out the window and nodded. The closer one came to the border, the deeper one fell into the nightmare domain of terrorists and criminals. He felt uneasy. He listened to the buffeting of the wind and an owl hooting in the darkness. He knew that out there lay a wild terrain of disappearing lanes and blown-up bridges, uninhabited farms and thick forests, a smuggler's paradise and the ultimate refuge for people traffickers. He picked up his jacket and stood at the door, wishing he could just walk out with her, but he knew that was too dangerous. He would have to organize something more cunning. His solution lay somewhere outside in the darkness of the border and in the shadowy corners of his past.

"Can you help me?" she asked.

"It will mean digging up some old comrades," he replied, half to himself. "It will cost me. And I'm not just talking about money."

He stared at her face. Was it his imagination or had her skin grown paler? For the first time, he noticed the dark rings under her eyes. He wondered who she was, this woman who made him want to risk all he had left behind in his life. She had a lovely body and a pretty face, but these attributes were common in the places he frequented. Although she held his gaze, he had the uncomfortable feeling he might be little more than a shadow to her, one of countless others that passed through the room. He began to suspect that she had deliberately revealed the bruises on her body, as a way to seek his protection. If he had any sense, he would leave now and never come back to this house, which offered nothing but pain and despair.

"I'll return in three days," he told her. "I should have a plan in place by then."

Before he left, he wrote down a mobile phone number on the back of a cigarette box.

"If anything happens before then, ring this number. It belongs to an old friend of mine. One with the right sort of connections. He should be able to help."

Afterward, she could not sleep. The promise of escape penetrated even her subconscious. She lay on her mattress waiting for his return, and in the darkness her mind turned to the plight of the other trafficked women. She drew up a list of the girls working in the brothel, along with the contact details of relatives back in Croatia. She asked them questions about Jozef Mikolajek, the man who had hoodwinked her into traveling from Croatia to Ireland. The name was familiar to all of them. He had promised each of them something; if not love, then work, or simply the opportunity to escape poverty. In return, he had taken each girl's whole world away. She felt the hairs stiffen on the back of her neck. Mikolajek was a predator, and they had been his prey. She had seen him on several occasions, walking through the farmhouse late at night, his face plunging by a crack in the doorway, his eyes shining like a wolf's as he weighed up the girls he had brought to ruin. The pent-up anger rose within her and threatened to fly off in all directions, harming anyone who was near—herself, the other women, the pimps and their clients, even her rescuer. However, her anger had only one real target, and that was Jozef Mikolajek.

At her bedroom window, she contemplated the blackness outside. This was a dark country, peopled by ghosts and dangerous men, she thought. She would not let herself become part of its painful history. The impulse to act burned within her. It struck her that she could not leave the farmhouse and all its terrible memories for good without taking revenge on the men who had robbed her and so many others of everything. She would concentrate and pounce at the right moment, she decided. Only then would her nightmare be over. She stared at her reflection, tethered in the blackness of the window like bait to the men who roamed border country. After a while, it started to snow. She watched the wind swathe her shadowy face with flakes. The thought of revenge thrilled her. It was easier to kill when a part of you was already dead.

The evening that Jack was due to return, Lena crept into the next-door room and sat down at the edge of the bed. When the girl lying there woke up, she held her hand.

"Have you decided?"

"Yes. I want to help you kill them. Now. Tonight."

"We have to wait our time. We have to be like hunters and lure our prey toward us."

She stroked the girl's cheek and handed her a small rag doll. Inside it was a piece of paper with the telephone number Fowler had given her, as well as the personal details of the women Mikolajek had trafficked. The girl hid the doll under her pillow.

"It's a horrible thing to do," she said to Lena.

"But we've been made to do horrible things."

"It has to be done, then."

A letter from the publisher

We hope you enjoyed this book. We are an independent
publisher dedicated to discovering brilliant books,
new authors and great storytelling. Please join us at
www.headofzeus.com and become part of our
community of book-lovers.

We will keep you up to date with our latest books, author
blogs, special previews, tempting offers, chances to win
signed editions and much more.

If you have any questions, feedback or just want to say hi,
please drop us a line on hello@headofzeus.com

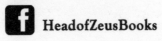 @HoZ_Books

HeadofZeusBooks

www.headofzeus.com

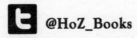 HEAD *of* ZEUS

The story starts here